Berkley Prime Crime titles by Jenn McKinlay

ON BORROWED TIME

Jenn McKinlay

BERKLEY PRIME CRIME, NEW YORK

THE BERKLEY PUBLISHING GROUP
Published by the Penguin Group
Penguin Group (USA) LLC
375 Hudson Street, New York, New York 10014

USA • Canada • UK • Ireland • Australia • New Zealand • India • South Africa • China

penguin.com

A Penguin Random House Company

ON BORROWED TIME

A Berkley Prime Crime Book / published by arrangement with the author

Berkley Prime Crime Books are published by The Berkley Publishing Group,
BERKLEY® PRIME CRIME and the PRIME CRIME logo are
registered trademarks of Penguin Group (USA) LLC.

For information, address: The Berkley Publishing Group,
a division of Penguin Group (USA) LLC,
375 Hudson Street, New York, New York 10014.

ISBN: 978-0-425-26073-9

PUBLISHING HISTORY
Berkley Prime Crime mass-market edition / November 2014

PRINTED IN THE UNITED STATES OF AMERICA

10 9 8 7 6 5 4 3 2 1

Cover illustration by Julia Green.
Cover design by Rita Frangie.
Interior text design by Laura K. Corless.

*This book is dedicated to my first best friend,
my brother, Jon (Jed) McKinlay. Through all of our
misguided adventures, major mishaps, and big life moments,
you have been the one constant in my life. You even taught
me how to drive! You understand me better than anyone else
and you love me anyway. I owe you for that. You are without
a doubt the best brother a girl could ever have and I'm
so glad you're mine. May the invisible cord between
us never be broken. I love you always!*

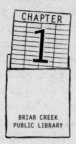

CHAPTER

1

BRIAR CREEK
PUBLIC LIBRARY

Lindsey Norris, director of the Briar Creek Public Library, strode across the library with her keys in hand. It was lunch hour on Thursday, which meant book talk, crafts and snacks, as their weekly crafternoon book club gathered in a meeting room on the far side of the building.

Out of all the activities the library hosted, this was by far Lindsey's favorite. She figured it was the book nerd in her that loved it so, but truthfully, these ladies had become her dearest friends since she'd moved to Briar Creek, Connecticut, a few years ago, and any afternoon she shared with them was time well spent.

"Lindsey, wait up!" a voice called to her from the children's department. She spun around to see an old-fashioned aviator charging toward her.

Lindsey squinted. Beneath the leather cap and goggles, she couldn't make out much, but she was pretty sure she recognized the upturned nose and stubborn chin as belonging to her children's librarian, Beth Stanley. But it was hard to say, as the rest of her was dressed in a white scarf, leather bomber jacket, black pants and boots. Not the typical wardrobe for a woman who spent most of her time doing finger plays, felt boards and story times.

"What do you think?" the aviator asked. She planted her hands on her hips and stood as if she were posing for a photo.

"I'm not sure," Lindsey said. "Who are you?"

"What? Oh!" The woman wrestled her goggles up onto her head. "It's me—Beth. What do you think of my steampunk outfit?"

"It's the bomb," Lindsey said with a laugh. Beth looked positively delighted with herself and with good reason. "You look like you could have stepped right out of Scott Westerfeld's *Leviathan*."

"Yes!" Beth pumped a fist in the air. "That's exactly what I was going for. My teen group worked on these at our meeting last night. You should see some of the stuff they made. We're all getting together at the Blue Anchor tonight to have our holiday blowout and show off our outfits."

"I love it," Lindsey said. Not for the first time, she thought how lucky the community was to have Beth, who truly brought reading to life for kids and teens.

"I think you look ridiculous," a voice said from the circulation desk. "Mr. Tupper never let his staff run around in costume, and certainly not out in public."

"No one asked you—" Beth began, but Lindsey cut her off.

"That will do, Ms. Cole," she said. "Beth has done amazing things to get our teens reading."

Ms. Cole sniffed but didn't argue, which Lindsey felt was a big improvement. Known as the lemon to the rest of the staff, Ms. Cole was an old-school librarian who longed for the days of shushing loud patrons and shunning late borrowers.

"Walk and talk," Lindsey said to Beth. "Crafternoon is starting soon, and I need to set up the meeting room."

"Who's bringing the food this week?" Beth asked.

"Nancy."

"Oh, I hope she baked cookies," Beth said. Nancy Peyton, who was also Lindsey's landlord, was known throughout Briar Creek for her exceptional cookie-baking skills. Since it was December and the holidays were just weeks away, Lindsey knew that Nancy had been giving her oven a workout.

"I think that's a safe bet," Lindsey said.

She glanced out the window as they turned down the short hallway that led to the crafternoon room. The town maintenance crew had been decorating the old-fashioned lampposts that lined Main Street with garlands of silver and gold tinsel, and hanging green wreaths with red ribbons just below the lamps.

The decorations added just the right amount of festive energy to the air and helped ward off the gloom that seemed to be descending upon them in the form of menacing, steel gray clouds, which were reflected by the water in the bay, giving everything a cold, hard and unforgiving appearance.

The crafternoon room had a small gas fireplace, and Lindsey had a feeling that they were going to need it today to fight off the wintery chill in the air.

"So I was thinking you should come and meet up with me and the teens at the Blue Anchor tonight," Beth said. "It'll be fun. I even have enough steampunk gear for you to wear."

Lindsey glanced at her friend. She could not picture herself looking like a souped-up Amelia Earhart; still Beth had spray-painted the goggles copper and stuck all sorts of knobs and gear and even a dragonfly on them. They were pretty cool.

"I don't like to leave Heathcliff alone for that long," she said.

"What alone?" Beth asked. "He's been mooching cookies off of Nancy all day."

"No doubt," Lindsey said. Nancy liked to have Lindsey's dog, Heathcliff, with her during the day. "Which is why he's going to need an even longer walk than usual tonight."

"Aw, come on," Beth said. "It'll be fun. Charlie's band is playing, and who knows? You might run into one of your admirers."

Lindsey gave her a bland look. "I have no idea to whom you could be referring."

"Sully or Robbie," Beth said. "You know they're both hovering around waiting for you to give any hint of encouragement."

"Did you finish the book for this week?" Lindsey asked.

"Nice conversational segue—not," Beth said. "Yes, I finished *The Woman in White*, but you didn't answer—"

"Did you know that the novel was so popular that Wilkie Collins had 'AUTHOR OF "THE WOMAN IN WHITE"' inscribed on his tombstone?"

"Fascinating, but you might want to save that tidbit for

when the other crafternooners start to grill you about your love life," Beth said.

Lindsey turned the key in the lock and pushed it open.

The room was dark, and she flipped the switch to the left of the door before stepping into the room.

Her gaze moved past the door to where she saw a man standing perfectly still. She felt a thrill of recognition surge through her, but the man shook his head from side to side and then put his finger to his lips. Lindsey knew immediately that he didn't want anyone to know he was there.

She quickly stepped back out of the room, bumping into Beth as she went.

"What's the matter?" Beth asked.

"It's freezing in there," Lindsey said. She shivered as if to prove it. "Even with the fireplace, there's no way this room will be warm enough to meet in. The heat must have been turned off, or maybe a window was left open. I'll check it out. In the meantime, could you set up one of the other meeting rooms for us?"

"On it," Beth said, and she hustled back down the hallway in the direction of the main library.

As soon as she was gone, Lindsey opened the door and hurried inside. She quickly shut and locked it behind her.

"Jack!" she cried.

"Linds!" he said in return.

The ruggedly handsome man met her halfway across the room with his arms open wide. Lindsey leapt at him, and he caught her in a hug that almost, but not quite, crushed her.

When he released her, Lindsey stepped back and stared at the face so similar to her own. She had many people in

5

her life whom she considered close friends, but the bond between siblings was one that could not be surpassed.

"Okay, brother of mine," she said as she crossed her arms over her chest in a fair imitation of their mother when she was irritated. "Start explaining."

CHAPTER

2

BRIAR CREEK
PUBLIC LIBRARY

Where Lindsey was all long blond curls and a face that was handsome more than pretty, Jack was short-cropped honey-colored curls with a face that was almost too pretty for a man. He had hit the genetic lottery with full lips and rich caramel-colored eyes, and Lindsey thought, not for the first time, how unfair it was. Paired with his muscular shoulders, lean hips and formidable height, Jack could have been a male model as easily as an economist, but where Lindsey's world revolved around words, Jack's passion had always been for numbers.

"What?" he asked, raising his hands in the air in a questioning gesture. "A brother can't surprise his favorite sister for the holidays?"

"I'm your only sister, but nice try," she said. "Of course, you can surprise me but why are you hiding in here?"

"Hiding? What hiding?" he asked. He turned away from

her and surveyed the room. "I'm just trying to keep my arrival on the down low for a while."

"What aren't you telling me, Jack?" she asked. He could try and fool her all he wanted, but she knew that whenever he was hiding something, he started to pace just like he was doing now.

"Nothing," he said. He crossed over to the bookshelves and then the fireplace. "I've just been doing the usual, you know, solving the business troubles of companies around the world."

"Then how come I haven't heard from you in a month, and why didn't you tell me you were coming? Do Mom and Dad know you're here? Where have you been anyway? Last I heard, you were in the Fiji Islands," she said.

"Ugh, so many questions." Jack groaned. "Can we do the catch-up thing later? Hey, is this a gas fireplace? Can I fire it up? It's chilly in here. I thought maybe I could catch a nap since I had almost no sleep last night." As if to prove his statement, he let out a jaw-popping yawn.

Lindsey fretted her lower lip between her teeth. There was only one person on the entire earth that she could never say no to, and that was Jack.

The building policy strictly stated that no one was to be in here without a staff member present, but he did look awfully tired and he was a responsible adult. Surely, Jack, a Cornell-educated economist, would be fine left to his own devices in the meeting room. Besides, she could keep checking on him as needed so she would sort of be in here with him.

"All right," she said. "But I still want an explanation. How did you get in here anyway? Because I know the door was locked."

"I am a man of many talents," he said in a bogus Houdini voice while waving his hands in the air like a magician.

"You found an unlocked window, didn't you?"

"Yeah." He dropped his arms, looking deflated. "You should really be more careful, Linds. You never know what kind of bad guy might come in and steal all of your precious books."

"Uh-huh." Lindsey switched on the gas fireplace, which clicked three times before it ignited.

Jack launched himself onto the squashy leather couch that faced the fireplace. As he settled in, he looked like a very big cat, finding just the right spot for his nap.

"You know my crafternoon group is supposed to be meeting in here," Lindsey said. "You owe me one for disrupting our meeting so you can have a nap."

Jack grabbed her hand as she passed by the couch, stopping her from leaving.

"I do owe you one, Linds, more than you know," he said. "It's really good to see you. I've missed you."

She could see the sincerity in his eyes, and she knew he felt the same way she did. The bond they shared, like an invisible cord, stretched as far as the globe could take them away from each other, but it never broke. They were always connected.

Lindsey bent down and kissed his head. "I've missed you, too, you big dope. We'll talk, and I mean that, when you wake up."

She checked her watch. She was going to be late for crafternoon, but that was okay. Her brother Jack was here, and suddenly the steely gray day outside seemed brimming with holiday cheer.

She couldn't wait to spend some time with him and

9

hear his latest adventures. Jack was like a crusty old penny with a heavy patina; he had lots of miles and lots of stories on him, and he always turned up when she least expected it.

" *T* he Woman in White was not what I expected," Nancy Peyton said while she arranged a tray of cookies on the end of the table. "Why do novels written in the eighteen hundreds always break up the happy couple? It's annoying."

"Oh, I don't know," Violet La Rue said. "It seems to me many novels separate the couple, especially if it's a series. I suppose we readers just have to read on, trusting the author and being committed to seeing it through."

"Not unlike most relationships," Lindsey said. "I suppose you have to decide if you're the committing type before you start a book, which if you think about it, is a relationship of sorts."

To Lindsey's relief, today's crafternoon actually worked out better in the smaller glassed-in conference room. Since they were recycling candles and were using little electric hot plates to do it, they had more access to outlets in the refurbished conference room than they would have had in the room she'd left to Jack.

"But that doesn't answer the question," Mary Murphy agreed. She added a bunch of half-spent candles to the pile in the center of the table. Then she looked pointedly at Lindsey and asked, "*Why* does the happy couple always break up?"

Lindsey shook her head. Captain Mike Sullivan, known to everyone one as Sully, was Mary Murphy's older brother, and Lindsey knew Mary well enough to know that she was asking why she and Sully were still broken up. Mary never missed an opportunity to fish for information, and since they both belonged to the library's crafternoon group, Mary always used it to work in an informal questioning, which felt like an inquisition, into the status of Lindsey's relationship with Sully.

"Because it's more dramatic that way," Charlene La Rue answered for Lindsey. "Right, Mom?"

Charlene La Rue turned to her mother, Violet, a former Broadway actress and the reigning queen of the local community theater.

"Exactly," Violet agreed. "The story would be over in twenty pages if Walter Hartwright won Laura Fairlie when they first met."

"And the fact that he's her poor drawing instructor makes it so much more romantic," Beth cried.

Nancy snorted. "My grandmother always said, 'It's just as easy to love a rich man as a poor one.'"

"True," Beth agreed. She was still wearing her steampunk cap and goggles, but had taken off the jacket and scarf. "But it just seems like there are so many more poor ones to choose from. You know, the unemployed, underachieving, living in his parents' basement population has really exploded."

"And thus, we remain single," Lindsey said.

"An actor is not unemployed," Violet said. "Their job prospects are just more eclectic than most."

Both Violet and Charlene hit Lindsey with their matching mother and daughter dazzling smiles. While Violet was retired from the stage and lived in Briar Creek, Charlene was a newscaster on the local station in New Haven. Both women were tall and thin with rich cocoa skin and warm brown eyes. Together they were a force to be reckoned with, but Lindsey was wise to their game.

The La Rue women were close friends with Robbie Vine, a famous British actor who had recently come to Briar Creek to star in a production of Violet's while getting reacquainted with his son. He had made no secret of his interest in Lindsey, but even though Robbie charmed her senseless, her heart was still knotted up over Sully, who had dumped her to give her space she had not requested. In a word, it was complicated.

"*Pffthbt.*" Beth made a scoffing noise. "You know, instead of pushing the head librarian with two beaus to make her choice—yes, I'm sure it's brutal, Lindsey, really—you all might consider canvassing the area for an available guy for me."

As one, they all turned to look at Beth in surprise.

"What?" she asked. "Just because my last boyfriend was stabbed to death doesn't mean I've sworn off men forever. Surely, there has to be a man out there who would like a short curvy gal who can recite Shel Silverstein from memory and knows every Mother Goose poem ever written by heart. I mean, honestly, is that asking so much?"

They all blinked at her. Beth was rarely anything but sunny in disposition, which was one of the many reasons why all the children in town adored her.

"She's right," Lindsey said. She smiled at Beth. "I'm taking up more than my share; you want one?"

"Sloppy seconds?" Beth asked with a grin. "No, thank you. But I'm sure the collective talent in this room can find me a guy that I won't be embarrassed to bring home to my mother. She's getting positively naggy on the subject of a husband and children. I'm going to have to make up an imaginary boyfriend soon if I can't manage a real one."

The others all exchanged a look, and Nancy said, "We'll get right on that."

"Absolutely," Charlene said. "Maybe there's someone at the station."

"Ian might know someone," Mary said, referring to her husband, with whom she owned the Blue Anchor, a café known locally as the Anchor.

"I can ask my nephew Charlie if he knows anyone," Nancy said. She and Lindsey glanced at each other and they both shook their heads.

In Nancy's three-story captain's house, Charlie lived in the second-floor apartment between Nancy and Lindsey. He worked for Sully seasonally, but was doggedly pursuing his dream of rock and roll stardom in his downtime. His musician friends, while interesting, were not exactly the bring home to Mom and show off type, as most of them slept all day, played out all night and didn't have a lock on the concept of regular pay as yet.

"Or not," Nancy said.

She finished putting out the food she had brought, and the group went back to discussing Wilkie Collins's novel while they continued melting the wax for their craft project. It was agreed that the novel was a worthy read, and they debated what exactly made it one of the original "sensation" novels.

The time sped past and Lindsey managed to make only two new candles. Using old canning jars, they had tied wicks to hang off a pencil into the jar and then melted the remnants of all their old candles by heating the bits in a small aluminum pan on a hot pot. Lastly, they poured the melted wax into the canning jar up to the top, leaving just enough space for the lid.

Lindsey was quite pleased to have created her candles in alternating red and green recycled wax, giving them a festive holiday look. She had thought to give them away as gifts, but now she wasn't so sure. They'd look nice on her dining table for the holidays.

As they packed up the room, leaving the candles to cool, Lindsey waved good-bye to the others before hurrying back to where Jack was snoozing. She hoped he'd had a good enough power nap, because she was itching to hear what had brought him to town earlier than expected and how long he was staying.

She really hoped he planned to be here for the entire holiday. With her parents coming down from New Hampshire, this would be the first holiday they had all been together in three years, and she found she was really looking forward to it.

Lindsey slipped the key into the lock and turned it. She didn't want to startle her brother, so she pushed the door open quietly.

Two things hit her immediately—a bitterly cold draft was blowing in from an open window, and it was dark. She stepped into the room. Maybe the lights had kept him awake and he'd gotten overheated because of the fireplace. It seemed unlikely, but she couldn't figure why else it was so cold and dark.

"Jack?" she called.

There was no answer. She hurried forward to see over the back of the couch where she'd left him. It was empty. The fire in the fireplace was off, and she shivered as the cold seeped through her sweater to her skin.

She glanced down at the floor in front of the hearth and gasped. A man was lying facedown on the floor. Lindsey raced forward.

"Jack! Are you all right?" she cried.

The gloomy midafternoon light made it hard to see, but Lindsey knew immediately from the bald head, the heavier build and the corduroy coat that this was not Jack.

She rolled the man over onto his back, trying to see what was wrong. His vacant brown eyes stared past her at the ceiling, and Lindsey felt a fist of dread clutch her insides in its meaty fist. The angry red marks around his neck, the lack of a rise and fall from his chest and the cold touch of his skin made it clear. The man was dead.

CHAPTER

3

BRIAR CREEK
PUBLIC LIBRARY

Lindsey met Police Chief Emma Plewicki at the main doors to the library. She had called Emma directly and told her about the dead stranger. She did not tell anyone on staff. She didn't want to cause a panic, plus if someone in the library had done the deed, she didn't want them to slip away.

She had no idea where Jack had gone or what he might know about the man in the room. The only thing she did know was that Jack was no murderer. She didn't care how bad it looked; she wouldn't believe it until she heard from Jack himself.

Emma Plewicki was built solid with glossy black hair that framed her heart-shaped face and big velvet brown eyes that, surrounded by long curly eyelashes, had beguiled more than one felon into confessing his crimes.

Emma stepped through the sliding doors and looked at Lindsey in question. Lindsey tipped her head to the side in a follow-me gesture. Emma turned to the two officers who had come with her.

"Cover the exits," she said. "Close the library. No one enters or leaves without my say-so."

"What happened?" Emma asked Lindsey. She whispered so as not to alert the other patrons in the building.

It was a wasted effort. Every head swiveled in their direction as they made their way to the back room. One officer checking out a book did not get noticed, but three officers with two blocking the exits were hard to miss.

Lindsey didn't want to lie to Emma, for not only did she like the chief in a professional capacity but she liked her personally as well. Still, she wasn't ready to bring her brother into it, so she decided to stick with the facts, just the facts.

"I opened the door to the room to check on the temperature," she said. "It had been too cold to use earlier, so I was following up. It was even colder this time. When I went in to see why, I found a man lying on the floor in front of the fireplace. When I checked him, I could see he had been strangled."

Emma snapped her head in Lindsey's direction. "You okay?"

"Yeah, I'm fine," Lindsey lied. She knew that Emma knew she was lying, but Emma nodded, accepting the big fib, and they hurried down the hallway to the back room.

Beth was standing outside the room. Lindsey had asked her to stay there until she returned with Emma.

She didn't tell Beth why she needed her to stand outside the locked room, and Beth didn't ask. They had been friends long enough that Beth knew that whatever it was, it was important.

"Okay, Beth," Lindsey said. "Thanks for keeping an eye."

Beth looked from her to Emma and back. She had taken off her steampunk hat and goggles and regarded Lindsey with a pensive expression.

"Is it a gas leak or something?" she asked.

"No, nothing like that," Lindsey said. "I'll explain later."

"Wait out here, please," Emma said as she pulled on a pair of blue latex gloves. Beth nodded.

Lindsey took out her key and unlocked the door. She pushed it open. It was still bitterly cold, as the window was still open. The body was exactly where she had left it.

Emma hurried to the victim's side. She glanced up at Lindsey. "Was this where he was when you found him?"

"Right here but facedown," Lindsey said. "I flipped him over to see if he was all right."

Emma nodded and confirmed what Lindsey had already discovered. "He's dead. I'm guessing strangled."

Her tone was dry, and Lindsey knew she was trying to sound as normal as possible, given the extraordinary circumstance. It just wasn't every day that you found a man strangled to death in the library.

Emma used her shoulder radio to call one of her officers, requesting he place a call into the medical examiner, then she continued examining the body. Lindsey didn't want to interrupt her, but she wasn't sure what to do about the library. Did she keep it open? Close it? What?

Emma left the body and was now studying the room. "Lindsey, can you tell if anything is missing from here?"

It was on the tip of Lindsey's tongue to say, *Yes, my brother*, but she held it in. She scanned the room. The collection of craft books were on the shelves. The fire was still out. The window was open but otherwise not even the cushions on the comfy couch seemed to have been moved.

Jack, where are you? Lindsey thought but didn't say. Instead, she said, "No, everything looks fine except for the window."

Emma crossed to the window and examined it. She checked the lock and then moved back and forth and from side to side as if looking for something. Lindsey watched her.

"We might get lucky with a set of latent prints on the glass. It doesn't appear to be broken," she said. "Could it have been left unlocked?"

"It's possible," Lindsey said, knowing full well that it had been.

She felt a twinge of guilt at not telling Emma about finding her brother in here, but how could she when she didn't know where he was or what had happened? She glanced at the dead man, and her knees felt weak with relief at the realization that it could have been Jack lying there. Then she felt bad about being relieved, as perhaps this man had a sister somewhere who would soon be mourning him.

A noise outside brought their attention to the door. The door banged open and Officer Kirkland stepped into the room.

"Sorry, Chief, but the ME is here," he said.

"Thanks," she said. "Show him in and then gather everyone in the library into another room."

"The story time room in the children's area will work," Lindsey said. She liked it for two reasons: One, it was big enough, and two, it was on the complete opposite side of the building from the crime scene.

"Excellent," Emma said. "Thanks."

"If you don't need me here . . ." Lindsey let her words trail off. She wanted to be the stalwart library director, but honestly, the dead body was giving her a severe case of the wiggins and she wanted out of this room in the worst possible way.

"Go ahead," Emma said. "I'm sure Officer Kirkland could use the assistance."

Lindsey did not wait for her to change her mind. She hurried out of the room, passing Officer Kirkland. He was a big-boned, redheaded farm boy newly minted from his public safety training, and he followed Chief Plewicki around like an eager puppy.

"Are you sure you don't need me, ma'am?" he asked.

"No, I'm good," Emma said. "I don't think our vic is going to put up much of a fight."

Kirkland narrowed his eyes. "It sure looks like he didn't at any rate."

Emma studied him. "What makes you say that, Kirkland?"

It was all the invitation he needed. Kirkland crossed the room to her side and pointed to the vic's hands. "There's nothing under his fingernails. If he'd put up a fight, there'd be blood or skin. He looks like he just had a manicure."

Emma raised her eyebrows. "What else?"

"His clothes aren't in disarray or torn. There are no scuffs on his shoes. If he'd kicked out at anything or anyone, there is no sign of it," he said. He pointed out the pristine shine on the man's leather shoes. "Since he doesn't appear to have put up a fight, it makes me wonder if he was unconscious when the person attacked or if the strangulation marks are postmortem, trying to throw us off the real cause of death."

Emma nodded. She clapped him on the shoulder, looking pleased. "That's exactly what I noticed. Nice work, Kirkland."

He beamed at her, and Lindsey was surprised he didn't start wagging. Lindsey bounced on her feet in the hallway. She was really ready to move away now and go search for her brother.

"Emma—" Lindsey began, but the medical examiner pushed past her into the room. "Hi, Dr. Griffiths."

He gave her a surly nod and Lindsey reminded herself that he wasn't a bad guy. He liked to read travel books about Europe and dreamed of backpacking there one day, but Lindsey suspected that his pteromerhanophobia held him back and "one day" might turn into "never" if he didn't get over his fear of flying.

"Go ahead and move the people in the library," Emma said to Kirkland.

He nodded, looking reluctant to leave. Dr. Griffiths, a small man with a bald head, which was surrounded by a gray fringe that stuck out all around his head just like the bushy gray mustache over his upper lip, gave Kirkland no choice as he elbowed the rookie out of the way.

"Again, Plewicki?" Griffiths asked as he snapped on his own blue gloves. "What is it you people don't get about being a sleepy coastal community?"

"Sorry, Al," she said. She held her hands wide. "What

can I say? Briar Creek has become a hot bed of murder and intrigue."

Griffiths snorted and the hairs on his mustache fluttered. Lindsey turned away. She had no interest in watching this. Kirkland was rooted to the spot, obviously fascinated to see what would happen next.

"Come on." Lindsey nudged him with an elbow. "You think this is interesting? We have patrons we have to disconnect from their Internet session. You may want to keep your Taser handy."

"Seriously?" Kirkland asked, his eyes wide.

"Haven't been in the library at closing, have you?" she asked.

"No, ma'am," he said.

"Well, follow me, you're in for a treat," she said. She wondered if he could tell she was being sarcastic. A glance at his face, which was eager, made her suspect that he could not.

Lindsey saw Officer Wilcox standing by the door and noted that he and Kirkland exchanged nods. Reassured that everyone was following the same game plan, she cleared her throat, preparing to address the library.

"Everyone, I'd like to have your attention," she said. A few people turned in her direction, but for the most part she was ignored. Lindsey sighed. She really needed to consider a public address system. "Everyone, please, we have a situation. I need you all to move into the story time room for a few minutes while we get everything sorted out."

Her voice sounded strained even to her own ears. She forced a reassuring smile. "The officers will escort you back there, and you should be free to go in a matter of minutes."

"What's going on?" demanded Peter Schwartz. He

was a crotchety older gentleman known for complaining about everything from the hardness of the chairs to the quality of the air-conditioning. And yet he came to the library every day to read the newspaper of which he was not a good sharer.

"The officers will explain in a moment," Lindsey said. "Please, if you'll follow me."

"No, I'm not going," Mr. Schwartz said. "Unless the building is on fire or there's a bomb in it, I'm going on with my day."

He snapped open the newspaper he'd been reading and returned to the sports page as if he were oblivious to the people around him moving reasonably to the back room.

"I'm sorry, sir, but our orders are to have everyone gather in the back room," Kirkland said.

Lindsey admired his diplomacy. She knew from several accidental fire alarms over the past few years that there was always one customer who refused to budge, as if whatever they were doing was so much more important than avoiding being burned to death. It boggled.

She glanced at the bank of Internet computers and saw that Beth was efficiently locking the sessions in order to get the people moving. Several of their regulars had already gone into the story room to await further instructions.

Ms. Cole and Ann Marie Martin, the part-time circulation clerk, were also helping to guide people in the direction of the story room. Not for the first time, Lindsey was grateful that she had such a crackerjack staff who did as she asked without question.

"My taxes pay your salary!" Mr. Schwartz rose out of his seat and stood up on his tiptoes, trying to intimidate Officer Kirkland.

"Excellent." Kirkland leaned forward, forcing Mr. Schwartz backward just a little. "Then while we're in the back room there, we can have a long discussion about why I deserve a raise."

Mr. Schwartz looked as if he was going to choke on his own spit. Lindsey stepped forward before he stroked out on the spot, not wanting to add another body to her quota for the day.

The next time someone made the observation that working in a library must be lovely because it was so quiet, she didn't think she'd be able to hold back her laughter.

CHAPTER

4

BRIAR CREEK
PUBLIC LIBRARY

"If you'll follow me, Mr. Schwartz," Lindsey said. "I know that having a senior member of the community present will be very helpful in our current crisis."

"Crisis?" Mr. Schwartz asked. He puffed himself up and walked beside her toward the back room. He shot Officer Kirkland a nasty look. "Well, anything I can do to help the police with their job."

Lindsey glanced over her shoulder at Kirkland. He gave her a small smile, and she wondered if they had a course about dealing with difficult people at the police academy, and then she wondered if she could audit it.

Once they were gathered in the room, Lindsey let Officer Wilcox take over mediating the situation. She assumed there was a police protocol that he would follow to let the people know what was happening without causing them to panic.

Meanwhile, she huddled in the corner with her staff.

"All right, Lindsey, spill it," Beth said. "What's going on?"

Ms. Cole and Ann Marie completed their circle, and Lindsey gestured for them to shuffle to the side out of earshot of the rest of the people.

"After our crafternoon meeting today, I went into the back room, where we usually meet," Lindsey began. She closed her eyes to steady herself as she recalled the horror of what she'd found. With a sharp exhale, she finished by saying, "When I opened the door, I found the window open and a dead body facedown on the floor."

"What?" squawked Beth. "You found a body in the library?"

"*Shh*," Ms. Cole hushed her and then glanced around to make sure no one had heard.

Beth gave her an annoyed look, but lowered her voice. "I just don't understand how it's possible. That door is always locked unless there is a meeting under way."

"Who was it? Was it a patron?" Ann Marie put her hand to her throat as if to steady herself.

"No, it was a stranger," Lindsey said. "I didn't recognize him nor did Chief Plewicki."

The other three visibly relaxed. And Lindsey understood that in a community this small there was a sense of looking out for each other, even for pesky people like Peter Schwartz.

"What's going to happen now?" Beth asked. "And why do they want us all in this room?"

"I think the chief wants to make sure no one knew the

26

man," Lindsey said. "Also she probably wants to know if anyone saw anything suspicious."

The others nodded. Officer Kirkland was taking down the names of all the other people in the room. He had just finished when the doors opened and Chief Plewicki walked in.

The room immediately erupted with questions, but she held up her hands, motioning for everyone to be quiet.

"Thank you all for your cooperation," she said. "Due to the nature of the event that has taken place out front, my officers and I will be taking you out of the room individually, starting with families first."

Mr. Schwartz's face screwed up into an unhappy knot, but Emma froze him with a look.

"Unless, of course, you'd rather we keep the children in here even longer."

As if on cue, a baby began to wail, and everyone agreed that its family should be the first interviewed. Lindsey and her staff were excused to return to work with the understanding that they would be interviewed last.

When Lindsey arrived out front, it was to see the medical examiner wheeling the stranger's body out in a body bag. She went directly to her office and called the mayor's right-hand man, Herb Gunderson, to let him know the situation.

Herb was a meticulous dot every *i* and cross every *t* man, who ran the town's department head meetings with a precision that left them all napping; still, she preferred breaking the bad news to him rather than the mayor.

"Herb Gun—" That was as far as he got before Lindsey interrupted.

"Herb, it's Lindsey, we have a situation at the library," she said.

"What sort of situation?" he asked.

She knew without seeing him that he had just sat up in his chair and smoothed his tie with the palm of his hand. He did that every time he was addressing an issue.

"Chief Plewicki is here with two officers as well as Dr. Griffiths, the medical examiner," Lindsey said.

"The ME?" Herb gulped. "Just what the heck is going on over there?"

Lindsey sighed. There was no gentle way to put this. "We . . . I found a dead body in the library."

"What? Where? When?" He fired the questions with the same sharp report as bullets out of a gun.

"Dead body, meeting room, half an hour ago," she returned fire.

"Who is it?" he asked.

"No idea," Lindsey said. "I'm just giving you a heads-up. I'm sure Emma will call with a full report as soon as she's done talking to the patrons and staff here."

Herb was silent for a moment as if meticulously choosing his words or maybe processing the bomb Lindsey had detonated on him.

"Is there anyone there that I should know about beforehand?" he asked.

It took Lindsey a second to get his drift and then she got it. "Peter Schwartz is here."

"Ah," Herb said. In one syllable he managed to convey the tortured anguish of the public servant when faced with a terminally whiny member of the public.

"I know he's quite the letter writer," Lindsey said. "He leaves us lots of helpful notes."

"Well, after this, I imagine he'll have enough to fill a book."

"Did you just tell a joke, Herb?" Lindsey asked in surprise.

"You know, I think I might have," Herb said. "Forgive me, obviously I'm not myself."

"No, it was funny," Lindsey said with a chuckle. "And quite appropriate."

"Unless you need me for anything else, Lindsey, I imagine I need to get the mayor up to speed."

"Good luck with that." She hung up feeling a bit sorry for Herb and the meeting he was about to walk into, then again, that was why he made the big bucks.

Lindsey took a moment to check her cell phone. There were no incoming texts or calls from Jack. She then called her apartment. Maybe Jack had gone there and hadn't had a chance to tell her. No one answered, so she hung up and checked her messages. There was one automated sales call for a home security system, but that was it. There was no word from Jack.

Despite the victim having been found in the library, Lindsey felt that ultimately the dead body was going to be Emma's problem more than hers, which was fine, because finding her brother was her number one priority.

Lindsey left her office to find the library cleared and Officer Kirkland talking to Beth while the other officer talked to Ms. Cole and Ann Marie. Emma Plewicki was talking on her cell phone, and Lindsey suspected by the set of her jaw that she didn't like what she was hearing.

"Fine, but call me the minute you learn anything," Emma said into the phone. She pressed the front of her phone and shoved it into a holder on her belt.

"Bad news?" Lindsey asked.

"Griffiths says there's a backlog of bodies at his office," she said. "Mine is in the queue but it may take them longer than usual to ID him."

Lindsey glanced around the library, noting that it was all but empty. It appeared that everyone but Mr. Schwartz, who had resumed his seat with his paper, had fled. She couldn't blame them. There was a part of her that wished she could escape the building, too, but then again, she wanted to be here in case Jack turned up.

"You ready for a few questions?" Emma asked her.

"Sure, fire away," Lindsey said.

"Why did you have your crafternoon meeting in a different location today?" Emma asked. Her tone was abrupt and no nonsense, and Lindsey had the paranoid thought that maybe Emma knew about Jack and was testing her. But no, that couldn't be.

"Um . . . it was cold in there, you know, our usual room," Lindsey said. She hated lying, but given that she had already told the same fib to her best friend, she couldn't really bust out the truth now, could she?

"Was the window open when you went in?" Emma asked. Her sharp brown eyes were studying Lindsey's face, making her feel uncomfortable.

Logically, Lindsey knew that Emma was just encouraging her to try and remember all that she could, but knowing that she was being less than truthful made Lindsey's skin prickle and she felt as if she had guilt written all over her face.

"Yes," she said. She rationalized that Jack had told her the window was unlocked, so it could be construed as being open and was therefore not a complete fabrication.

"Then what did you do?" Emma asked.

"I decided to switch the location for our meeting and locked up the room, planning to check back later," Lindsey said. Truth. "And when I went back, I found the body." Also, truth.

Emma frowned at her. "The first time you were in the room, did you close the window?"

Lindsey refused to lie as it could only lead to more lies so instead, she went for vague, which judging by the politicians she saw on the news these days, was probably the best way to handle it.

"I don't know," she said. "I meant to, but it must have slipped my mind what with rushing off to change rooms and such."

Emma didn't look convinced and Lindsey couldn't blame her. An awkward moment passed between them, which mercifully was interrupted by the front doors sliding open and two men rushing into the building.

"Lindsey!" they cried her name in unison and hurried forward.

Emma glanced from them back to Lindsey and then grinned at her. In a teasing voice, she said, "Yeah, well, I could see how you might forget to shut a window when you have so much on your mind."

Lindsey gave her a weak smile in return and had to squash the urge to hug the stuffing out of both Robbie Vine and Mike Sullivan as they hurried toward her. They were saving her hide more than they would ever know.

"Are you all right?" Sully demanded. He reached her first and hugged her close.

"We heard there was a nasty incident in the library," Robbie said as he waited for Sully to release her and then hugged her himself. When he would have lingered, Sully pulled him off by the back of his collar.

"No taking advantage of the situation," Sully said to Robbie. "We agreed."

"Sorry, mate, it's in my nature," Robbie said in his charming British accent.

"Change your nature," Sully said. It sounded more like a threat than a suggestion.

Lindsey glanced between them and frowned. "What do you mean, you agreed?"

"We were both having lunch over at the Blue Anchor," Sully began.

"Not together," Robbie added.

Sully rolled his eyes and continued, "When Terry Lucas said she heard a man was shot while trying to rob the library, we agreed to come over together but not promote our own agendas, didn't we?"

"Not my idea," Robbie said, pouting. "I say when a bloke sees an opportunity, he should exploit it."

"Nice," Sully said in a tone that made it clear that it wasn't.

"Shot?" Lindsey asked. She glanced at Emma, who shook her head as if she was not at all surprised that the story had been warped from traveling on too many tongues.

"That's a ridiculous rumor. Who would rob the library?" Ms. Cole asked with an indignant sniff.

Lindsey had to give her that. She didn't know anyone who would take on Ms. Cole over her cash drawer, not willingly.

The two officers had finished questioning the other staff, and Lindsey looked at Emma. "Did you have any more questions?"

"Not right now," she said. "But I'll be in touch if I do. The room has been cordoned off, and it goes without saying that no one should go back there until we take the crime scene tape down."

"Got it," Lindsey said.

"Crime scene tape? Well, blimey, Lindsey, if you weren't robbed, what happened?" Robbie asked.

CHAPTER
5

BRIAR CREEK
PUBLIC LIBRARY

Lindsey looked at Emma, who gave her a small nod. Obviously, now that the preliminary investigation was done, the facts could be revealed.

"A man was found dead in one of the back rooms," Lindsey said. "We don't know who he is yet, but it does appear that he was murdered."

Sully's gaze narrowed on her face. Nothing much got by Sully, and he asked, "You found the body, didn't you?"

A shudder rippled from the top of Lindsey's head all the way down to her feet. For as long as she lived, she was never going to forget the chilling moment she realized the man was dead.

"Oh, love, you poor thing," Robbie said. He opened his arms wide as if to scoop Lindsey close and comfort her. Sully blocked him, intercepting his move and leaving Robbie hugging him instead.

Robbie dropped his arms and stepped back with an irritated twist to his lips. "Now was that necessary?"

"Yes," Sully snapped.

In spite of the trauma of the day, Lindsey felt the corners of her mouth curve up. This sort of thing had been going on for a while, ever since Robbie had arrived in town to help Violet with her community theater production of *A Midsummer Night's Dream* a few months before. The play was long over but Robbie remained.

Tall, with reddish-blond hair, green eyes and a pair of roguish dimples, Robbie Vine, a famous stage and film actor from England, had charmed his way into the Briar Creek community and made it more than plain that he was interested in Lindsey.

Meanwhile, Sully, a local boat captain with a sailor's strong build, sea blue eyes and a head of thick reddish-brown curls, had alternately won Lindsey's heart and then broken it. Not one to quit, however, Sully was now in the process of trying to win her affection back.

Lindsey adored them both, but she had declined any offers of a romantic nature, wanting to have more than a passing acquaintance with her own feelings before she made any rash decisions. It had made for an interesting few months with both men under foot, and just as Emma had noted, it had certainly kept her mind occupied.

"Unless the mayor tells me otherwise, I'm going to close the library to the public for the rest of the day," Lindsey said. "Staff can stay and catch up on clerical work if they choose, but I think it will be easier for the investigators if we close."

"I can call the mayor and request it," Emma said. "It certainly would make our job easier."

"Let's do it," Lindsey said. She put one hand through Sully's arm and the other through Robbie's as she began to walk them to the door. "Thank you so much for checking on me. It was very considerate of you both."

"She's giving us the boot, isn't she?" Robbie asked Sully.

"And how," he agreed. "Are you sure there isn't anything we can do to help?"

"I can't think of anything," Lindsey said. "But I'll let you know if I do."

She gave them a gentle push out the door and then stepped back as the automatic doors whooshed shut.

Beth strolled over to her side. "Decisions have to be made."

"No, they don't," Lindsey protested. "I don't know what I want yet. Honestly, aren't I allowed to take my time and figure it out? I mean, is there some invisible relationship countdown clock of which I'm unaware?"

"Um, I was talking about whether I should cancel the teens' party tonight or not," Beth said.

"Oh." Lindsey puckered her lips. "Since it's not in the library, I think you should forge ahead. There's no reason for the teens to miss out on wearing their steampunk gear."

"Excellent," Beth said. "They've all worked so hard, I'd hate to disappoint them. I'll send out a status update on our social media page that we're a go."

She disappeared into the children's department while Ms. Cole and Ann Marie manned their positions at the circulation desk. Lindsey scanned the library one more time, futilely looking for her brother with no success. Where could Jack have gone?

This was only one of many questions plaguing Lindsey. Had Jack been in the meeting room when the man came in? What happened between them? Or was Jack gone before the man entered? If so, who had strangled the man to death?

Lindsey felt her stomach knot up. If it was someone else who harmed the man, and it had to be because she knew it couldn't have been Jack, then where was that person? And was he looking for Jack? Or even worse, had he found him?

"Lindsey, are you all right?" Emma paused beside her and studied her face.

"Yeah, I'm good," Lindsey lied. Again.

"You know, what you saw in there would make a veteran police officer puke on his shoes," she said. "It's okay to be rattled."

"Oh, I'm more than rattled," Lindsey assured her. "But I'm still functional."

Emma nodded. "Let me know if you need to talk."

Lindsey squeezed her friend's arm in silent thank-you. She watched Emma go back to the crime scene while Officer Kirkwood escorted Peter Schwartz out of the building to much complaining.

She took the opportunity to go back to her office, hoping that this time she'd find a message from her brother on her phone. No such luck. Lindsey hovered by her office phone and her computer for the rest of the day, but there were no messages or calls from Jack.

The police cleared out an hour before closing, so it was just Lindsey and her staff meeting at the back door to exit the building.

Beth came running down the hall in her steampunk aviator costume with a big paper bag in her hands. As Lindsey set the alarm, they stepped out of the building into the bitter December air.

Ms. Cole gave them a stiff nod as she headed to her car while Ann Marie waved and gave them a small smile, her usual cheeriness subdued by the events of the day.

Being environmentally minded, Lindsey and Beth usually rode their bicycles to work even in winter, so they headed toward the bike rack at the side of the building. Lindsey was wrapping her scarf about her face and making sure her gloves reached up under her coat sleeves so a sneaky chill couldn't creep in between her layers.

"I think you should come to the Blue Anchor tonight," Beth said. "In fact, I insist."

Lindsey gave her a tired smile. "I would, really, but I'm just not up for it tonight."

Beth held a folded piece of paper out to her. "No, really, you need to come."

Lindsey frowned and took the paper. She opened it and caught her breath as the familiar scrawl of Jack's handwriting filled the small space.

Meet me at the Anchor tonight. Love, J

"When? How?" Lindsey asked. "Is he okay?"

"He was fine, a little mysterious, but fine."

"Why didn't you tell me earlier?" Lindsey asked.

"He asked me not to," Beth said. "I went into the storage area about an hour ago to gather my steampunk stuff, and there he was. He said he has to talk to you and that you'll know what it's about."

Beth gave her an assessing look. She may play with children all day, but Beth was no one's fool. She had to suspect that the dead body and Jack's arrival were not unrelated.

"He's not in trouble, is he?" she asked.

"I don't know," Lindsey said.

She could barely focus, given the relief that was pounding through her. Jack was okay. Only now could she admit to herself that she'd been dreading the worst, that somehow Jack was involved with the dead man and that he was hurt or harmed or had even been killed.

Lindsey clutched the paper to her chest and sucked in a gulp of the frigid evening air.

"What's going on, Lindsey?" Beth asked.

"I wish I knew," Lindsey said. "I only saw Jack for a few moments today and then he disappeared. I won't know any more until I talk to him. So it looks like I'm going with you."

"Excellent," Beth said. "I figured you would and, of course, you'll need this to fit in."

She opened her bag and rummaged through it. She pulled out a black top hat that was covered with knobs and gears and a purple lacy scarf. She glanced at Lindsey's wool skirt and lace-up boots and nodded.

"Unbutton a few buttons on your blouse and you'll look like a nice Victorian steampunk chick," Beth said.

"I don't get to be an adventurer?" Lindsey asked. "I wanted jodhpurs and a monocle."

"Beggars can't be choosers," Beth said. She clapped the hat onto Lindsey's head and draped the lacy scarf around her neck. "Besides, Jack already helped himself to my cool gear."

"Jack's in costume, too?" Lindsey asked.

"Yes," Beth said. She looked delighted. "He was so enthusiastic when I mentioned the party. Much more so than you. He even kissed me."

"What?" Lindsey asked.

"Don't worry. It was very sisterly," Beth said and

wrinkled her nose, letting Lindsey know that it was a disappointment. "Why didn't you tell me he was coming to town early?"

"I didn't know," she said. "You know how uncommunicative he is."

At least, that was the truth. She tried to ignore the sparkle in Beth's eye. Beth had fostered a crush on Jack since the first time she'd met him when she and Lindsey had been in grad school in New Haven.

When it came to Jack, whom she loved, and her friends, Lindsey always felt like she was standing out in a storm wildly waving to oncoming cars that the bridge was out. It never worked. Every friend she had ever had, had plunged headfirst over the abyss that was falling in love with Jack Norris.

So far, Jack had not stood still long enough for Beth to lose her heart to him completely, but Lindsey knew the signs. The giddy smile, the blush that colored her cheeks, the wild light in her eyes, yeah, Beth had it bad. Oh, no.

They climbed onto their bikes and pushed off the curb toward the Anchor. Lindsey's hat was heavy and she tipped it back so that she could see. With her lacy scarf blowing in the wind, she had to admit she felt a bit like a Victorian lady and, boy howdy, did she ever feel sorry for them.

They parked their bikes by the café, locking them up on the rail at the side of the building. The faint strains of Charlie Peyton's band could be heard through the door. Judging by the full parking lot, it was a rocking good time at the Blue Anchor tonight.

Lindsey and Beth blew into the building with a strong wind at their backs. The restaurant was standing room only, but Beth's teens had already taken over the corner by the band. Beth grabbed Lindsey's hand and hustled her across the room to the waiting group.

The band finished their song to much applause. Lindsey saw Charlie, her downstairs neighbor, standing off to the side with his guitar. She'd seen him play a million times, but every time, she was amazed at his skills and his natural affinity for the stage. Catching her eye, Charlie pointed at her and winked.

As she hurried by, he yelled, "Nice lid."

Lindsey adjusted the enormous hat on her head and gave him a rueful smile.

"Okay, now that the ladies are here," Charlie said into the mike, "it's time to slow things down a bit."

The band broke into a ballad and the teens they had just reached surged past them. Dylan, one of their older teen workers, grabbed Beth as he went past and Lindsey found herself alone, facing a youth in an explorer's jacket, a pith helmet and a monocle. He winked at her with his available eye.

"Jack?" she asked.

"Shh," he said. "It's Sir Tarryton at the moment."

He held out his arm to her, and much to Lindsey's bemusement, her brother led her out onto the dance floor amid the throng of similarly clad teens. To Lindsey, it appeared to be a crush of cogs, gears, wool coats, flouncy skirts and fancy hats.

She had to admit there was a certain appeal to the tricked-out clothes, but at the moment, she was much more concerned with her brother and the dead guy in her library.

Jack spun her into the funky waltz the teens were all

attempting, and when they were face-to-face, she began her interrogation.

"What happened to you today?" she asked. "When I went back to check on you, there was a dead man on the floor."

"I heard," Jack said. He adjusted his monocle before putting his hand back on her waist. "Are you okay? That must have been horrible."

"Not as horrible as it was for him, I'd imagine," she said.

She thought over the past two years and the number of bodies she'd seen, and she hated to think she was actually getting desensitized to it, but there was no question that today's corpse hadn't rattled her nearly as badly as it would have a few years ago.

She noticed Jack studying her face as if curious about what she meant, and she shook her head.

"Enough about me. What about you? What happened in there? You didn't . . . it wasn't . . . oh, Jack, what happened?"

Jack leaned in close to her and whispered, "You know I had nothing to do with that man's death."

He said it like a statement and Lindsey nodded. She knew that. She did. All the way down to her soul, she knew her brother could never harm another living being.

"I was asleep on the couch when I heard someone opening the window. I must not have locked it as well as I thought, but nothing good ever comes from people who use windows instead of doors," he said.

"Present company excepted?" Lindsey asked.

Jack gave a small smile and nod. "Anyway, I rolled off

of the couch and onto the floor and then scuttled my way behind one of the chairs in the corner."

"Who was the man? Why was he sneaking into my library?" Lindsey asked.

Jack's mouth was in a tight line, his expression grim. "When I woke up, I assumed he was after me. I was sure he was sent to kill me."

CHAPTER

6

BRIAR CREEK
PUBLIC LIBRARY

66 "Kill you?" Lindsey cried.

"*Shh*," Jack hushed her.

She lowered her voice and asked, "But why?"

"Would you believe for my love of coffee?" he asked.

He was being cryptic and it was annoying. Lindsey opened her mouth to say so when she saw the front door open and Sully entered the café.

"Is that the boat captain who broke your heart?" Jack asked, following the line of her gaze. He looked like he was going to go over and bust a Three Stooges eye gouge on Sully.

"We're friends now," Lindsey said. "Stand down."

Jack made a growly noise in his throat and Lindsey huffed an exasperated breath.

"Really?" she asked. "My broken heart is more of an issue for you than a man trying to kill you?"

"Well, he didn't," Jack said. "Primarily because another man climbed through the window after him and the two of them started to fight. One of them yelled for me to run, and I didn't need to be told twice."

"Did you see the man get murdered?" Lindsey asked. She was horrified.

"No." Jack shook his head and his too-large pith helmet swiveled on his head. Lindsey reached up to straighten it and met his gaze. He looked distraught.

"I would have stayed and helped if I'd known it was going to go that way. One of the men was my contact, but having never met him, I didn't know which one. I figured the best thing I could do to help would be to get away and then they'd have no reason to fight. Obviously, I was wrong and a man is dead because of it."

"Contact? What do you mean? Why were you meeting a contact here? Why is someone trying to harm you?" Lindsey asked. "You're an economist; how is that a life-threatening occupation?"

"I work for people who have a lot of money, a lot of power, and not that many scruples," Jack said. "One of them might be the teensiest bit unhappy with me right now."

"Then they sue you, they don't kill you," Lindsey said. She was going to say more but Jack spun her away and then pulled her back.

While spinning, Lindsey saw Sully leaning against the bar watching her. She felt her face flame hot at the thought that he might think she was flirting with teenagers. Then she shook her head. It really did not matter what Sully thought. Jack was obviously in serious trouble and her number one concern had to be helping him.

As she was swept back into Jack's arms, she frowned at him. "Tell me who's after you."

"Sorry, Linds, it's too dangerous," he said. "The less you know, the better. In fact, I was planning to spend the holiday hiding out here, but now that they've found me, I'm gonna have to bounce."

"No, you need to go to the police," Lindsey said. "Chief Plewicki is amazing and she'll help you, especially if you can help identify the dead man or at least give her a lead. I know she will."

The corner of Jack's mouth turned up in a half smile. "Linds," he began but she interrupted. She knew that look. He was about to completely blow her off.

"No, Jack, you listen to me—"

"Can't," he said. "You've got a new partner."

With that, he spun Lindsey right into Sully's arms while he snagged Beth, who looked delighted, and twirled her away from Dylan. Lindsey kept her eye on them, making sure Jack didn't disappear without telling her again.

The fact that he had dumped her into Sully's waiting arms when he'd wanted to stomp Sully just minutes before indicated to her that he was avoiding her suggestion to talk to the police.

"Problem?" Sully asked.

Good manners forced Lindsey to take her attention off Jack and look at Sully, whose blue eyes were narrowed with concern.

"It's not what you think," she said. She returned her gaze to Jack, following Sully's movements from sheer memory of the days when they had gone dancing while they were dating. Mercifully, not being a power dancer, Sully had always kept it to a simple two-step.

"Should I be worried that you have such a fascination with one of Beth's teens?" he asked. "I mean I really thought the flirting Englishman was enough."

Lindsey was only half listening. Jack leaned close to Beth's ear and whispered something that made her eyes go wide and then she tipped her head back and laughed with abandon. Oh, no! He was not working his charm on her best friend. Lindsey frowned. If anyone was going to get a butt kicking tonight, it was going to be her brother Jack.

"I'm not fascinated," Lindsey said, still watching Jack. "Irritated, more likely, and he's not a teen. He's a big, grown-up jackass."

"And you're irritated with donkey boy, because . . ." Sully prompted her.

"I just . . . I don't think he's a very good influence on Beth," Lindsey said. "She's always had a soft spot for him and he's, well, unreliable."

"Please do not tell me he is another ex-boyfriend," Sully said. "Really, what is it about Briar Creek and ex-boyfriends?"

This brought Lindsey's attention to him. Over the past few months, they had tiptoed around this particularly thorny bush in the garden of their relationship.

"Do you really want to discuss that now?" she asked.

He glanced around the room. "Well, it's the first time I've been able to get you alone in months, so it seems as good a time as any."

"You know, for a former Navy man and a boat captain, your timing is singularly awful," she said.

"Is it because of the body in the library?" he asked. "Is that too much on your mind right now?"

"Among other things," she said. Truth be told, she was

47

a little alarmed that she wasn't more fixated on the dead man in the crafternoon room. She blamed Jack.

"Well, if you could just let me plead my case," Sully said. "Before you get caught up in another murder case, I just want to tell you that I miss you. I miss us. And I'd like a do-over."

Now he had her attention. She stared into the face that had captured her heart so many months before. Oh, she had missed him, too, more than she had thought possible. Still, he had cut her loose. He had decided that she had feelings for her ex, when she did not, and he had stepped out of their relationship with no discussion, no input from her, nada. How did she know he wasn't going to do that again?

"No," she said.

Sully looked surprised. His voice was low and full of regret when he asked, "So you're calling it for good?"

"No," she said.

At this, Sully heaved the sigh of the beleaguered male and said, "No what? Are you trying to torture me?"

"No," she said again. Then she laughed. "I'm sorry!"

"For?" Sully asked.

"I don't want to call it quits," she said.

"Okaaaay." He drew out the word as if by the end of it, he would understand what she was talking about.

"But I'm not ready for a do-over either," she said.

"So that leaves us where exactly?" he asked.

"Friends," she said.

"Friends." He wrinkled his nose like he smelled something bad. "Isn't that what we've been doing?"

"Sort of," she said. "But real friends tell each other everything, their innermost deepest, darkest, hairy-scary thoughts and feelings. If we can learn to do that as friends,

48

then we'll have a relationship where no one will bail. At least, I hope *they* won't."

"Um, in case you haven't noticed"—he paused—"I'm not much of a talker."

"That's okay, it gets easier with practice," she said. She gave him her brightest smile, and he looked momentarily blinded.

"All right, I'm in," he said. His tone was grudging. "So long as I don't have to fight off that other guy, too. The tea tippler is bad enough."

"The tea tippler has a name," she said.

Remembering her brother, she glanced over Sully's shoulder but didn't see Beth or Jack on the dance floor. She twisted around and glanced behind her.

Charlie was up onstage and he was grinning like an idiot at the two of them. He even gave Sully a thumbs-up. Lindsey shook her head and spun back around. She stopped dancing, causing Sully to stop, too, which caused another couple to bump into them, creating the dance floor version of a four-car pileup.

"Come on," Sully said. He led her off the floor.

Lindsey was scanning the café, hoping to see Jack and Beth holed up at their table. No such luck. Beth was sitting there all by herself. Lindsey hurried across the room, praying that Jack had only gone to use the restroom.

Beth looked glumly up from the table, where she was contemplating the bottom of her mug of root beer. "Yes, I did it again."

"Did what?" Lindsey asked.

"Drove yet another man away from me as far and as fast as his feet could carry him," she said. "It's a gift, truly."

"Where did Jack go?" Lindsey asked.

"I don't know," Beth said. "One minute we were talking and laughing and then *she* came in."

"She? Who is she?" Lindsey asked.

Beth shrugged. "Don't know. She was all big hair and bodacious curves. She was definitely not dressed like a steampunk virgin."

Lindsey could hear the lack of self-confidence in her friend's voice, and it made her want to kick her brother's patoot.

"Well, I think you're stunning," Sully said. "But then I tend to go for that whole female adventurer thing."

Beth gave him a watery smile. "You're not just saying that, are you? Don't answer that. If you are, please continue to lie to me."

"I'm not. Captain's honor," Sully said with a salute. "You're a smokin' hot aviator chick."

"Did Jack know her?" Lindsey asked, forcing them back to the more pressing subject.

"He seemed to," Beth said with a frown. "Come to think of it, he really did not want to go with her, but she whispered something in his ear that had him moving out that door pretty quick. I assumed it was a proposition, but now that I think on it, he looked pretty worried." Beth's eyes went wide. "Maybe she threatened him."

Lindsey had the horrible thought that Jack's mystery woman had something to do with the dead guy in the library.

"I think you're right. I don't think Jack left by choice," she said. With that, she spun on her heel and hurried toward the door.

Sully caught her arm. "Lindsey, what are you doing?"

"Going after him," she said.

"I thought you didn't like him," he said. "I thought you didn't think he was good for Beth."

"I don't think he's good for Beth," she said. "But as crazy as he makes me, the truth is, I love him."

Sully sucked in a breath as if she'd punched him in the solar plexus. Lindsey shook her head.

"No, not like that." She waved her hand as if she could wipe away the thought. "Sully, Jack is my brother."

CHAPTER

7

BRIAR CREEK
PUBLIC LIBRARY

"And when were you planning on sharing that with me?" he asked.

"I'm sharing it now," she said. She pushed through the door into the frigid night air. "Besides, it's complicated."

"So I gathered," he said. She didn't have to look to know that Sully was frowning and probably rolling his eyes, too.

The wind coming off the water whipped down the pier and shoved the hat back on Lindsey's head. She took it off and cradled it under her arm.

She scanned the surrounding area and the parking lot beyond. She didn't even know if Jack had a car here. It was too dark to see very far. She glanced down the pier, which had security lights overhead all the way down to the end.

She could see the silhouettes of two people in the distance. She wondered if one of them was Jack, and then she saw the overhead light glint off the tip of the pith helmet Jack was wearing. She began to hurry toward the end of the pier and Sully fell into step beside her.

They crossed the weatherworn uneven planks. Lindsey wobbled in her low-heeled boots, and Sully steadied her with a hand on her elbow. From this distance she couldn't make out much about Jack and his companion. She saw him step back and she saw the woman raise her arms. He then crossed his arms over his chest.

"It might be a wild guess here," Sully said. "But it seems that they're having a tiff."

"No, not a wild guess," Lindsey said. "Jack has a long line of angry women trailing after him. I don't think he means to hurt them, and in fact, he's told me that he tells them he isn't the type to stick around, but he's charming and they all think that it will be different with them, that they're the one who makes him want to stay."

"And he never does," Sully surmised.

"His longest relationship was with a beautiful Swedish woman named Anita that he got snowed in with for four months when he was working for a company in Kiruna that wanted to know how to market its hotel made out of ice."

"Seriously?" he asked.

"I don't think he was as snowed in as he led us to believe," Lindsey said with a smile. "But yeah, she was the longest of all his relationships. He still speaks fondly of Sweden and her."

Sully looked bemused, and Lindsey felt the need to clarify the situation on Jack's behalf.

"He's an economist," she said. "He works for a company in Boston and is hired by businesses all over the world to come in and evaluate their current processes and develop a plan to sustainably grow their profit margins. He's taken companies on the brink of disaster and gotten them back into the Forbes top one hundred."

"So he's smart," Sully said.

"About business," Lindsey said. "Relationships? Not so much."

She glanced back at the couple. The woman was wearing a coat, but Lindsey could see her long dark hair streaming on the wind. Even from a distance, Lindsey could tell that she was beautiful. Jack specialized in beautiful women.

"I don't want to embarrass them," she said. She paused about fifty yards away, unsure of whether to continue or not.

She shivered, regretting that she'd left her coat in the café. Sully noticed and quickly put an arm around her, pulling her close. He didn't have his jacket on either.

"Body heat will have to suffice," he said. He didn't sound bummed by this at all.

Lindsey gave him a dubious sideways glance at which he blinked innocently. Since her fingers were freezing into claws around the brim of the hat she still held, she gratefully accepted his warmth and didn't argue the point.

She glanced back at her brother just in time to see the woman slap Jack. Her open palm connected with his face in a hit that cracked like a gunshot. Jack staggered and his pith helmet fell to the ground. All thought of the chill or Sully's delightful warmth vanished and Lindsey was running down the pier as fast as she could.

It was that sibling bond again. She might take issue with Jack and his life choices, but she would not tolerate anyone else doing so, especially in front of her.

The low hum of an engine sounded, and Lindsey wondered at the noise. Still, she was focused on Jack and the woman, who looked angry enough to strike him again.

"Jack, what have you gotten yourself into now?" she muttered as she continued jogging, the cold air feeling like icicle spears in her lungs.

She pounded down the pier with Sully at her side. "What's the plan?"

"Get him away from her," she panted. "Any way we can."

They were halfway there when the humming noise grew louder and Lindsey saw a speedboat approaching the dock at a breakneck pace.

"Isn't that a no wake zone?" she asked.

"Yeah," Sully said. He was frowning, and he poured on the speed to reach the couple.

Lindsey could hear the woman shrieking at Jack. She went to hit him again, and he held up his hands to ward off the blows.

"How dare you betray me?" the woman screeched. Using both hands, she shoved Jack off the pier.

"Ah!" Lindsey shrieked, and the woman turned to look at her. She was just as breathtaking as Lindsey had suspected. She noted that even Sully stumbled when he saw her.

The woman met Lindsey's gaze, and with a malicious smile and a wave, she jumped after Jack. Lindsey sprinted the distance to the end of the pier with Sully right beside her. When they reached the end, the speedboat they'd heard coming in shot out from under the pier.

Jack was lying on the floor while the woman stood over him. Lindsey shouted Jack's name, but there was no way he could hear her over the roar of the engine. Lindsey watched powerlessly as the boat smacked across the top of the water as it headed out into the bay.

She turned her stunned face to Sully. "I think my brother has just been kidnapped."

"Not yet he hasn't," Sully said. He grabbed her hand and they raced over to his office. Sully owned and operated a water taxi and tour boat company that serviced the one hundred–plus Thumb Islands out in the bay.

"I'm on call for the taxi tonight," he said. He took his keys out of his pocket and unlocked the glass door to his office. They hustled through the office and out the back door to the private dock that led to his boats below. The water taxi was bobbing in the water. Lindsey tossed her hat into it then bent down and began to unfasten one of the ropes holding it while Sully undid the other.

She jumped in and Sully pushed off the dock. The boat rocked and Lindsey grabbed the back of one of the seats to steady herself. Sully fired up the engine and shot away from the pier, going faster than she'd ever seen him drive amid the islands. In a matter of seconds, they were giving chase after the speedboat that had taken Jack away.

"Isn't this dangerous?" she cried over the wind that clawed at her hair and clothes.

"More so for them than us," Sully shouted. "I know where the rocks are!"

The speedboat was gaining speed and disappearing around Clover Island, named not for its shape but for the first family to live there. Sully cursed under his breath and yelled, "Hang on!"

He didn't have to tell Lindsey twice. She clutched the back of the seat as he cut the wheel hard to the left. The boat lifted half out of the water with the sharpness of the turn, and Lindsey forced herself to lean against it in an effort to keep them from capsizing.

The spray from the water was icy cold and soaked them both all the way to their bones. Lindsey could feel her teeth chattering, but she couldn't hear the clacking over the roar of the engine, the wind and the waves.

Sully leveled out the boat and gunned the engine. Lindsey realized he was trying to take a shortcut around Clover Island that would allow him to cut off the other boat. As they cleared the far end of the island, the speedboat was just coming around the other side.

The driver saw Sully and panicked. He sped up and turned away from them, narrowly avoiding colliding with a rocky outcropping. Shouts were heard from the speedboat, and wisely, the driver slowed down.

Sully followed them, trying desperately to catch up. The water taxi wasn't built for speed, however, and only Sully's cleverness had kept them in the game this long. He maneuvered around another smaller island, trying to close the distance between them. No luck.

Lindsey's fingers were numb, but still she clung to the seat. She stared doggedly at the speedboat as if she could will its engine to stop or mentally eject her brother from the boat so that they could scoop him up out of the water.

The faster boat steered into a chain of smaller islands. Both boats slowed down, as they had to pick their way between the islands or risk running aground on one of the submerged boulders surrounding them.

"So stupid!" Sully muttered. "Nobody takes a boat through here. It's suicide."

Still, his familiarity with the islands gave him an edge, and Sully was able to almost overtake the faster craft.

They were just ten yards away, and Lindsey could see Jack arguing with the woman, who was gesturing wildly. It was then that Lindsey noted two other men in the craft. They were both large, hulking figures. One drove the boat while the other carried what looked like a high-powered rifle, cradling it across his chest like a baby.

"Sully," Lindsey said.

"Yeah, I see him," he said.

Jack must have said something the woman didn't like because all of a sudden the woman turned and yelled at the man with the rifle. In seconds he had the hilt at his shoulder and the muzzle pointed at Sully and Lindsey.

Jack shouted at the man and was ignored.

"Oh, shit!" Sully cursed. He cut the engine and snapped off the boat's deck lights. Then he grabbed Lindsey by the shoulder and shoved her down on the cold wet floor. "If he pops the boat, we're sunk. Not to mention what will happen if he hits one of us instead."

"But—" Lindsey would have stood back up, but Sully wouldn't let her. "No, stay down."

She could hear Jack shouting over the idling engine of the speedboat. He sounded crazy mad and she was afraid he was going to get himself killed. She couldn't stand it anymore. She shoved away from Sully, who anticipated the move and blocked her, pinning her to the floor with his body.

"Lindsey, you'll get yourself killed," he said.

"He's my brother," she argued. "You'd do the same for your sister Mary."

They stared at each other for a moment. Lindsey could see Sully struggling with the truth of her words.

"All right," he said finally, but he did not look happy about it. "Together but stay low."

In one fluid motion they popped up on their knees and peeked over the water taxi's dashboard to see what was happening.

In the speedboat's floodlights, Lindsey could see the woman and Jack arguing. The driver looked nervous as the woman tried to take the rifle from the other man while she yelled. Apparently, this was too much for the driver because all of a sudden he sped up, obviously determined to keep the woman from getting the rifle and shooting them all.

The woman stumbled at the sudden motion. Jack went to pounce on her but the big man kicked him aside and trained the rifle on him, making it clear he would have no problem shooting him if he attacked. Jack raised his hands in surrender. They were moving faster and faster away.

Lindsey saw Jack glance her way and with his right hand he quickly formed the American Sign Language sign for *I love you*.

"Jack!" she cried. She jumped to her feet, feeling impotent rage flood her. She held up the sign in return, hoping he could see it in the darkness.

Jack had come up with the *I love you* sign when she had been terrified about starting middle school. A year ahead of her, he'd see her in the hall or in a class and send her the sign. It had always made her feel safe and pro-tected. It was a habit they had kept up ever since. When Jack texted her pictures of himself from all over the globe, he always made the *I love you* sign.

"Jack!" She said his name again, but the wind carried

it away. She lowered her arm, feeling her insides twist with the panicked thought that she would never see the sign from him again.

"Damn it!" Sully cried. He punched the dashboard. "He's going too fast and heading straight for the rocks! I can't pursue him or I could get them all killed."

Sully flipped a switch on the dashboard and snatched a radio microphone out of its holder. He clicked the button on the side and his voice was amplified over the water.

"Alter your course, you are headed straight for rocks!" His voice boomed out over the water. The boat ahead slowed and Sully repeated his command.

Lindsey watched as the pilot flipped on a searchlight. Illuminated ahead of the speedboat was an enormous boulder. The pilot swiftly turned to the right, away from the treacherous area. Once he was clear, the boat picked up speed. Sully maneuvered his way through the rocks, while Lindsey watched as the speedboat with her brother aboard disappeared around another island.

The fact that Sully's warning had worked and the driver hadn't smashed into the rock was cold comfort. Lindsey didn't think there was any way they could catch them now, but still, Sully pressed on.

"Who knows?" she asked. "Maybe their boat will break down and they'll need us."

"I just hope they don't shoot us and take our boat," he said.

Lindsey gave him an alarmed look and he frowned. He turned back to the controls, driving the boat faster as he rounded the island. They now had a straight shot out into Long Island Sound, and Sully pushed the water taxi to go as fast as it could.

Lindsey was scanning the water, looking for the speedboat even though she knew it had probably rocketed out of the area and the odds of catching it were slim to none. Frustration made her ball her hands into fists, which was a bad idea, as her frozen fingers exploded with painful prickles.

"We lost them, didn't we?" she asked.

"Maybe," Sully said. Clearly he was not ready to give up. His narrowed gaze searched the darkness.

A light in the distance flickered over the water. Sully headed for it.

"That's not good," he said.

"Why, what is it?" Lindsey asked.

Sully was still for a moment and then he cursed. He pushed the throttle hard and shouted, "Hang on!"

Lindsey grabbed the seatback just as he jerked the wheel in a hard turn. Out of the darkness, a boat the size of a whale, a really big whale, was coming right at them. Just before it neared them, its lights all came on and Lindsey felt her jaw drop. The boat was huge! And on the helm, with the captain, she saw the woman and her brother Jack. He was pressed up against the glass as if he could break through and save her.

Lindsey yelped and clenched her eyes tight. The impact she was waiting for never came. Sully managed to get them out of harm's way and the yacht missed smashing into them by a salty sea air kiss. Its waves smashed against them, drenching them and leaving a large puddle in the bottom of their boat, but they were intact.

When Lindsey unclenched, all of the breath that had stalled in her lungs came out in a whoosh. Sully glanced over his shoulder at her as they continued speeding away from the yacht.

"You didn't think I was going to let them harm my favorite boat, did you?" he asked.

Lindsey gave him a shaky smile.

As the yacht moved out into the big water, Sully slowed their significantly smaller craft down and Lindsey knew what he wasn't saying. There was no way they could catch them now.

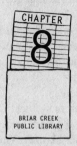

CHAPTER

8

BRIAR CREEK
PUBLIC LIBRARY

He opened his arms to Lindsey, and she did not need encouragement. She dove at him, partly for his warmth and partly for the affirmation that, yes, they were alive and also for comfort. In Sully's arms, she found that she could fight off the fear that she would never see her brother again. With Sully, she felt safe.

She was soaked and shivering and Sully was, too. She didn't think they had enough body heat between them to stave off hypothermia. She wiggled her toes just to see if she could feel them. She could not.

Sully let her go and Lindsey immediately missed the little warmth there had been. He lifted off a seat cushion and opened a hatch. Mixed in with some life jackets were a couple of bags. Sully pulled them out and tossed one to Lindsey.

"I just bought these," he said. "I've been dying to give

them a try. I didn't realize that death would be so imminent when I did."

Lindsey's stiff fingers had a hard time with the drawstring, but she managed to get it open. Fuzzy fleece wrapped itself around her hand and she snatched the blanket out of the bag.

"Warmth!" she cried.

"Oh, it gets better than that," Sully said. He knelt down and foraged on the floor for a moment and then he plugged a hose into her blanket. Warmth from the boat's heater filled her blanket and Lindsey practically purred with how good it felt.

It took her a second to realize that Sully just had a blanket with no heater. She opened her blanket wide, imagining that she looked like a big fleecy bat, and said, "Come on."

Sully didn't hesitate, and she wrapped her arms around his shoulders, trying to cover him with the blanket, too. It felt as if they were in a heated cocoon. Lindsey gave in and rested her head on his shoulder. His hands moved around her back and pulled her close. It took several long minutes but Lindsey finally stopped shivering and so did Sully.

He leaned back to look at her face and said, "I think we're going to live."

She laughed. "Thanks to you. When that yacht appeared out of nowhere, I figured that was it."

They were both quiet for a moment, letting the fact that they had survived sink in. Lindsey became overly aware of the silence, especially as Sully was so close.

She had read about the aftermath of near-death experiences. People tended to react with abandon and have wild, life-affirming sex. She had to admit she could see the appeal. Sully kissed the top of her head and stepped out of the blanket. Or not.

"I think they abandoned their speedboat. I want to find it," he said. He picked up the other blanket and wrapped it around his shoulders while he started up the boat again.

"Do you think it will give us a clue as to who they are?" Lindsey asked.

"If we're lucky, they may have left paperwork or personal effects or maybe even fingerprints behind," Sully said. "We can tow it in and let Emma take a look at it."

He flipped on the searchlight. Lindsey moved in beside him and offered to take the controls so he could sweep the water with the light.

"Just keep it slow and steady," he said. "The current would have pushed it toward shore. If we get lucky, we'll be able to catch it before it smashes into a rock."

Lindsey moved the boat forward at what felt like a doggy paddle. She stared at the water ahead of them, but it seemed to be nothing but unrelenting liquid black. If it weren't for the stars above them and the tiny distant lights onshore, she would have thought they were lost in a shadow.

The heat was still pumping into her blanket, and she was feeling toasty warm. She felt badly that Sully had only a blanket, but he seemed oblivious as he scanned the water, looking for any trace of the abandoned boat.

"Turn to the right a bit," Sully said.

Lindsey turned very slowly, trying to see what he might have seen. And then she saw the white hull reflect the searchlight's glow.

"That's it!" she cried.

"Switch positions," Sully said.

Lindsey took his spot and he took over the controls. The speedboat was riding the low waves in toward the islands. Without bodies for ballast or anyone at the controls, it bobbled like a buoy cut loose and Sully had to maneuver around it, trying to anticipate which direction it would go so that it didn't slam into them.

They were close to the islands now, and several rocky outcroppings jutted out of the water. The empty boat got caught on one and Sully couldn't get close to it for fear of bottoming out his own craft on the rocks.

They watched as the speedboat rode a wave and slid over a pile of rocks, slipping effortlessly away from them as if it had planned its escape route all along.

Sully heaved a sigh. "Looks like we'll have to go around the island and meet it on the other side. I can't risk following it through the rocks."

Lindsey nodded. She'd always had a fear of water over her head, and dark water in particular freaked her out. She didn't like not being able to see what was in the water around her. She had no desire to wreck their boat. Swimming to safety through the dark, cold ocean held zero to no appeal.

"Sounds like a plan," she said.

She braced herself while Sully took over the controls and fired up the engine. They were just picking up speed when a horrific explosion sounded behind them. Sully grabbed Lindsey about the waist and dove for the floor.

He threw his blanket over both of their heads for protection from any debris as they huddled on the cold wet floor.

"Are you all right?" he asked.

"Yeah, I think so," Lindsey answered. Her voice came

out in a croak and she knew it was a combination of shock and fear that had seized hold of her throat. "What was that?"

"I'm not positive," Sully said as he poked his head out from under the blanket, "but I think it was our evidence."

Lindsey shoved the blanket off her head and joined him as he cautiously knelt on the floor, easing his way up. He reached for the controls and cut the engine. They both glanced back over the stern at where they had left the speedboat to wind its way through the rocks.

There was no question. The speedboat was now no more than a floating bonfire.

Lindsey could feel the heat from the flames consuming the boat all the way across the water. If there had been any clue as to who'd taken Jack, it was gone now. As the waves battled with the flames, Lindsey felt her hope for finding her brother evaporate just like the hisses of steam rising from the charred hull of the boat.

"They blew it up so we wouldn't be able to trace them, didn't they?" she asked.

"Among other things," he said.

Lindsey gave Sully a questioning glance.

"That was a timed detonation," he said. "They didn't blow it up when they abandoned it, which means they left it behind, hoping we would do exactly what we did. Go after it in the hopes of finding a clue as to who they are."

"Meaning that we'd either be towing it or be on it when it blew," she said.

"Yeah."

Despite her cocoon of warmth, Lindsey shivered. This proved to her beyond any doubts or hopes she'd been clinging to that whoever had taken Jack meant to do him harm.

"Now what?" she asked.

"Same thing," he said. "We pick up what we can of the boat on the other side of the island, and we go to the police."

Sully didn't wait for her response, but restarted the boat and began to motor around the island. As the smoking hull disappeared from view, she hoped there was enough of the boat left to give them something, anything, that might lead them to Jack.

It was a wet, exhausting and complicated process to catch the remnants of the flaming boat. But after dousing it with an extinguisher Sully had on board and using a long lead of rope with a grappling hook, they managed to haul the boat's sorry carcass into shore.

Lindsey jumped out of the boat and tied it up while Sully shut it down. He then stood on the end of the dock and hauled what was left of the speedboat in. While the bottom was intact enough to float, the top of it was a charred mess and the instrument panel had been blown to bits, making Lindsey think that was where the bomb had been located.

"Lindsey!" a voice cried from the pier above. "Lindsey! Where have you been?"

Beth came running down the stairs to the smaller dock below. She was still wearing her bomber jacket and scarf but had lost the pilot cap and goggles.

"Oh, hey, Beth," she said. She glanced at Sully. How was she supposed to explain this? "Something happened."

"So I gathered when you left two hours ago and never came back for your purse." Beth held up Lindsey's bag as if she were showing her evidence. She then turned to Sully and the rope he still held in his hands. "What is that?"

He tied up their catch as if they had just gone on a fishing trip and caught a whale.

"Long story," Lindsey said.

"My favorite kind," Beth said. She looped her arm through Lindsey's and led her to the stairs. "Come on, you look like someone drowned the steampunk right out of you."

"They did," Lindsey said. She dragged her feet until Sully fell into step behind them.

At the top of the steps, Lindsey was surprised to find the lights on, the office open and Sully's office clerk, Ronnie Maynard, sitting at her desk. At a tick of the clock past eighty years old, she was as spry as a woman half her age. She wore her cranberry red hair in a puff on top of her head and accessorized her look with big, plastic rings and bangles that reminded Lindsey of polyester and macramé.

Mercifully, Ronnie had let the rest of the seventies go and dressed in stylish corduroy gray slacks and a black turtleneck with matching Uggs. Lindsey's frozen toes had serious Ugg envy.

"Ronnie, my darling, what are you doing here this late at night?" Sully asked.

"Drama queen here"—she paused to gesture at Beth—"saw me at the Anchor and asked me to open up the office to see if you were inside," Ronnie said. She was pouring hot cups of coffee from a stand in the corner as if she had fully expected Lindsey and Sully to be stone cold when they arrived.

"Well, they just vanished," Beth said. "One minute they're all owning the dance floor"—she paused to give Lindsey a significant we'll-talk-later look, and then said—"and then they were gone, and when I saw that the boat was gone . . ."

"You panicked," Ronnie said.

"Yeah, that's true," Beth admitted. Then she looked at Lindsey. "I thought Jack would be with you. Did he go somewhere with *her*?"

Lindsey looked at her friend. Subtle, she was not. Beth was fishing to see if Jack had taken off with the woman, and he had. Although not in the way Beth thought, which put Lindsey in the tricky position of trying to figure out how much to say. She didn't want to encourage Beth's crush on Jack, but she didn't want to send her into a panic about him either.

"Well, now that you're all accounted for and seemingly just fine, I'm going to get back to my date," Ronnie said. She was just shrugging on her coat when the phone on her desk rang.

"Who is calling the main line this late?" Sully asked. "I thought the phones were rolled over to my cell for late-night taxi calls."

"They were, but since you didn't answer your cell . . ." Ronnie's voice trailed off and Sully dug his cell phone out of his pocket.

"Battery died," he said.

"Yeah, I figured," Ronnie said. "This had better not be my date canceling. I had him on the hook for a lobster roll."

"He wouldn't dare," Sully said. Which was true. Ronnie was a fearsome woman and Lindsey couldn't imagine anyone canceling on her.

"Thumb Island Tours and Taxi," Ronnie answered the phone. "How may I help you?"

She listened for a moment and then frowned. She held out the phone to Lindsey. "It's for you."

CHAPTER

9

BRIAR CREEK
PUBLIC LIBRARY

"Me?" Lindsey asked as she put her coffee mug down and reached for the phone. She watched Ronnie give them all a little finger wave as she tucked her purse under her arm and trotted out the front door into the night.

"Hello?" Lindsey said into the phone.

"Linds, it's me," Jack said.

"Jack!" she cried. Both Sully and Beth gave her wide-eyed looks. "Are you all right? Where are you? Are those the people who killed the man in my library? Who are th—"

"Linds, I don't have time," he interrupted her. "Are you all right? I saw the explosion and I told them if anything happened to you . . ."

His voice trailed off as if he couldn't even bear to finish the sentence.

"We're fine," she said. "We were far enough away."

Jack made a sound like he'd been holding his breath for a very long time and was finally able to let it go.

Lindsey lowered her voice and asked, "Jack, who were those people? What's happening?"

"You have to let this go, Linds, for me. Don't worry. It's not like I've been taken to Camazotz—" His voice was cut off and a scuffle sounded. Lindsey got the sense the phone had been forcibly taken away from him.

"Jack!" she cried. "Jack!"

"He can't talk to you now," a voice said. It was a woman's voice. Deep and sultry with an exotic accent, the woman sounded nonchalant, as if this sort of thing happened to her every day. "Do not call the police. Do not call anyone."

"Oh, I'm calling the police, the Coast Guard, the FBI, you name it, I am calling them," Lindsey snapped. "I want my brother back—now."

"If you do that"—the woman's voice dropped in tone, sounding suddenly weary—"your brother will die."

"If you hurt him . . ." Lindsey growled through gritted teeth.

"Not me, my husband," the woman said. She paused as if giving Lindsey a second to absorb that. "Your brother and I are lovers. We are on the run from my husband. He is a very jealous man. He has already killed once, as you know, and you saw how he blew up our boat. We were lucky to get away. He will kill us if he finds us. Do you understand?"

Lindsey was speechless. This was like something out of one of her favorite Robert Ludlum novels. This was not real life. How could this be happening? What sort of *married* woman had Jack gotten himself involved with?

"Do you understand?" the woman asked. Her voice was now urgently imploring. "Your brother's life is at stake."

"Yes, yes, I understand," Lindsey said. Although she really didn't, not even a little.

"Good. I know you don't want to do anything that will help my husband find us." The woman hung up.

Lindsey stared at the receiver in her hand. The message was clear. Jack could be killed if she went for help. So there would be no police, Coast Guard or FBI, and she was left with no idea where her brother was or when she might see him again.

"Well?" Beth cried, throwing her hands up in the air. "Obviously, that was Jack. What did he say? What's going on? Who was that woman?"

Lindsey looked from Beth to Sully and back. What could she say? Could she say anything? The woman on the phone hadn't said she couldn't tell her friends. That seemed like a technicality, but still.

She slowly replaced the receiver, giving herself a second to think. She didn't want to put Beth in jeopardy by telling her about Jack being kidnapped. Then again, Beth had already seen the woman at the Anchor, and Lindsey didn't want Beth to stumble into something she shouldn't by not knowing what was going on. *Gah!* This was impossible. She decided to go with her gut.

"Jack was kidnapped," she said. Whether he and the woman were lovers or not, the woman had taken him forcibly, and as far as Lindsey was concerned, that was kidnapping.

Beth gasped but Sully didn't even flicker an eyelash,

which told her more than words that he had suspected as much. It also told her that he had expected her to let Beth into the loop and that he would have done the same, which made her feel better about her choice.

"But he was just here, and he went with that woman. Oh, is she the kidnapper?" Beth asked. "What does she want? Is she a stalker?"

"I don't know," Lindsey said. The fight went out of her, and she slid into a nearby padded chair, feeling as if she could not be upright for one more second.

Beth took the seat opposite her while Sully retrieved her coffee cup and handed it to her before taking the seat beside her.

"What did she say exactly?" Sully asked.

Lindsey glanced at him. How did he know she'd spoken to the woman?

"When you yelled, I figured she took the phone from Jack once he knew you were safe," he explained. "Probably he was refusing to cooperate until he knew you weren't hurt in the explosion."

"Explosion?" Beth cried. "Is that why you brought that charred wreck in? It exploded?"

"We were hoping to turn it over to the police," Lindsey said. "That can't happen now."

Sully nodded as if he expected as much. Beth shoved her hands into her short spiky black hair as if yanking on her follicles would make all of this clearer.

"Explain," she ordered. She let go of her hair. "From the very beginning."

Lindsey glanced at Sully. Even he didn't know the very beginning—that Jack had been at the library before the dead guy showed up. Oh, well, there was no turning back now.

She took a long sip from her coffee and started at the very beginning with finding Jack in the crafternoon room and cataloged the day's events all the way through to the phone call. No one said anything when she was finished. She didn't know if she'd offended them by not telling them about her first contact with Jack or if they were just dazed by the info dump she had unloaded onto them.

"Jack's in big trouble, isn't he?" Beth asked.

"I'm afraid so," Lindsey said.

"We have to help him," Beth said.

"We can't go to the police," Lindsey said. Sully looked like he was going to protest, but she cut him off. "I won't put him at risk."

"Noted," Sully said. "What I was going to suggest was that we hire an independent outfit to check out the wreckage, maybe an investigator with an insurance agency. They wouldn't be 'the authorities,' but they might be able to give us a lead."

"That's brilliant," Lindsey said. Sully gave her a small smile, and she was suddenly very glad she had told them everything. She would have hated to try to figure this out alone.

"I'll call some of my old Navy contacts and see what they suggest," he said.

"What should we do in the meantime?" Beth asked.

"Nothing," Sully said. "If what this woman says is true and her husband killed the man in the library, then we want to make sure we stay off of his radar, especially you, Lindsey. If this jealous husband figures out that Jack is your brother, you could be his next target."

Lindsey nodded. She couldn't help but glance at the windows, wondering if someone was watching them even now.

Sully walked them back to the café, where they loaded up their bikes into the back of his truck and he drove them home. He dropped off Beth first, helping her unload her bike and waiting until she was safely inside before leaving.

Lindsey noted the cat tree in her large bay window was fully loaded with her three felines, Skippyjon Jones, Slinky Malinky and Pete the Cat, all named for Beth's favorite picture book cats. After Pete arrived a few months ago, Beth had made Lindsey promise not to let her acquire any more cats for fear that she would become a spinster cat lady, but as Lindsey pointed out, there were plenty of men who adored cats and she would be just fine. But after watching Beth practically swoon at Jack's feet, Lindsey was rethinking. The girl needed to get a boyfriend stat.

"We need to hook Beth up with a date," she said when Sully got back into the cab of the truck.

He gave her a sidelong glance. "I might know someone," he said.

"Really?" she asked. "Who?"

"He's a charming British bloke, new to the area," he said. "The ladies all love him or so I hear."

She smiled. "Don't tell me, let me guess, Robbie Vine?"

"You have to admit they'd make a cute couple," he said. "Of course, it would help if he wasn't besotted with you."

"I wouldn't say he's besotted," Lindsey said.

"Oh, yeah, he is," Sully said. He turned onto the road

that led to Lindsey's third-floor apartment. "Otherwise why would he stick around here?"

"Because it's his son's senior year of high school and he's missed so much of Dylan's life already," she said.

"*Hmm*," Sully hummed, which Lindsey figured was his less rude version of *whatever*.

Sully wheeled her bike into the garage, and Lindsey followed him, closing the side door after him. Together they walked to the house. During the time they'd spent in Sully's office, their clothes and hair had dried out, but Lindsey doubted she'd ever truly feel warm again.

It was too bad she and Sully weren't still dating. He made the best hot chocolate in the world, and on a night like tonight, she could really use a mug or four.

The front door opened as soon as they stepped onto the porch, and a black ball of fur charged at top speed right for them. Heathcliff, Lindsey's rescued puppy who was now almost full grown, stood on his hind legs while he wrapped his front paws about her knee. Lindsey knelt down and scratched his head and sides while he wiggled and waggled. No one was ever as delighted to see her as Heathcliff. She felt her heart pinch at the thought that Jack would have loved her furry baby and Heathcliff would have adored Jack.

"He has been squirrelly all night," Nancy Peyton said as she followed Heathcliff out the open door. "About two hours ago, he just started barking and pacing and then he calmed down, but then he got so excited about ten minutes ago. I swear he can tell when you're almost home."

"That's because he's the best dog ever," Lindsey said.

She straightened up and Heathcliff ran over to Sully to give him the same effusive greeting.

"How are you, boy?" Sully asked, squatting down and giving him the same rubdown Lindsey had.

Lindsey had no doubt that Heathcliff was overjoyed to see his buddy.

"So how did Beth's steampunk shindig go?" Nancy asked. "I know Charlie was looking forward to having a built-in crowd for his gig. Did the band sound all right?"

Sully and Lindsey exchanged a look. She was not about to put her landlord in jeopardy by telling her about Jack. Sully gave her an imperceptible nod, letting her know that he was thinking the same.

"The band sounded great," Lindsey said, which was true. "Charlie sure does own a stage."

Nancy beamed with pride. "Well, don't stand out here, you two, I just finished my famous fruit cake cookies, and I have all the fixings for Sully's hot chocolate if he's willing?"

Nancy's sparkling blue eyes twinkled at Sully, and Lindsey got the feeling that Nancy had been quite the looker in her day. Despite the gray hair and preference for sweat suits, she still knew how to flirt, and Lindsey had yet to see a man resist her wiles.

"I'm game if you are," he said.

Lindsey nodded. She had no desire to be alone in her apartment, where she'd undoubtedly just brood about her brother all night. Nancy had a fire going in the fireplace, and Lindsey sat down on the hearth and let the heat pour into her. Sully and Nancy disappeared into the kitchen while Heathcliff stretched out on the floor, propping his head on her feet.

She absently stroked his fur while she wondered where Jack was right now. Was he warm? Was he safe? She felt her throat get tight and her eyes burned as she tried to push down the question that bobbed to the surface like an apple in a water barrel: Would she ever see him again?

CHAPTER

10

BRIAR CREEK
PUBLIC LIBRARY

Lindsey did not sleep that night. Not a big surprise, she supposed. It seemed like every memory she'd ever had of Jack converged in her head in a cheesy montage just to torture her. She remembered him helping her learn to ride a bike and beating up a bully who was picking on her. He'd gotten a fat lip for his effort, but as he told their parents with the beginnings of his future swagger, "You should see the other guy."

She remembered him showing her the shortcut through the woods that led to a convenience store on the main road where they emptied their piggy banks on candy and made themselves sick. Together they discovered the best climbing trees, made the best skateboard ramp, and when they were older, he taught her how to drive a stick shift by parking the car at the bottom of a hill and making her drive up it.

Jack was a free spirit, the last of the rogues, with a brilliant brain for business and a weakness for the ladies. He'd knocked around the globe, circling it at least six times, and always coming home with exotic tales and strange gifts.

Lindsey rested on her side, looking at the enamel lotus charm that hung on the wall beside her bed. Jack had sent it to her from Tibet right after she had moved to Briar Creek to start her life anew. It was supposed to symbolize good fortune, like the lotus flower, which rises out of the mud to bloom, he had explained in his note. She thought about her life in Briar Creek. She didn't know if the enamel lotus blossom was responsible, but she had definitely found happiness here in her new life.

Heathcliff let out a yawn from his blanket at the foot of the bed. She nudged him with her foot, and he grumbled under his breath even as he rolled over so she could rub his belly. Heathcliff preferred to sleep in on chilly mornings and frequently stayed in bed while she went and made her coffee. Usually, only the sound of the front door opening, which signaled outside time, got him moving.

"You are a slug," Lindsey said as she pushed back her covers and shoved her feet into her slippers.

Heathcliff growled something unintelligible, and Lindsey suspected it was a good thing he couldn't talk. She had a feeling she didn't want to hear what he had to say, especially as she suspected that he could be a bit of a sassy pants.

Once the morning routine was finished, which included a long walk for Heathcliff, Lindsey tried to muster the energy to get ready for work. Today was her day to go in a bit later, as she would close the library in the evening.

She glanced out her living room window to try and get

an idea of what to wear. She noted it was another flannel day outside. She always thought of gray days as flannel days partly because she wanted to burrow in her flannel jammies and not go out and partly because it looked like a big sheet of gray flannel was blanketing her world.

Her third-story apartment overlooked the bay, and she could see the outline of the islands dotting the land-scape, or rather the waterscape, all the way to the horizon. There was no sign of a big yacht, however, which depressed her to no end.

For the millionth time, she wondered where Jack was, whether he was safe, and how he had gotten involved with a married woman with a psychotic husband. She was just turning to freshen her coffee when her cell phone rang. She snatched it off the table where it sat in its charger.

The display showed a library number. She frowned. Not Jack then.

"Hello?" she answered.

"Lindsey," Beth said. "You have to get down here right now."

"Why? What's happening?" Lindsey asked.

"Detective Trimble is here and he's asking for you," she said. She sounded like she was whispering.

Lindsey wasn't surprised. Beth had gotten up close and personal with the state investigator, and Lindsey was pretty sure she had some emotional scars from the encounter.

"What does he want?" Lindsey asked. "Did he say?"

"No, and I didn't ask. In fact, as soon as he came in, I hid under my desk. That's where I'm calling you from," Beth said.

"Wait, you're under your desk?" Lindsey asked.

"It seemed best," Beth said. "Ann Marie is chatting

with him at the circulation desk. She's using her best dimples and everything."

"Good plan," Lindsey said.

Ann Marie, their part-time clerk, was the mother of two precocious young boys who were notorious in Briar Creek for their shenanigans, like the time they decided to have a snack at their old preschool in the Lutheran church, disregarding the fact that the church was closed and the kitchen locked up.

The church alarm could be heard throughout the small town, and Ann Marie had left the library at a run, knowing as only a mother does that her two were somehow responsible. She found them sitting in the church kitchen munching on animal crackers. They'd had to make a formal apology to the pastor and do a week of chores around the preschool in repentance. Needless to say, Ann Marie had been using her dimples to charm irate neighbors, teachers and law enforcement officials since the boys had been born.

"Tell Ann Marie to tell him I'll be right there," Lindsey said. "And please don't mention *anything* else."

"Got it," Beth said. "You don't have to worry about me. My lips are sealed with superglue, no, Gorilla Glue. You can't pry that stuff loose even with a banana, I tell you."

"Uh-huh." Lindsey hung up and flew into her bedroom as if she'd been shot out of a canon.

"Detective Trimble," Lindsey said as she extended her hand in greeting to the man in the sharp navy suit. "Good to see you again."

"You, too, Ms. Norris," he said. His grip was firm and warm. "I wish it was under a better circumstance."

"Me, too," she said. "How can I help you?"

"Chief Plewicki called us in to help investigate her John Doe," he said. "Since her resources are limited, she was hoping the state police might give her a few more avenues of inquiry and identification."

Lindsey nodded as if this all made sense, which it did except that she was concerned that her brother was connected to this mess and that the police might already know this and be looking for him as well.

Detective Trimble pushed the gold-rimmed glasses up on his nose and studied her. He hadn't changed much since she'd met him a year and a half ago. He still had the same precisely cut short black hair, same glasses and impeccable suit and the same intelligent gaze. Just as before, she felt as if he knew more than he was saying. It was very unnerving.

"So I'm assuming you want to reinterview me and see the scene of the crime?" she asked. She was pleased that she sounded so matter of fact.

"If it's no trouble," he said.

"None at all," Lindsey assured him. Meanwhile in her head, she kept saying, *Just the facts*. Surely, she couldn't blow it if she kept to the facts.

"If you'll follow me," she said.

She led him down the hallway to the cordoned-off room. The door had been kept locked to keep away the curious. Lindsey opened the door and they both stepped under the yellow crime scene tape and into the room.

"Now what happened the day that you found the body?" Trimble asked.

Lindsey told him the same information she'd given Chief Plewicki. She had a spasm of guilt for omitting the part about finding Jack, but she couldn't risk it. Not knowing whom Jack was running from, she didn't feel like she could mention him at all and risk drawing attention to him, which, according to the strange woman who had taken him, might get him killed.

Trimble asked many of the same questions that Emma had asked. He walked around the room while he listened to her answers. He clarified points about how the body had been positioned when it was found and about the open window.

Lindsey tried to look like she thought she would if she didn't know anything else. It was hard to make her features blank, however, when she knew more than she was telling and she'd gotten no sleep last night.

When Trimble finally seemed satisfied with the information, she turned to go. Relief welled up inside her, and she felt like she was stepping off the hangman's platform in a stay of execution granted just in the nick of time.

"Oh, there's one more thing, Lindsey," Trimble said. "One thing that doesn't make sense to me."

"Yes?" Lindsey felt a prickle of unease tingle the back of her neck.

"You said that it was too cold in here to have your craft club meeting—"

"Crafternoon," she corrected him. She didn't mean to be picky but a crafternoon was a book discussion, a craft and a shared meal, which made it so much more than a craft meeting.

"Pardon me," he said, "crafternoon meeting." He said the words as if trying them out. He lifted his eyebrows as

86

if it wasn't so bad and then he continued, "So why would the window be open?"

"Beg pardon?" Lindsey asked as her heart knocked around in her chest, probably trying to dodge the surge of panic that was rocketing through her and would undoubtedly cause her heart to seize up in a paralyzed knot of anxiety.

"Why was the window open?" he asked. "It seems to me if you'd found the room too cold earlier, you would have shut and latched it, correct?"

Lindsey didn't know what to say. Was this it? Was the open window like the single hair or clothing fiber found on a murdered corpse that identifies the killer? Her throat went dry. She mentally begged for a rescue, in any form, even if it was Ms. Cole arriving to chew her out for something ridiculous.

She glanced at the door. Trimble raised his eyebrows as if he knew she was considering a run for it.

"Uh . . . well . . . I don't remem—" she began when a male's voice, an unhappy male's voice, interrupted her.

"What's this I hear about you and that salty dog dancing at the Blue Anchor last night?" Robbie Vine asked as he ducked under the crime scene tape and stepped into the room. "I thought we had an agreement."

CHAPTER

11

BRIAR CREEK
PUBLIC LIBRARY

Lindsey was so relieved to see Robbie that she opened her arms wide and dashed across the room to hug him tight.

"Oh, Robbie, it's so good to see you," she said. "Have you met Detective Trimble from the state police? He's investigating our John Doe."

Robbie gave her a curious glance, and Lindsey knew he was sensing her panic. Being the consummate actor that he was and a genius at improvisation, he picked up on her cue without a misstep.

"Nasty business that," he said. He extended his hand to Trimble for a handshake and Lindsey glanced at the detective, who looked like he'd just been slapped upside the head.

"You . . . you're . . . I'm a huge fan, Mr. Vine," he said. He took Robbie's hand and pumped it furiously, looking more like a kid than Lindsey could ever have imagined.

"Oh, well, thank you," Robbie said. He was charmingly humble, and Lindsey could tell he was pleased by the worship.

"That *Detective Inspector* series you did on *Masterpiece Theater*, it was genius, pure genius," Trimble gushed.

Lindsey looked at Robbie, who was frowning in thought. He was rocking back and forth on his feet, a habit Lindsey had noticed that he employed whenever he was mulling over a character or how he wanted to deliver his lines.

"Do you really think so?" Robbie asked. "I had a devil of a time trying to get inside that character's head. D.I. Gordon was quite challenging."

"Oh, you nailed it," Trimble said. "I especially loved the part where you, er, Gordon took down that murderer when he was escaping through the London underground."

"Mind the gap," Robbie quipped with a wink.

"You really brought the complexity of the policeman's life into the part you played," Trimble said. "It's rare that an actor can capture the true essence of what it is to work in law enforcement."

"You don't say," Robbie said. He threw an arm around Trimble's shoulders and the two of them began to walk out of the room together. "I was afraid I was underplaying it, but it seemed to me that a detective is a thinker and needs to keep his emotions tightly in check."

"Exactly!" Trimble said.

They disappeared out the door and Lindsey followed in bemusement. She would have to thank Robbie later for his spectacular timing. She ducked under the crime scene tape and locked the door behind them.

She thought about asking Trimble if there was anything else he required, but he was so animated in his conversation with Robbie that she hated to interrupt. Really, she did, so she watched as they walked right out of the library, chatting as if they were long-lost friends.

"Robbie to the rescue?" Beth asked as she joined Lindsey by the window that overlooked Main Street, the small town park and the bay beyond.

"And how," Lindsey said. "Apparently, Trimble is a huge fan and the two of them caught on like a house on fire."

"I'm glad," Beth said. "Robbie was none too pleased when he arrived, muttering something about you and that waterlogged wanker dancing the night away at the Anchor."

Lindsey burst out laughing. She could just see Sully's face if he heard what Robbie had called him.

"Well, I don't suppose I can deny it, given that the rumor is a good cover for what Sully and I were really doing," Lindsey said.

"And what, pray tell, would that be?"

"Yip!" Lindsey yelped and jumped, spinning around to find Robbie standing behind her with his arms crossed over his chest and a glower on his face.

"Outta here," Beth said. She scurried off but not before Lindsey caught her smiling. Some friend.

"It's not what you think," Lindsey said.

"Really?" Robbie asked. "Now whatever would I be thinking? Last I heard, you had issues with me being married and issues with sailor boy being too quick to cut you loose, so you were refusing to date either of us. And yet I hear you were dancing with the dodgy blighter. Explain yourself."

"Did you know your accent gets thicker when you're irritated?" Lindsey asked.

Robbie took a step forward, and she took a step back. He took another step forward, and she turned sideways and slipped her hand through his arm.

"Did I thank you yet for saving me from the inquisition?" she asked.

"No," he said. "And just what was that all about? What does the detective with the most excellent taste in television dramas want with you?"

"You're not going to be derailed, are you?" Lindsey asked.

"Not even a little," he said.

"He was reviewing the events of the morning prior to finding the body," she said. "No big deal."

"Then why were you lying to him?" Robbie said.

"I wasn't lying," Lindsey protested.

"Oh, love, I'm a student of human behavior and mannerisms," he said. "I know your tell."

"What?" Lindsey gasped. "I don't have a tell."

"Your nose crinkles right here when you're less than truthful," he said. Lindsey gave him a dubious look and he said, "It's true, when you fib, you look like you smell something bad but you're trying not to let anyone know."

"It's true, you do," Ms. Cole said from behind the circulation desk.

Lindsey looked at her and then fingered the bridge of her nose. Was she really that bad of a liar? Would Detective Trimble have noticed?

"No, only people who know you very well would be able to recognize it," Robbie said as if reading her mind.

"I didn't lie," she protested. Then when she noticed

Ms. Cole was leaning closer in an attempt to hear better, she hissed, "Not on purpose anyway."

Robbie just looked at her as if he had all the time in the world. "You may as well tell me what is going on, because I'm just going to keep asking until you give in. In case you haven't noticed, I am nothing if not tenacious."

Lindsey rolled her eyes. He would badger her and bug her and pester her until she gave in or pleaded for mercy. She had no doubt of it.

"Come on, I'll make you some tea and explain." She turned and raised her voice so that the lemon, a not nice but very appropriate nickname for Ms. Cole, could hear her as well when she said, "And we can discuss that new play you're auditioning actors for next week."

Robbie tsked as he followed her into the back room. "You're trying to throw off Ms. Cole by distracting her with more theater opportunities."

"Maybe." Lindsey shrugged.

"Ha, there it is again!" he cried. He tapped his nose and then pointed to her.

Lindsey pursed her lips. She was obviously going to have to practice fibbing in the mirror. She led the way to her office. She had taken to keeping a kettle and a tin of loose leaf tea around for when Robbie popped in, which seemed to be quite regularly. She told herself it was just because his son, Dylan, worked in the library, shelving books, but she suspected there was more to it than that.

She and Robbie had become friends, good friends, during the production of *A Midsummer Night's Dream*. Robbie had made it pretty clear that he liked her, but as he had mentioned, one of her many issues with him was the fact that he was married.

She thought about Kitty, his wife, while she filled the electric kettle from the water cooler outside her office. Yes, his marriage was in name only, but still, Lindsey was not about to get involved with someone whose personal life was a train wreck. Friendship was the best she had to offer, so he could take it or leave it. And since that was the case, he really had no say about her dance partners.

She reentered her office and plugged in the kettle to find Robbie lounging in one of her visitor's chairs with his feet up on the other vacant chair while thumbing through the latest celebrity rag to which the library subscribed.

He looked awfully at home in here, and she cringed at the thought of what Mayor Henson would think if he found him here. Of course, Mayor Henson loved having Robbie as a resident of their little coastal community. He'd probably encourage him to put in his own desk if he so chose. Lindsey frowned. Maybe it was time to establish some new boundaries in their friendship. She was winding up to tell him just that when her phone rang.

"Lindsey Norris, Briar Creek Library, may I help you?" she answered.

Robbie wagged his eyebrows at her over the top of his magazine as if to tell her that he found her phone manners attractive. Lindsey turned her back to him.

"I certainly hope so, Ms. Norris." It was a man's voice, one that she didn't recognize. He had a lilting accent that made his low voice sound exotic.

She could tell by the sharp tone that he was not a happy customer. She flitted through the reasons that she usually fielded calls from the cranky. He had an overdue fine that he felt was unfair. He lost a book, movie, what have you, and wanted to argue why it wasn't his fault.

He wanted them to buy an obscure and undoubtedly expensive book, movie, magazine subscription that only he was interested in. He didn't like that they had time limits on the Internet computers. He didn't like their hours. He felt someone had been rude to him by not letting him in the building after they were closed.

Really, when a patron was cranky, it could be a myriad of issues. Of course, it could also be a justified complaint such as Ms. Cole being overzealous in her shushing or he was fined for a book that he had actually returned, both of which had been known to happen.

"I'll certainly do my best," Lindsey said. "What is it that you need?"

"Your brother," he said.

CHAPTER

12

BRIAR CREEK
PUBLIC LIBRARY

Lindsey went utterly still. The only sensation of movement in her entire body was from her heart doing a free-falling plummet into her feet like a rock into the sea.

"Excuse me, I'm not sure I understand," she said. She must have misunderstood him. "What was your name again?"

Something in her tone must have alerted Robbie to her distress because he was on his feet and standing beside her before she blinked.

"I don't believe my name is relevant," the man said. "However, your brother's whereabouts are."

"If you're asking for my brother, then, yes, your name is most definitely required," Lindsey said. "Privacy issues being what they are and all."

Robbie nudged his head in beside hers so he could listen in on the call. Lindsey would have shoved him away, but she didn't want to miss a word the man said, and it was reassuring to have someone witness to the call.

"Your brother is in grave danger," the man said. "I know he came to see you."

He waited, and Lindsey realized he expected her to say something.

"I have no idea what you're talking about." It sounded lame even to her, but she didn't know what else to say. She had no doubt her nose was crinkling.

The man made an impatient noise, and she could hear him cover the receiver and talk to someone else. Maybe it was the beautiful woman's husband, and he was sending his goons after them even as they spoke.

"It is imperative that I talk to Jack," the man said. "His life is in danger."

"From you?" Lindsey asked. "Are you the one who is hunting him?"

"No, you misunderstand—" the man said.

"I don't think I do," Lindsey said. "I don't know where my brother is, and even if I did, I would never tell a man who won't even give me his name."

"It would put *you* in danger if I was to tell you," the man said.

"Really?" she asked. "Or would it give a killer a name?"

"I am not a killer," he protested. "I am a friend."

"Without a name?" Lindsey asked. "I don't think so."

Lindsey refused to feel guilty for being harsh when for all she knew this was the strange woman's husband who was looking for Jack and would like to kill him for having a fling with his wife.

"I wish I could tell you more," the man said. He sounded sincere but Lindsey was pretty sure all bad guys mastered that at a young age. She bet this man, whoever he was, could lie without a tell.

"I'm sure you do," she said. She couldn't mask the sarcasm in her voice.

The man's voice grew intense. "Listen, I have to go, but I'll be in touch."

The man hung up and a chill scurried down Lindsey's spine like a runaway spider.

"Bloody hell!" Robbie swore. "What the devil was that about?"

The kettle in the corner began to whistle, and Lindsey hung up the phone and unplugged the kettle. She poured the boiling water into the teapot, which already held the stainless steel infuser full of tea. She covered the pot and let it steep.

She could feel Robbie staring at her, but she didn't know how much he had heard and she didn't know what to say about the surreal conversation. She found herself looking anywhere but at him.

"Sit," he barked, and Lindsey did.

She was ridiculously glad to have someone tell her what to do because honestly she was kind of freaking out.

"Look at me," Robbie ordered. "Lindsey, eyes up here."

Lindsey forced her gaze up to his. He had the piercing sharp glance of the born observer. She found she could maintain contact for only a brief moment before her gaze shot off in another direction.

"Just as I suspected," he said.

"What?" she asked.

"You're hiding something, something huge," he said. "Now spill it."

"I'm not hiding anything," she protested. "Do you think the tea is ready?"

"No." He stared at her with one eye narrowed as if they were in a chess match and he was trying to determine his next move. "Why was that man asking about your brother? Who was he? What does he want with you?"

"No idea," Lindsey said. She couldn't help but feel her nose. Crinkled. Damn it.

Robbie stared at her without blinking. It was quite unnerving.

"All right, maybe my brother showed up here yesterday right before the body was found in the library, and maybe my brother was kidnapped by a beautiful woman last night," she said.

"What?" Robbie squawked. "That's huge! And you didn't tell me? I have to tell you, Lindsey, I'm hurt. Really hurt."

"It wasn't my story to tell," she said. "My brother showed up out of the blue. He said he needed a place to hide out, so I gave him the craft room. When I went back to check on him later, the window was open, Jack was gone and there was a dead man on the floor. What was I supposed to do?"

"Confide in your boyfriend," Robbie said.

"You're not my boyfriend," Lindsey argued.

"Did you tell that manky mariner all of this?" he demanded.

"No," she said. "At least not until Jack was snatched from the Blue Anchor last night and we set off after him in Sully's boat."

"Oy, so he got to play hero, did he? Driving you all

over the bay in his boat?" Robbie asked. He looked quite put out.

"It was actually cold and wet and we were damn near blown up," she said. Robbie's inability to focus on the bigger problem was beginning to annoy her.

"Blown up?" he asked. "All right, that's it. I demand to know everything that happened from the very beginning and none of this dodgy hole-ridden storytelling either. I want the tale in its entirety."

Lindsey glanced at the teapot, and Robbie shook his head. There would be no evading him with menial tasks. "The beginning," he repeated and set about pouring their tea himself.

With no choice left, Lindsey told him about the events of the day, starting with finding Jack in the library and ending with the phone call that he had just overheard. Robbie sipped his tea in thoughtful silence while he listened.

"You and the scalawag are damn lucky you didn't get blown to smithereens," he said at the end. "Just wait until I see him. I have a few things to get off my chest. What was he thinking going after the abandoned boat?"

"That it would give us a lead as to who took Jack," she said.

"Don't muddy the argument with logic," Robbie said. "You're lucky you survived."

Lindsey nodded. She took a deep drink from her mug and let the tea's soothing warmth heat her up from the inside out.

She glanced at Robbie and said, "I don't know what to do. Emma isn't just the chief of police, she's my friend and I know she'd want to know about this, but Jack's my brother and telling the police could get him killed."

"Very true," Robbie said. "You really have no idea who you're dealing with and that's always a dicey proposition."

"And that man on the phone, I don't know who he is or what he wants, but he sounded like he knew a lot more than I did," she said.

"Not that much," Robbie disagreed.

"What do you mean?"

"Think about it—the mere fact that he called you means he's fishing for information," Robbie said. "If he is the jealous husband, he doesn't know where they are; otherwise why call you?"

"So Jack might be safe," Lindsey said.

"For now," Robbie agreed.

A knock sounded on the door. It was Violet and Nancy. They took in the scene at a glance and Violet gave Lindsey a broad grin while Nancy frowned. The two women were best friends, but when it came to Lindsey's love life, they had differing viewpoints on with whom Lindsey should be spending her time.

Violet, being one of Robbie's oldest friends, naturally wanted things to progress between Lindsey and Robbie. Lindsey knew it was more because Violet hoped Lindsey would give Robbie a reason to stay in Briar Creek than it was because she felt they were suited to each other.

Lindsey frequently argued the point that Robbie had a trail of broken hearts a mile wide behind him, and she had no intention of being one of those hearts. And yeah, he was still married, and whether it was in name only or not, Lindsey didn't see herself taking up with a married man. The mere thought of trying to explain that to Jack or her parents was extremely unpleasant.

As for Nancy, she was firmly on Team Sully. This was not a big surprise either, given that Sully was a native "Creeker" just like Nancy, and to cap it off, he was a boat captain just like her late husband. It had been clear from the day Lindsey had seen Sully and Nancy together that they shared a bond. Sully had worshiped Nancy's late husband, Captain Peyton, and Lindsey knew that in many ways Sully kept Jake's memory fresh for Nancy, especially when he talked in his sailor's jargon.

"Oh, you're busy," Violet said. "Well, we won't interrupt."

"I'm sure we're not interrupting," Nancy said, pushing her way around Violet. "We just wanted to see how you were doing."

"I'm fine," Lindsey lied. "But thanks for checking up on me."

She wasn't up to an inquisition today, but judging by the lack of movement on the two ladies' part, they weren't taking the hint to skedaddle.

"So this is cozy," Nancy said. She glanced from Robbie to Lindsey. "I didn't realize you'd taken to having afternoon tea."

"She hasn't," Robbie said. "Not properly. We really need some scones, don't you think, Violet?"

"With clotted cream and marmalade," she agreed with a sigh. "Do you remember when we were treading the boards at the Prince Edward Theatre in London and then we'd dash over to the Soho Hotel for afternoon tea?"

"How could I forget?" Robbie grinned at her. "I think we gave the best performances of our lives so that the show would be extended for a longer season so we didn't have to give up our high tea." He turned to Lindsey. "You have to come to London with me on my next trip. I'll take you to the best tea in town."

He gave Lindsey his most charming grin, and she noticed that Nancy was scowling at him.

"Is it true that you and Sully were dancing at the Anchor last night?" Nancy asked.

Now Robbie frowned and Nancy looked sly. Lindsey had no doubt that this was the real reason for Violet and Nancy's visit. To confirm the rumor that was no doubt spreading through their town with the speed and destruction of a wildfire.

"Yes, I was," Lindsey said. She saw Violet stiffen and Nancy looked vanquished, which Robbie managed to squash.

"Only because he cut in, or so I'm told," Robbie said. "Rather clumsy of him if you ask me."

"No one asked you," Nancy snapped.

"Hey, now, I might have asked," Violet said.

Seeing that this was going nowhere pleasant, Lindsey decided to end the conversation posthaste.

"As much as I'd love to continue this charming chat," she said, giving them a look that told them she was finding it anything but, "I really have to get back to work."

"Of course," Violet said. She hooked her arm through Nancy's. "We were just passing through. I have a book on hold and Nancy's supposed to be picking up a movie for us tonight. A comedy."

"Action adventure," Nancy said, allowing herself to be dragged from the room.

"Fine but it better be funny," Violet said.

The door closed behind them with a snap. Then it opened again with Nancy giving Lindsey a look like a disapproving chaperone before she disappeared.

"And I thought the paparazzi were a bunch of nosey parkers," Robbie said. "Small town living is, well, small, isn't it?"

"Quite," Lindsey agreed.

She gathered their mugs and the teapot to rinse out in the break room. Robbie took the teapot from her hands and followed her out of her office. In the break room, he happily dried while she rinsed.

"I know I don't have to say it, but . . ." Her voice trailed off.

"You're welcome," he said.

Lindsey laughed. "I was going to tell you not to tell anyone about our conversation. But just to clarify, what exactly would I be thanking you for?"

"For taking your mind off of your troubles—it's a specialty of mine," he said with a wink as he draped the dish towel over his shoulder.

"Oh, is that so?" she asked. She couldn't help but notice how handsome Robbie was. He had a certain energy about him that was almost palpable, and his reddish blond hair, green eyes and muscular build were not so easily ignored either.

"Yes, but also, for giving you my insight into the fact that I really do think your brother is okay."

"For now," Lindsey said.

They were standing side by side, and Lindsey felt the urge to lean into him for comfort coming on a bit too strong, so she made herself back up a step. Robbie grinned at her, letting her know he'd noticed.

"What's your next move?" he asked.

Lindsey gathered the teapot and mugs to return to their shelf in her office. Again, Robbie took the teapot out of her hands and fell into step beside her.

"Well, it appears I have no choice," she said. She arranged the delicate pot and matching cups on the shelf. When she was satisfied, she turned to face him. "I think it's time I called my parents."

CHAPTER

13

BRIAR CREEK
PUBLIC LIBRARY

Lindsey had not expected that statement to act like rocket fuel on Robbie, but the man fled the building so fast she was pretty sure he was shooting sparks out his behind. So the mention of parentals caused the Englishman to flee the scene as if it were a crime and he was holding a bloody dagger. Good to know.

She found her cell phone in her purse and closed her office door while she called her father's office. Both of her parents were professors at a small college in New Hampshire.

Big thinkers on the subjects of literature, they spent their days teaching their students how to do the same. They were devoted professors who had carved out a comfortable life together in the academic town they had lived in since her dad had gotten his first teaching job there. Lindsey's mother had joined him as a professor as soon as Lindsey and Jack were of school age. Lindsey had no doubt that they would teach right up until they drew their last breaths.

"How do, pumpkin?" John Norris answered the phone in his usual jovial way.

"Hi, Dad, what's the good word?" she asked. They started every conversation in the exact same manner, since one of her father's most favorite classes to teach was etymology, the study of words, specifically, their history and change in usage over time.

"I don't know that it's a good word," he said. "But it's a doozy of a mystery. Are you ready?"

"As I'll ever be," she said.

"Would you call that young rascal of yours a dog or a hound?" her father asked.

Lindsey considered before answering, "Well, in common vernacular, he would be a dog."

"Ah, yes, but there is our mystery," her father said. She could practically hear him rubbing his hands together. "According to the *OED*, the word *dog* has no reference prior to a specific breed reference in 1050, which was *dogca*. Then it appears to replace the already well-used *hund*, or *hound* as we know it. But there is no specific point of origin."

"How long have you been chewing on this?" Lindsey asked.

"Like a dog with a bone on and off for years," her father said. "But enough about me—how is my favorite daughter?"

"I'm your only daughter," she said.

"That doesn't make it any less true," he said.

Lindsey smiled. He sounded just like Jack.

"I was just wondering what day you and Mom think you might arrive," she said. "I know we left it loose, since none of us knew, er, know what Jack is doing."

"Mom and I were thinking we'd pop on down a few days before Christmas," he said. "We'll have finished with finals by then and hopefully Jack will do the same and we'll get to spend a few days together before he has to dash off to who knows where next."

"So you haven't heard from him?" Lindsey asked.

"No, not yet," he said.

This was why Lindsey had called her father. When it came to the family, he was the less detail oriented of her two parents. Her mother would have asked straight out if Lindsey had heard from Jack, but her father would assume that if she had, she would mention it. Since he didn't ask, she was spared having to lie to him.

For a moment, she wondered if she should tell her father about the mess Jack had gotten himself into, but she couldn't help but remember Jack's warning, the fewer who knew about him the better. If a deranged husband was hunting for him, he would no doubt check and see if his parents had heard from him. Telling her parents what was happening could put them in danger as well as Jack.

She changed the subject by asking about one of their neighbors, and her dad got busy recounting the gossip from town. Lindsey used to get homesick when she heard about who had gotten married, who had kids and who had passed away. Growing up, she had never really thought she'd move away and stay away.

But now that she'd planted some roots in Briar Creek, she really couldn't imagine living anywhere else. She liked the quirky shore town. She also liked that she was a short train ride from Boston and New York. It really felt as if it was the best of all worlds.

"Drat, I have a faculty meeting to get to," her father said. Lindsey could tell by his tone that he was already late and contemplating skipping it.

"I'll let you go then," she said. She didn't want to be the reason he got into trouble. "Give Mom my love."

"Will do," he said. "Love you, peanut. See you soon."

"Love you, too. Bye, Dad."

Lindsey hung up the phone, feeling lousy for having pulled the old lie of omission trick on her dad. She hadn't had to do that in years, and she really didn't like it.

Of course, this time, just like when they were younger, it was to spare Jack. Once he had taken the family station wagon out for a joy ride, and when her father asked her if she had seen her brother, she'd said no. Not a total lie, as she was forced to point out later. She had heard Jack leaving in the station wagon but she hadn't seen him, thus not a lie. Her parents hadn't really seen it that way then and she doubted they would see it that way now.

But what choice did she have? She didn't want to put Jack or her parents in danger. She didn't know what was going on or whom she could trust. The man on the phone had sounded seriously scary. She knew that whatever she did, she had to be extremely careful.

When she did see Jack again, she thought she should demand payback for all of the times she had covered his butt with their parents. She was thinking a week's vacation on a tropical beach with a stack of books might be just the ticket. Of course, first she had to get Jack back, but that was just a detail. She fully intended to find out where her brother was and to get him home in time for the holidays. She refused to give in to her fear. Failure was not an option.

Lindsey spent the rest of the day trying to concentrate on work. There were orders to place and meetings to prepare for. The town was hoping to launch a new website that promoted tourism, and the mayor's right-hand man, Herb Gunderson, had been tasked with nagging all the department heads for their input in regards to the website. Because the library's website was so much more interactive than the sites for the other departments, much of the burden of usability was on Lindsey.

About an hour before closing, Lindsey got a case of the yawns that made her jaw pop. Suddenly there was nothing more appealing in the world than putting her head down on her desk and taking a power nap.

When her eyes started to blink shut, she knew resistance was futile. She got out of her seat and strode to the front door. A gust of cold winter air slapping her across the face ought to do the trick.

She stepped on the rubber mat that triggered the automatic doors. The day was gray again, and the air was brisk. It was getting dark really early now, and she could see that it would be fully dark well before they closed. She moved to the side of the doors and stared out at the naked trees in the park across the street.

The briny smell of the bay at low tide filled her nostrils. She inhaled deeply, hoping it would act like a spark plug on her weariness and ignite some wakefulness. She shivered. She rubbed her hands up and down her arms. She stared past the park at the pier. She was sure she could see Sully in his office all the way at the edge of the pier.

This made her pause. He had said he was going to keep looking for the yacht that had carried Jack away. The thought that he might get hurt in the process made Lindsey's heart hammer hard in her chest. She couldn't bear it if anything happened to him while he was looking into Jack's disappearance. The guilt would be a crushing weight from which she'd never recover. She had to stop him.

She turned around and headed back into the library. Now that she knew she was going to have to run an errand after work, she was fully awake and ready to face the argument that she knew was coming.

Lindsey hurried home to get Heathcliff before she headed to the pier. The dog needed a good walk, she reasoned, and besides, his canine charm might have more sway with Sully than she did.

"What, no tights-and-tutu-wearing thespian with you?" Sully asked when they appeared in his office.

Heathcliff didn't hear the censure in his voice and skidded across the tile floor to get to his friend. Smacking into Sully's shin, he stood on his hind legs and wrapped his doggy paws around Sully's knee. As expected, Sully made his "*aw*" face, and scooped Heathcliff up as if he were a toddler, giving his back a good scratch before setting him back down.

"I assume you're referring to Robbie?" she asked.

"Charlie told me he had tea in the library today," Sully said with a shrug of nonchalance that was anything but. "I just assumed he'd still be shadowing you."

"How did Charlie know that Robbie was there?" she asked.

"I believe he said that Nancy mentioned it in passing," he said.

"Uh-huh," Lindsey said. Robbie had been right. Small towns were definitely *small*. "We did have tea, but last I heard, he and Dylan were running lines for their next production. And I don't think they're wearing tutus."

Sully blinked at her as if he knew he'd been out of line but was not about to take it back.

"So what brings you and the boy by?" he asked. He sounded as if he was trying for a more casual tone. "Has there been any news about the John Doe?"

"No." Lindsey shook her head. "As far as I know, there's been no ID on the body."

"What about Jack?" he asked. "Any word from him?"

"That's what I wanted to talk to you about," she said. "I think it would be best if you don't look for the yacht he disappeared on."

Sully studied her for a moment and then he frowned. "What aren't you telling me?"

Lindsey wondered if a lie of omission would work for her in this instance. Sully was not her distractible dad. Full disclosure might be the only way to get him to see reason.

"Nothing really," she said. "I just think it's too dangerous, and I can't in good conscience have you getting involved in something that could be, well, deadly."

Sully stared at her for a moment then he moved around her. Shutting off lights, checking the coffeepot, he was moving toward the door before Lindsey registered that they were in motion.

"I'm thinking we need to have a longer conversation," he said. "But I have stew in the Crock-Pot that won't wait much longer."

He was dismissing her in order to go eat his dinner. It was perfectly reasonable, and yet Lindsey could feel a tiny bubble of hurt float up inside her, which was ridiculous. It was late. The man needed his dinner. They could talk another time. Yeah, all very logical and she still felt a severe case of the pouts coming on.

CHAPTER
14

BRIAR CREEK
PUBLIC LIBRARY

"Oh, of course," Lindsey said. She was pleased that she sounded so incredibly mature. "We won't keep you."

"No, but you'll join me for dinner, right?" he asked. "Believe me, I made enough to feed twenty."

"Oh, I don't want to impose—" Lindsey began but Sully interrupted her as he took her arm and led her out of the building.

"You're not," he said. He glanced at her sideways before adding, "I even have those small sourdough loaves of bread from the bakery."

"Oh, well, that changes everything. You know I can't turn down a bread bowl," she said. It was ridiculous how relieved she felt that he wasn't sending her away.

"Yeah, I know," he said. His voice was gruff with affection, and Lindsey wondered if maybe this wasn't the best idea.

She and Sully had been very careful around each other for the past few months as if neither of them wanted to lose the fragile friendship they had been able to rebuild.

Sully gave her little time to reconsider, however, as he locked the door and led the way up the pier to Main Street, where he parked his truck. Heathcliff jumped in without hesitation and Lindsey followed.

It was fully dark now and the streetlights had come on, illuminating patches of the street. Lindsey burrowed into her coat, nudging her nose under her scarf as she sat beside Sully. He didn't wear gloves and his coat was unbuttoned. She wondered how he could not be frozen, but then, working out on the water driving passengers to and from the islands had probably thickened up his blood.

He started up the truck and drove a half mile then he turned off Main Street to follow a narrow road that wound its way back out toward the water. This was an older neighborhood of small beach houses built in the fifties. They were the original vacation cabins that the wealthy residents of New Haven had used during the summer.

Sully's small three-bedroom house was halfway down the street. Weathered to a pearly shade of gray with a crisp white trim, it was boxy in shape but it sported floor-to-ceiling windows that offered a view of the bay, a thick stone fireplace, and was surrounded by hedges of summer roses on both sides, keeping it private from the neighbors. It had a small front yard enclosed by a white picket fence, with a side garden that was now dead cornstalks and pumpkin vines. Lindsey had always thought that Sully's house was just perfect. She was surprised to find how much she had missed it.

Sully parked in the drive and led the way to the house. Heathcliff followed with his nose to the ground. Sully unlocked the door and flicked on the lights. The tiled foyer led through the kitchen to the living room, which had two full-sized leather couches with the fireplace on one side, a big screen television on the wall beside it and windows that looked out over the water, completing the cozy room.

The rich hearty smell of a thick homemade stew cooking perfumed the air. Lindsey felt her stomach cramp and realized that she'd had nothing to eat since tea with Robbie.

Sully went over to the fireplace and switched on the gas, causing the fire to ignite in a bright burst of warm flames.

"Make yourselves at home," he said. "I'll dish the food and be right back."

Heathcliff took that to mean that Sully needed an assist and he followed him into the kitchen. Lindsey heard the low rumble of Sully talking to the dog and she smiled. When she and Sully had been dating, they had spent a lot of time at Sully's house, and Heathcliff had settled in like it was his second home.

She stood by the fire to warm up, but the lure of the view caused her to wander over to the window. She had to look past her own reflection on the glass, but when she leaned close, she could see out into the darkness and pick out some of the Thumb Islands by the pinpricks of light that sat just above the water. Only a few of the islands had electricity, and those usually had year-round tenants, like Sully's parents on Bell Island.

She thought the idea of living on an island year-round was romantic, but she didn't know if she could do it.

115

Maybe if she had family or neighbors on the island with her, but by herself she was afraid she'd become a hermit who refused to leave her island and Sully would have to deliver all of her food and goods. She'd probably become feral and lose all of her social skills and start living off the land like a wild woman.

It had a certain allure, like not shaving her armpits or legs, but then it had a dark side as well—no toilet paper. Yeah, she was out.

Sully was back in a few moments with a loaded tray. Two plates heaped with stew inside a small hollowed loaf of round bread, a perfect defense against the December chill, and when paired with a bottle of Shiraz and two glasses, it almost felt like a date.

Lindsey looked at Sully. Did he look like a man who considered this a date? He was clean shaven, he smelled good, and she was pretty sure he had just combed his hair. His unruly head of reddish brown curls always looked wonderfully wind tossed after a day of working on his boats. Yes, he had definitely paused to comb it. Hmm.

"What?" he asked as he handed her a glass of wine.

"What what?" she returned. She had to keep herself from smacking her forehead. Man, she sounded dumb.

"You're staring at me," he said.

"You combed your hair," she said. She let out a pained sigh. Did she really just say that out loud? This was agony. She sounded dumber than dumb; she sounded like an idiot to the tenth power.

"Mom always taught me to clean up before dinner," he said. His tone was easy and light. "Thanks for noticing."

Lindsey felt her face get hot. This wasn't working. Being here with him in his house like they had so many times when they were a couple, it was blurring the lines, and she wasn't sure if she was Lindsey the friend or Lindsey the ex-girlfriend or Lindsey who wished they could get back together.

The thought made her toss back a gulp of Shiraz, which was not the mellowest of wines to chug. She sputtered a little, and when she glanced at Sully, she was almost certain she saw him trying not to laugh.

As was their old habit, they sat on the floor in front of the fire on big square cushions that gave them just the right elevation to eat at the large glass coffee table. Sully had even brought a bowl of stew for Heathcliff, which sat on the table until it was cool enough for him to eat.

"I have an ulterior motive for mellowing you with food," Sully said.

"Oh?" Lindsey asked. She felt her pulse pound, but she strived to sound casual. "What's that?"

"It's bad news," he said.

Lindsey felt her chest clutch. "How bad?"

"The scorched wreck that we hauled in last night is gone," he said.

"What?" Lindsey asked. "When? How?"

"It had to be last night after we docked," he said. "I called a Navy buddy with some experience in forensics, but when he came out this morning and we went to check out the boat, we found the tie had been cut clear through. Someone didn't want anyone looking at that boat. We searched for it but no luck. I don't know if they hauled it away or sank it, but it's gone. I'm sorry, Lindsey."

He looked genuinely regretful and Lindsey knew he thought he'd let her down, which was ridiculous.

Lindsey shook her head. "It's not your fault. There are

more players than we realized in this little drama. I'm just beginning to understand how much trouble Jack is in."

Sully nodded. "Yeah, I got that feeling when the boat was gone. Now it's your turn. What were you not sharing with me back at the office? And more importantly, does the British bit player know what's going on?"

Lindsey dipped the top of her bread into the stew. It was savory and seasoned to perfection. She took her time chewing while she considered what to tell him. As if there was really any option. Briar Creek was too small a town to keep secrets, at least not for long, which reminded her that any day Chief Plewicki was going to find out about her brother.

"I received a phone call today from a man," Lindsey said. She could tell by the way Sully had gone completely still that she had his full attention.

"Go on," he said. He took a sip from his glass as if to brace himself.

Lindsey picked up her spoon and fiddled with her stew. "He didn't or wouldn't identify himself. He asked where my brother was, and when I said I didn't know, he sounded very irritated with me."

"Do you think it was the jealous husband?" Sully asked.

"I don't know," Lindsey said. "On the one hand, that makes the most sense, but then again, he didn't sound jealous. He sounded concerned right up until he told me he'd be in touch."

"What?" Sully asked. "And you're just mentioning this now?"

"I'm not sure he meant it like it sounded," she said. "Robbie heard him, too. He could verify that it wasn't like a threat."

"Oh, the mincing mime was in on the call, was he?" Sully asked.

"He just happened to be there when the call came through," she said. She took the opportunity to shove a spoonful of savory stew into her mouth. Delicious.

"Fine, moving on," Sully said. "If it wasn't a threat, what did it sound like?"

As if he could stand it no longer, Heathcliff gave a whimper from his spot on the floor then he barked and rolled over as if he would expire if he didn't get to eat his stew right now.

"Oh, sorry, boy," Sully said. He checked the temperature of Heathcliff's bowl. "The ice has melted. You're good."

He put a placemat on the floor and put the bowl on top of it. Heathcliff leapt to his feet and slammed his muzzle into the bowl with absolutely no regard for manners of any kind. He wagged while he ate.

"Compliments to the chef," Lindsey said as she pointed at his tail.

"The dog has good taste," Sully said.

"Yes, he does, the stew is excellent," Lindsey said. She took a sip of wine before she answered his question. "I think the man on the phone was trying to warn me."

"About what?" Sully asked.

"I don't know," she said. "Maybe the jealous husband or it could be something else entirely. That's why I want you to stop looking for any trace of the yacht. Whatever Jack is mixed up in, one man is already dead. I really don't want you to make yourself a target as well."

"Given that I had no luck tracing the boat, I think I'm fine," he said.

"Except for the fact that you know everyone in the

119

area, and if you start asking questions, it will draw the bad guys' attention back to you and you could get hurt," Lindsey said. "I really would feel much better if you didn't look around or ask questions or anything."

"But what if someone saw something?" Sully said. "We might be able to find your brother."

"I know," Lindsey said. "But Jack was very clear when he said that the fewer people who knew about him, the better. As it is, too many of you know, and I really couldn't stand it if something happened to any of you."

"Who exactly is too many of us?" Sully asked.

"You, Beth and Robbie."

"How does he know everything that is going on?" he asked.

"After he heard the phone call, I had to tell him," Lindsey said. "I couldn't risk him asking the wrong person and getting everyone gossiping."

Sully grumbled something unintelligible and tucked into his stew. Lindsey did the same. Heathcliff obviously considered it a race and was the first one done, which he announced by standing on his hind legs and propping his front paws on the table as if looking for seconds.

"No," Lindsey said. He wagged. She shook her head. He pushed off the table with a grunt.

"He's mad at you," Sully said.

"He'll get over it when I take him O-U-T," she said. Heathcliff's ears perked up at her words and Sully laughed.

"I think he can spell," he said.

"He's too smart for his own good," she said. "More accurately, he's too smart for my own good."

They finished eating and Lindsey helped Sully with the dishes. She could tell he was thinking, mulling over what she had told him about the phone call. She refused to feel guilty for including Robbie in the loop. His input had been very helpful, and she'd been pretty rattled to get the call and was grateful for his calming presence.

A mournful cry sounded from the living room, and Sully and Lindsey exchanged amused looks.

"Nice to know some things don't change," Sully said. "The boy still makes it clear when he needs to go out."

"Yes, he does," Lindsey said.

Together they shrugged on their coats, and Sully flipped on the outside spotlight that illuminated the small yard and the beach beyond. The minute Lindsey opened the door, Heathcliff shot out the door and rushed through the tall grass over the sandy hill to the water.

Sully and Lindsey followed at a slower pace, and when they crested the hill, it was to find Heathcliff racing at the water, barking at the waves and running when they chased him back up the beach.

The wind tugged at her hair, sending it swirling about her head. Lindsey pulled up the hood on her coat and shoved her hands in her pockets.

"Want to walk a ways and wear him out?" Sully asked.

Lindsey nodded.

They set off on the firm dry sand, staying clear of the waves while Heathcliff sprinted down the beach and back. It wasn't long before his tongue was hanging out but still he barked and chased the waves.

Lindsey had thought Sully was going to take this time in the fresh air to talk, but to her surprise he didn't say anything. She wondered what he was thinking but then she suspected he had a whole lot of unhappy going about her telling him not to look for the yacht. Sully was the original fixer. When he saw a problem, it was ingrained in his nature to fix it. She knew it chafed him for her to tell him to stop.

Deep in thought, she yelped when Sully abruptly draped his arm about her shoulders and pulled her close. His mouth was next to her ear, giving her all sorts of shivers and not the kind that come from the cold, when he said, "Don't panic, but someone is following us."

It took her a moment or two to get his scent out of her head and replace it with his words. *Following them?*

CHAPTER

15

BRIAR CREEK
PUBLIC LIBRARY

Naturally, Lindsey's first reaction was to look over her shoulder and see who it was. Sully anticipated her move, however, and pulled her in even closer, blocking her from turning around by pressing his mouth right below her ear.

"No, don't look," he whispered. "We don't want him to know we're aware of him."

His voice was gravel rough and managed to turn Lindsey's insides to hot mush even while she felt an adrenaline surge of fear pump through her. She closed her eyes, trying to focus, and asked, "Who is it?"

Sully's breath brushed across her cheek when he answered, "Don't know. I don't recognize him, but we can't get back to the house the way we came without passing him. I'm thinking we need to hike into the tall grass and lose him at the old red shack."

"Sounds like a plan," she said.

Sully took her hand in his, and within three steps they had disappeared into the marsh grass that separated his small neighborhood from the next. As if sensing their urgency, Heathcliff was right beside Lindsey as they picked their way through the phragmites.

Before they disappeared over the small hill, she glanced back. She gasped when she saw the shadow of a large man backlit against the light coming from Sully's house. He was making his way down the beach, headed straight for them.

"He's coming!" Lindsey whispered, because yeah, Sully might have missed that fact.

He gave her hand a firm squeeze and then he bent down and scooped Heathcliff up into his arms. He shifted their speed into high gear, using his elbow to lead them through the spiky grass. Lindsey followed, hoping that in the darkness the man would have a hard time following Sully, who knew every inch of the terrain from his boyhood spent running wild.

They broke out of the grass and found themselves beside an old shack that had stood on this unpopulated part of the bay for as long as anyone could remember. Up on stilts, it had been painted red over the years, but was still weatherworn and tired looking. In the dark, Lindsey couldn't make out much more than the fact that it looked abandoned.

"It's the local hangout for high schoolers," Sully said. "At least, it used to be."

"Are we going in?"

"No, but we hope he thinks we are. Come on." Sully pulled her past the shack and into a small copse of evergreens. He handed off Heathcliff to her and said, "Don't move. I'll be right back."

Lindsey clutched Heathcliff close, which was no mean feat, since he weighed a solid thirty-plus pounds. He struggled a bit as if he wanted to go after Sully, but Lindsey hushed him and talked softly to him.

"It's okay, boy," she said. "Sully knows what he's doing."

The wait was excruciating. Lindsey edged closer to the edge of the trees. She just wanted to peek and see that Sully was okay.

In the darkness, she couldn't make out anything. Just shadows layered against shadows. Her hair blew across her face and she tossed it back. Heathcliff whined and she shushed him. He was a solid bundle, and she shifted him in her arms as she leaned out from behind a long branch.

She heard the noise of something slamming and then footsteps were fleeing toward her. She stiffened. She had no way of knowing in the dark if it was Sully or not. Heathcliff's ears perked up but he didn't bark so she assumed it must be him, but just to be on the safe side, she backed up into the tree, letting the branches cover her.

"Lindsey," a voice hissed. It was Sully and he sounded a little panicked. She stepped out from the tree and he took Heathcliff from her arms.

"I wasn't sure it was you," she explained.

"Good thinking," he said. "I've bought us some time, but we'd better hurry."

"What did you do?" she asked.

"Impeded his progress," he said. "I hope."

He led the way onto a narrow path in the high grass that was mercifully hard-packed dirt and not marshland mud. In a few spots where it looked soggy, someone had put down narrow wooden planks. They hurried through the high grass. Lindsey looked behind them twice, but there was no sign of anyone following them.

Only once when they were nearing the edge of the marsh did Sully stop. He ducked down and pulled Lindsey with him. Crouched low, Lindsey saw the sweep of a flashlight illuminate the tips of the grass above their heads.

She felt her heart race and she broke out in a sweat. Who was looking for them? What did they want? Was it the woman who had taken Jack? Maybe she should stand up and ask them. Even as the idea flitted through her head, she rejected it. She didn't want to put Heathcliff and Sully, yes, in that order, at risk.

As the light flared over them on its second sweep, she glanced at Sully. He was frowning, but when he turned to glance at her, he gave her a small smile and a wink.

"Don't you worry," he said. "I've got the home court advantage here."

Lindsey didn't doubt it for a second.

They waited several long minutes in the cold before Sully gave the signal to start moving. When they neared the edge of the high grass that led to the road, Sully put Heathcliff down. The dog was happy to be free, and he barked once in approval. Lindsey hushed him but a neighborhood dog barked in response so she fervently hoped that whoever was looking for them thought it was just the local dogs reacting to strangers in the neighborhood.

They were down the street from Sully's small house, and he gestured for Lindsey to follow him. They strolled through his neighbors' backyards, thankfully not running into anyone who wanted to stop and chat.

On the edge of his yard, Sully again had Lindsey and

Heathcliff wait while he checked the perimeter of his house to make sure no one was inside or waiting for them out front. When he waved the "all clear" to Lindsey, she and Heathcliff hurried inside.

"Stay away from the windows," he said.

He quickly checked the house and then came back and drew the thick curtains over the glass panes. He kept the outside lights on, but turned out all the lights in the house, save one very dim twenty-five-watt lamp that Lindsey had always thought was decorative.

"What did you do, back at the shack?" she asked. A shiver ran over her skin and she wasn't sure if it was from the cold or residual fear.

Sully switched on the fire in the fireplace and warmth immediately flared out from the hearth. Lindsey sat on the floor in front of it and let it toast her back to her normal temperature. Sully sat beside her, and Heathcliff wedged himself between them, rolling onto his back so his belly was in the air, perfectly positioned for a tummy rub.

"First, I hid on the back porch," he said. "Then when the man got closer, I walked loudly across the boards, hoping he'd think we were inside. He did. Then I hurried around the front, slammed the door and wedged a board under the knob so he'd have to work at it to let himself out. I figured it would buy us enough time to get away from him."

"Do you really think he was following us?" she asked.

"No," Sully said. Lindsey felt her shoulders drop in relief. Then he added, "I think he was following you."

"Aw, man, I really only liked the first part of your answer," she said.

Sully shrugged. "Just calling it like I see it."

"What should I do?" she asked.

"Go to the police," he said. Lindsey started to protest but he held up his hand to stop her. "These people are not your garden-variety bad guys. They've killed one man and kidnapped another and now they're following you. What do you think they'll do when they catch you?"

"Invite me to tea?" she asked. She didn't mean to be so flip, but she was scared and she didn't know how else to respond.

"I don't think you're their Darjeeling," he said.

Lindsey blinked at him. Then she laughed.

"Very clever!" she said and he smiled.

Sully pulled a cushion off the couch and propped it against the stone hearth. He shifted so he was lying down on the pillow with his legs stretched out in front of him.

It was so cozy here with him that Lindsey almost forgot that there had been someone following them. She wondered if their imaginations were getting the best of them since seeing her brother abducted. Then again, had Jack really been abducted or had the woman who'd taken him away saved him from her estranged husband? The whole thing made Lindsey's head pound.

She wondered if the man who'd followed them had been the woman's husband. "Did you get a good look at him?"

"No, I tried, but he was backlit," he said. "Judging by the size of him and his lack of stealth, I'd say he had some defensive lineman in him."

"That big?" Lindsey asked.

Sully nodded. Being a big man himself, if he considered the other guy on the large side, well, it certainly gave Lindsey pause. She shivered but not from the cold.

"Sit tight," he said. He disappeared into the kitchen and

she could hear him banging around in there. In moments she caught the faint scent of simmering cinnamon and her mouth watered. One of the first evenings she'd ever spent with Sully, he had made her his patent-worthy hot chocolate. She hoped that's what he was brewing now.

He returned in minutes bearing two mugs with steam pouring out of their tops. He handed one to Lindsey, and she gratefully clutched the warm ceramic in her hands. She took a delicate sip, checking the heat. It was the perfect temperature.

"You still make the best hot chocolate," she said.

"Thanks," he said, resuming his seat by the hearth. "I tweaked my mom's recipe by adding the cinnamon and nutmeg. She thinks it's over the top, but I like the oomph."

"I like the oomph, too."

They were both quiet. Lindsey rubbed Heathcliff's belly while she pondered what to do next. It wasn't long before the dog was emitting soft snores. She had thought that the fright would make her jittery and wide awake, but as the adrenaline ebbed from her system, baked out by the heat of the fire and the richness of the cocoa, she felt her head get heavy. She knew she needed to get home while the getting was good.

"I'd better call it a night," she said.

"Not a good plan," Sully said. "They could still be out there."

"I don't know," she said. "It's awfully cold to be sitting out there, and I'm sure one of your neighbors would have noticed a strange car parked on the street."

"Maybe," he said. "I'd feel better if we waited just a bit longer. We're safe inside and have nothing but time. I don't see any point in rushing out there to be a target."

Lindsey nodded. That was reasonable.

"When you say 'target,' do you think their intent is to do harm?" she asked. Her voice sounded a bit fainter than she'd like, but it would be pointless to deny the fact that she was scared. They'd just been chased down the beach by an ogre; any sane person would be scared.

"I think their intent is to find your brother," he said. "And I think they'll do whatever it takes to achieve that goal."

"Oh."

He held out his hand, and Lindsey gave him her empty mug. Sully rose from his reclined spot and disappeared down the hallway. Lindsey heard a cupboard door open and shut, and Sully reappeared with two heavy comforters and two big fluffy pillows.

"We can sack out on the couch until the coast is clear," he said.

Lindsey gave him a look.

"Separate couches," he clarified.

The thought of burrowing under a thick blanket was too tempting to resist. Sully's couch was shaped like an L, so they put their pillows in the corner where the two sides met and then they both stretched out on their own side of the couch. Not to be left behind, Heathcliff jumped onto the couch and wedged his way in between their pillows.

With the fire on low and the lone light glowing, Lindsey felt as snug and safe as a caterpillar in a cocoon. It felt as if nothing could get her here. She wondered how much of that had to do with Sully's presence, and she tried to imagine if she were home alone whether she would feel this safe. Yeah, no, it was him.

There was something inherently good and strong and

safe about Sully. He radiated a certainty about life and his place in it that she had never known in another person. It made her feel secure. She liked that.

She thought about what had driven them apart. It wasn't Sully's propensity for silence. He was not the world's biggest talker—major understatement—but that wasn't it. No, she could handle that because when he did speak, it was worth listening to. Rather what had driven the wedge between them was his inability to express his feelings. It was one thing to be quiet; it was another to be an emotional withholder.

She knew he didn't do it on purpose as some twisted form of manipulation. That wasn't Sully's style. From what she knew about him, his inability to articulate his thoughts and feelings came from a serious lack of practice and quite possibly an emotional trauma in his past.

As a Navy man turned boat captain, he was a solitary soul. She doubted he'd had much cause to voice his concerns in his relationships, since he was always away. So instead of having a normal dialogue about things, he just took matters into his own hands and made decisions without consulting the person who would be most affected by his decision. Now how she was supposed to school him about that, she had no idea.

"Lindsey, you awake?" he asked.

"Yep," she said.

"Ah, I wasn't sure if that was you or Heathcliff snoring," he said.

"I don't snore," she protested.

"You sure about that?" he asked.

Lindsey felt her face grow warm. When they had been dating, he had never mentioned that she snored.

"Yes!" she snapped. "Quite sure. You must have me confused with some other girl."

Ha! Let him chew on that, she thought.

"Could be," he said. His tone was so matter-of-fact that Lindsey sat straight up and turned to look at him. When she did, she found him propped up with his chin in his hand, grinning at her.

"Oh, you—"

"Shh," he said. "You'll wake the baby."

Then he pointed to Heathcliff.

"Do not try to hide behind the furry boy," she said. She looked him straight in the eye. "Are you seeing someone?"

CHAPTER

16

BRIAR CREEK
PUBLIC LIBRARY

"No," he said. "I'd like to be, but I get the feeling she's not ready yet."

"Maybe she's just waiting to see if you can learn to communicate more effectively," she said. Lindsey could not believe those words had just flown out of her mouth. She wanted to smack herself in the forehead. Honestly, she sounded like a corporate chucklehead.

"Well, it's hard to find an opportunity to express myself what with that annoying, limelight-hogging Brit always circling her," he said.

Lindsey knew him well enough to know he was making his voice sound grumpier than he actually was.

"He's married," she said. "So I believe that locks him firmly into the just friends category."

Sully stared at her for a second, and Lindsey felt like they were coming to an understanding. She settled back down on her pillow, shifting on her side so she could still see him while they talked.

"There is one other small detail," Sully said.

"What's that?" For a panicked moment, Lindsey wondered if he had some secret bombshell to drop on her.

Was he married, too? Did he have a gambling, drinking, drug problem? Maybe he had an offspring from a previous relationship that he had neglected to mention. Lindsey felt her palms get sweaty as random thoughts flitted through her head, but she couldn't latch on to anything specific. It was all white noise.

"You may not have noticed, but I'm not a big talker," he said. "The communication thing is challenging."

She looked at him. That was it?

"Shocking, I know," he said.

Lindsey couldn't help but smile. She supposed she could have rolled her eyes or made a sarcastic noise, but she was too afraid of derailing him when he was actually sharing to risk mucking it up.

"The thing is, just because I don't tell people how I'm feeling doesn't mean I'm not feeling anything," he said. He stared into the fire for a moment. "I always thought it was obvious that if I showed up every day, I cared."

"Sometimes people need a little more to go on," Lindsey said.

"So my sister has been telling me," he said. "And telling me and telling me."

The harangued look he gave her told her more than words that his sister Mary had a lot to say about his relationship status.

"Sorry," Lindsey said. And she was. Sully was a private man and she knew he had to be uncomfortable with everyone being up in his business.

"No, it's my own fault," he said. "I should have talked to you before I cut things off between us. I should have given you a chance to explain what you were feeling before I walked."

Lindsey would have disagreed just to be polite, but since he was right, it seemed silly not to agree with him. Over the summer when her ex-fiancé had arrived in town in a misguided attempt to win her back, they had gotten embroiled in a murder investigation that had nearly gotten them all killed.

Lindsey had naturally felt responsible for her ex's role in the situation and had felt terrible about what could have happened to him. Sully had misconstrued her concern for her ex as something more and had broken up with her to give her time to figure out her feelings. Lindsey had pretty much been mad at him ever since.

"It was a preemptive strike," he said.

"You don't say," she said. This time she couldn't keep the sarcasm out of her voice.

He flopped over onto his back and stared at the ceiling. "Couldn't I just drop and give you twenty and we could call it even?"

"You owe me at least fifty," she said. "And no."

"I could run five miles in the rain with a knapsack full of books on my back," he said.

"Relationships are not boot camp," she said. She had to look away so he didn't catch her smiling and mistakenly think she might give in.

"No, they're a lot harder," he grumbled. "Fine. It was

my first year in the Navy and I was stationed in San Diego. I met a girl, a gorgeous girl."

While he paused to collect his thoughts, Lindsey chided herself for the spurt of jealousy that was wreaking havoc with her insides.

She wanted to ask how gorgeous and demand a description, but her good sense prevailed and she kept her mouth shut. She also promised herself that she would interrogate his sister Mary at their next crafternoon and see what she knew about the gorgeous girl from San Diego.

"We spent all of my free time together," he said. "Her family was all career Navy, so I knew she understood the life. I really thought she was the one."

"How old were you?" Lindsey asked.

"Twenty-two," he said.

Lindsey nodded. It was all coming into focus now. That age was never kind to relationships. While old enough to drink, vote and go to war, picking a mate in the early twenties was fraught with hormone-induced disasters. The relationships that survived from those early years were the stuff of legends.

"I shipped out, a low-ranking officer on my first time out to sea. We were out in the Pacific on a guided-missile frigate. While there was a lot of excitement, a ship full of sweaty men sure does make whatever you left behind seem even more lovely in comparison.

"We stopped in Tahiti, which was unlike anything I had ever seen, and I found a pretty black pearl ring. It was set in gold nestled in a ring of diamonds. I knew I had to buy it for her. It wiped out all of my pay and my one credit card. But it was worth it because I was sure she was worth it."

Lindsey had a feeling this wasn't going to end well. A part of her wanted to tell him to stop. She didn't need to know, but then, wasn't this what she had wanted from him? To know how he felt and why he felt that way? She hadn't expected that hearing the hurt in his voice would hurt her as much as it did.

She forced herself to buck up. "What happened?"

"When I got home, I called her up and asked her out to dinner," he said. "I told her I had something to tell her and she said she had news, too."

"When I picked her up, she threw herself at me," he said. "It was a pretty passionate reunion."

Again, Lindsey felt the green-eyed monster roar in her chest. She shook it off like a dog shedding rain off its fur.

"Over dinner I gave her the ring and asked her to marry me," he said. "She hesitated for just a second. I knew I had surprised her, so that was all right. I was enthusiastic enough for both of us. I outlined my dreams for us, you know, big wedding, me moving up the ranks in the Navy, a houseful of kids, the whole shebang. She was quiet and looked like she was going to cry. For the first time, it occurred to me that maybe she didn't want all that. I braced myself for a solid rejection and then she said yes."

Lindsey was shocked. He had never mentioned being engaged before. She knew she shouldn't feel like it was a sort of betrayal, but that sort of thing was supposed to come up in the first few weeks of dating. That's what all those awkward meals over sourdough and linguine were made for—to discover the other person's previous engagements, marriages, time spent in jail and communicable diseases. How could he not have mentioned it?

"So you were engaged?" she asked. Her voice sounded faint and she cleared her throat.

"You would think so, wouldn't you?" he asked.

Lindsey turned and propped herself up on her elbows while Sully was still lying down. She stared at the top of his head, waiting for him to explain.

"I'm not following," she prompted him, and Sully heaved a long sigh.

"My girl neglected to tell me one thing in her letters to me," he said. "While I was gone, she had managed to catch herself a higher-ranking officer and married him."

CHAPTER

17

BRIAR CREEK
PUBLIC LIBRARY

"She didn't!" Lindsey gasped. Out of anything he might have said, that she did not expect.

Sully looked rueful at her outrage.

"Yes, she did," he said. He reached up and rubbed Heathcliff's ears. "Believe it or not, it gets worse."

"She was pregnant," Lindsey guessed.

"No," he said.

"She already had a child?"

"No," he said.

"What could possibly be worse?" she asked.

"She managed to conceal her marriage from me for two weeks," he said. "So while I was walking around all hearts and flowers, she was running a covert op to rival the skills of a CIA operative to make sure I didn't find out the truth, which naturally, I did."

Lindsey noticed that he didn't call *her* by name. She

139

wondered if it was just habit or if there was a reason, like it was too painful for him. She was a librarian, an information gatherer of the first water, and details could not be ignored. She swallowed hard and then posed her question as simply and directly as she could.

"What was her name?"

"Kelly O'Laughlin," he said after a thoughtful pause. "She was my wild Irish rose."

Lindsey had to force herself not to let her eyebrows shoot up at the affectionate note in his voice. She frowned instead. Sully sounded almost fond of the woman who had tossed him aside so callously. Surely, he could not still be in love with her.

"Well, I should clarify that was the name I knew her by," he said. "Her married name was different."

Sensing that would cause him pain, Lindsey did not ask for her new surname.

"How did you find out?" she asked.

"An officer from my ship was childhood pals with her husband," he said. "He'd heard that Kelly and I were out together romantically and he called me out for hitting on his friend's wife."

Lindsey cringed. That could not have gone well.

"A fistfight ensued, which ended with me at Kelly's house confronting her about her marriage," he said. "It wasn't pretty. I was hurt and angry. I said things I shouldn't have. She was from a military family, and the man she married had been a friend of the family forever. While I was gone, they started dating and their wedding had been a spur-of-the-moment idea right before he shipped out."

He was quiet for so long that Lindsey was sure he

wasn't going to say another word. Really, she couldn't fault him. It was much worse than her walking in on her fiancé while he was fornicating with one of his grad students. At least, her ex hadn't lied to her about it. He hadn't had the chance.

"She was having second thoughts about her marriage when I showed up. The man she married was significantly older and had already done the kid thing and didn't want any more. When I pitched my idea of the perfect life, I caused her to doubt her choice. She was feeling utterly confused, and I didn't help," he said. "When I asked her why she said yes, she said she couldn't bear the thought of losing me."

His voice sounded as if every word cost him, and Lindsey felt terrible that he'd had to go through such a horrible time and that in order to prove himself to her, he was being forced to relive it.

"I'm sorry," she said. "It sounds like it was rough all around."

"Mostly for her. I wasn't very nice or understanding about the situation," Sully said. "I was immature and angry. I lashed out at her and said some truly awful things."

He sounded as if this was the part that bothered him the most. Lindsey couldn't imagine why. Kelly had lied to him; she had betrayed him. Why did he feel bad because he was angry about it? It seemed perfectly reasonable to her. Of course, she'd had visions of running her ex over with a car, repeatedly, when he had cheated on her, so maybe she wasn't the best judge of post-relationship niceness.

"Kelly begged me to give her a chance to figure it out.

She said she needed time," he said. "I told her I was through wasting time on her and that she wasn't worth it."

Lindsey could hear the raw pain in his voice, and the hair on the back of her neck tingled with dread. In a flash of understanding, she knew there was more here, much more.

Her voice was just over a whisper when she asked, "What happened?"

"A couple of days after our argument, she fell asleep at the wheel of her car, exhaustion they said, she hit a tree head on and died instantly."

Lindsey felt as if the bottom had dropped out of her stomach. Kelly's death was a punch to the chest. She felt small and petty for feeling jealous of a woman who had made a disastrous choice and died too young to fix it.

Lindsey knew Sully, and if she felt blindsided by the story's end, she could only imagine how he felt having lived it. He was not someone who lost his temper. Ever. In fact, the most negative emotion she'd seen rise up out of him was annoyance or irritation, and a person had to push him pretty hard to get either of those reactions.

To have spoken harshly to someone even if she deserved it, well, if Sully cared about the person, and obviously he had since he'd wanted to marry Kelly, then to have hateful words be the last words between them would dog him mercilessly.

Finally, finding her voice, she said, "Oh, Sully, I am so sorry. It must have been awful."

"Her husband forbid me from going to the funeral. He blamed me for her death," he said. "I did, too. If I hadn't been so hard on her, if I had been more understanding and given her the time she asked for . . ."

"Sully, you can't take the blame on that one," Lindsey said. "I know that the tragedy surrounding her death makes you feel obliged to, but truly, if she had told you the truth from the start, none of those tragic events would have played out the way they had."

"Or we would have argued earlier, and she could have died earlier," he said. "I never should have bought the ring."

"That's a lot of woulda, coulda, shouldas," she said.

"She was wearing the ring when they found her body," he said. "Not her wedding ring but the engagement ring I'd bought for her. It was another reason I was barred from her funeral."

"That must have been brutal," Lindsey said.

"I shipped out the morning of the service so I wouldn't be tempted to gate crash. I figured she deserved better than that," he said. "I took the first available post and bugged out all the way to the Philippines."

Lindsey didn't know what to say. She couldn't imagine how awful it must have been. Sully was the sort who would feel responsible for Kelly's death. It didn't matter that it was a chain of events that he only played a small part in; he would still think that if he had never asked her to marry him, she would still be alive today.

"It wasn't, you know," she said.

"What?" he asked.

"Your fault," she said.

He made a grunting noise that she figured would translate into *yeah, right* in word form, a big blow off from any absolution. She had expected as much. She knew it wouldn't do any good to argue with him. He would believe what he chose to believe and he wouldn't be swayed, not about his responsibility at any rate.

"Thank you for telling me about this," she said.

"You're welcome," he said. He looked up at her. "It was important to me to help you understand why I did what I did between us."

"You didn't want to get burned again," she said.

"No question," he agreed. "But it was more than that. I didn't want you to feel pressured to make a choice that you weren't ready to make. When I said I was walking away to give you time, I meant it." After all these months, it finally came into focus why Sully had stepped back from their relationship when her ex had reappeared.

"So you were just trying to make sure you didn't put me through what Kelly went through?" she asked.

"Yeah," he said. His voice was gruff, but Lindsey couldn't tell if it was exhaustion or emotion making it deeper than normal.

She rolled onto her back and thought about all that he'd shared with her. This was by far the biggest glimpse into the inner workings of Mike Sullivan than he had ever given her. While she felt badly that it was obviously hard for him, she couldn't help but be awed that he had willingly shared such a personal story.

"You are a brave man. I really admire you for telling me all of this," she said. He didn't say anything, so she took it as encouragement that he didn't grumble in denial. "I mean, I know it wasn't easy for you to open up, and I know this experience must have been particularly painful to share."

Still he was quiet, so she wondered if he was feeling that vulnerable ickiness a person feels when they've overshared. Yeah, she hated that feeling. She hurried to reassure him.

"You don't have to worry. I will never tell a soul what you told me. And I don't want you to feel badly for telling me all of this. Even before we were dating, I considered you a close friend and you can tell a good friend anything. I hope you know that."

He said nothing and Lindsey feared she had offended him by calling him a friend. Oh, why were words so hard for her? She had spent the better part of her life with her nose in a book; surely she should be able to articulate how she felt or at least rip off someone who knew what to say better than she did.

Her brain did a quick scan of snippets from Emily Dickens, "Each life converges to some centre," and W. H. Auden, "Let the more loving one be me." *No, no, no! These would not do.*

"Listen, Sully, I just want you to know that I truly appreciate what you told me, and I feel that I understand you and your actions better than I did before, and it truly helps me to rethink everything that happened . . . between us . . . before."

At this point Lindsey really expected him to say something, anything, or to at least acknowledge what she was saying. But in usual Sully fashion, he had gone silent. A flash of irritation lit up inside her.

She sat up and turned around. She glanced over Heathcliff at Sully and found him dead asleep. She nodded. Well, at least that made sense. The poor guy had obviously taxed himself by speaking way more than usual and had plum tuckered himself out.

Lindsey put her hand on his soft wavy hair and leaned forward to whisper, "Good night, Sully, and don't worry, I have your back. Always."

A soft exhale was his only response. Lindsey burrowed under her blanket and contemplated all that Sully had told her. She couldn't help but feel sorry for Kelly. Obviously, she had loved Sully, but she had wanted the status of wife to a higher-ranking officer more.

Lindsey couldn't pretend to understand that. Anyone could see that Sully was a great guy who would be successful at whatever he worked at, and if he had chosen to be career military, Lindsey had no doubt he would have been promoted right to the top.

Then she reminded herself that Sully and Kelly, and didn't those two names go together like salt and pepper, were very young. Navigating a long-distance relationship was hard at any age, but in the twenties it was particularly tricky.

That made her think of her brother and the beautiful woman who had absconded with him. Had long distance made her miss him so much that she felt the need to kidnap him? Or was her husband really so dangerous that she had to snatch Jack to protect him?

Lindsey felt the same sick dread she always felt when she thought about that moment at the pier when Jack was in the bottom of the boat speeding away. What had he gotten himself into? The dead man at the library made her feel like there was more going on than anyone was telling her.

Why had that man been following her and Sully tonight? Were they just being paranoid, or did he want something from them, okay, more accurately from her because she was Jack's sister? And if so, what?

A yawn crept up on Lindsey and she realized that

despite the crazy events of the past few days, she was snug and cozy with Heathcliff and Sully beside her. Her eyelids drooped and she felt the woozy abyss open up before her. Without any hesitation, she fell fast asleep.

Morning was unkind to people who slept on couches in their clothes, Lindsey decided as she examined her reflection in Sully's bedroom mirror. She borrowed his hairbrush and luckily he had a spare toothbrush. Really, she could not face the outside world without a good scrubbing of the pearlies.

Once they had fortified themselves with a pot of coffee, a stack of toast and some fluffy scrambled eggs, they bundled up in their coats and scarves and headed out into the crisp December morning.

Neither of them had broached the topic of last night's discussion this morning. Lindsey didn't because she didn't know what to say. She suspected Sully had said all he could muster, and she didn't want to be one of those women who talked a subject to death. Although she could easily discuss his past at greater length, she was pretty sure he had shared as much as he could for now.

She wondered if this new chattier version of Sully was going to stick around. She certainly hoped so, but she wasn't going to get all tangled up with him again until she was sure. She glanced at him as he opened the passenger door to his pickup truck for her. He sure was handsome, even rumpled and unshaven and looking like he'd slept in an awkward position on a couch.

"Thanks," she said.

"Anytime," he answered.

Lindsey got the feeling he knew she was talking about more than the lift home. She smiled and he returned it, and for a moment it felt as if they had never broken up. Then Heathcliff bounded into the truck with a bark and a wag, interrupting the moment.

Lindsey climbed up after him and Sully closed the door. As he walked around the front of the truck, Lindsey scratched Heathcliff's ears.

"Remind me to work with you on your timing, big boy," she said. "You pretty much ruined the moment there."

Heathcliff, with his mastery of the English language, glanced at her from underneath his bushy eyebrows and then he licked her cheek as if in apology.

"It's okay," she laughed. "I'm taking it slow."

Sully climbed into the truck just as Heathcliff barked in approval.

"He sure does love to ride in the truck," he said.

Lindsey nodded as she scooted over in her seat, so Heathcliff could have the window. Despite the cold, she rolled down the window so the puppy could stick his head out and enjoy sniffing the air. His tail kept a constant happy rhythm against her shoulder as he wagged the entire ride back to Lindsey's apartment.

When Sully pulled into the drive, Lindsey turned in her seat to face him.

"I owe you dinner," she said.

"I'll take you up on that," he said. "Tonight?"

Lindsey laughed at his eager expression. "I'm working tonight, but soon. I suppose I owe you a night's sleep, too. I don't know that I would have slept well after that episode on the beach."

"Hmm, how does one repay a night's sleep?" he asked, sounding intrigued.

"You leave the poor man alone," she said with a laugh.

"How disappointing."

"You don't suppose the man following us was just someone out taking a walk who happened to be going the same way we did, do you?"

"No, otherwise why would he go into the shack in the dark?" Sully asked. "And why was someone sweeping the tall grass with flashlights, looking for us?"

"Good points," she said.

"Lindsey, I know you are worried about putting your brother at risk, but last night upped the ante," he said. "I really think it would be a good idea to tell Emma what you know."

Lindsey turned away. She didn't want to have this conversation again.

"Well, thanks for the ride," she said. She opened the door and hopped out before he could continue the discussion.

To her surprise, he got out of his side and walked her to the door. "I want to know you're safe inside before I leave."

"I'll be fine," Lindsey said. They walked through the front door. Her landlady's door was open and she gestured to it as they passed. "See? Nancy's home."

Heathcliff darted inside Nancy's, which was his daytime play place, and Lindsey followed after him.

"Come here, buddy," she said. "I'm off this morning. Nancy's not babysitting you."

Heathcliff ignored her and rounded the corner, heading straight for the kitchen. It was hard to stop a puppy when he knew who was generous with the cookies.

Lindsey stepped into the kitchen and her feet faltered, causing Sully to slam into her back as they both stumbled into the room.

"Well, hello, love," Robbie said from his seat at Nancy's kitchen counter. "Late night?"

CHAPTER

18

BRIAR CREEK
PUBLIC LIBRARY

"Robbie!" Lindsey cried. "What are you doing here?"
Robbie was looking past Lindsey with a glower at Sully, who she noticed had a decidedly pleased look on his face.

"The lovely Nancy saw me come calling on you, and when you didn't answer, she invited me in for breakfast," he said. He gave her a pointed look, and Lindsey was suddenly very aware of how the situation looked given that she was wearing the same clothes she'd worn yesterday.

"It's not how it looks," she said. "We went for a walk."

There was a beat of silence and Robbie said, "Must have been a long walk."

Lindsey noticed Robbie was still looking past her at Sully when he said this, and he was still glaring. She glanced over her shoulder at Sully, who was smirking. Smirking!

151

"You've got the wrong idea," she said.

"Reeeeally?" Robbie asked. "What idea would that be?"

"I spent the night at Sully's—" she began, but he interrupted.

"Oh, I'd say that was the exact idea that I have," he said. "How about you, Nancy, same idea?"

"Well, they do look a bit rumpled," she said. The twinkle in her blue eyes was full of mischief.

"Do I?" Sully asked in a mock tone of surprise. "Well, now how could that have happened?"

"You are not helping," Lindsey chided him.

"Helping with what?" he asked.

"Helping yourself to the goodies apparently," Robbie muttered.

Sully shrugged and Nancy coughed in a way that Lindsey suspected she was trying to mask a laugh and failing miserably.

"Oh, for gosh Pete's sake!" Lindsey cried. "I went to the pier to tell Sully not to look into identifying the yacht because I don't want to see him get hurt."

"Isn't she the sweetest?" Sully asked Nancy, who nodded.

"Hush!" Lindsey ordered in a stern voice. Heathcliff gave her a concerned tip of the head. She reached down to rub his ears in reassurance while she continued.

"Sully had soup made so Heathcliff and I joined him for dinner and a walk on the beach, where we discovered someone was following us."

"What?" Nancy and Robbie spoke in unison. They both straightened with concern and looked to Sully for confirmation.

Lindsey glanced at Sully. Gone was the teasing; instead he looked suitably grim.

"He wasn't from around here," he confirmed. "At least, I'd never seen him before. I don't know that he intended any harm, but I didn't want to take any chances, so we ditched him at the old red shack."

"Define *ditched him*," Nancy said.

"I encouraged him to investigate the shed and then I shut the door after him," he said.

"So it's not like you bludgeoned him over the head or wrestled him to the ground or got an ID on him or anything?" Robbie asked. Lindsey wasn't sure how he did it, but he managed to make it sound like Sully was lacking.

"I was more concerned with getting Lindsey and Heathcliff out of there safely than I was about taking down someone who might be completely innocent," Sully said. "Priorities."

"If you want to call it that," Robbie said. His look was taunting. Sully opened his mouth to protest, but Lindsey cut him off.

"In any event, we got back to Sully's house, and fell asleep," she said. Sully smiled. Robbie frowned. Lindsey clarified, "On the couch."

Robbie was still frowning.

"On separate ends with Heathcliff in between us."

Robbie snatched a slice of bacon off his plate and held it out to Heathcliff, who devoured it in one swallow.

"You really are man's best friend, aren't you, mate?" he asked as he tousled his ears.

Heathcliff licked his hand, either cleaning up the grease or looking for another slice.

"Bacon bribery won't help you," Sully said. "Heathcliff loves everyone."

"Not bribing, just rewarding," Robbie said.

"Oh, please, that was a payoff if I ever saw one," Sully said.

"Zip it, you two," Nancy said. She leaned across the table and stared at Lindsey. "Why would Sully think that man was following you? Does this have something to do with the dead man in the library? Is there something you haven't told me?"

Lindsey met Nancy's gaze. The woman was too shrewd for her own good.

"Hey! I saw that!" Robbie shouted.

"Saw what?" Sully asked.

"You just snitched a piece of bacon off the counter and gave it to the dog!" Robbie accused.

"I don't know what you're talking about," Sully said innocently—too innocently.

Lindsey took the opportunity to avoid any more questions from Nancy.

"That's it!" she said. "Come on, Heathcliff, upstairs before these two make you too fat to fit through the door. No more spoiling my dog—either of you!"

She gave them a dark look and then hurried through the door before anyone, namely Nancy, could stop her. She hit the stairs at a jog, thinking Heathcliff probably needed to work off the bacon anyway.

She reached the second-floor landing when the door popped open and Nancy's nephew Charlie poked his head out.

"Oh, hey, Lindsey, I didn't expect to see you up this early," he said.

"Don't you start," she chided him.

"What?" he asked. He rubbed Heathcliff's head and asked, "What did I say?"

"Just because I didn't sleep at home last night doesn't give everyone the right to comment on my behavior," she said. "It's not what you think."

"What am I thinking?" he asked in confusion. He blinked at her and Lindsey noted that he was still in his pajamas, a pair of black and red checked bottoms with a matching long john black top.

"That just because I spent the night at Sully's, something happened. Nothing happened."

"Wait." He shook his stringy black hair as if he was trying to wake himself up. "Did you just say you weren't home at all last night?"

"That's what I said." Lindsey tried to keep the sarcasm out of her voice. Yeah, big fail. "But it doesn't mean that we're back together, and it certainly doesn't mean everyone can gossip about us. We're just friends. That's it."

"So you weren't home at all last night," Charlie said. "Not even at three o'clock in the morning?"

"Let it go, Charlie," she said. She made to move around him and continue up the stairs.

"No!" Charlie shouted and grabbed her arm.

"What is wrong with you?" she asked in exasperation. "I know you want Sully and me to get back together, but these things take time, and we'll just have to see what happens."

"No," he said.

"Excuse me?" she asked.

"Sorry, what I meant was this isn't about you and Sully, although that would be totally cool if you and the boss man hooked up again."

155

Lindsey gave him a pointed look.

"Okay, okay," he said. He let go of her arm and palmed the sides of his head as if trying to squeeze his brain into proper functionality. "I've had no caffeine, and when I'm trying to converse, that never goes well."

"It's okay." Lindsey patted his arm. "When you figure it out, you let me know."

She moved past him and began up the stairs to the third floor.

"Three fifteen," Charlie called after her.

Lindsey paused and looked back at him. "Explain."

"At three fifteen this morning, I know because I looked at my clock, there was a lot of noise coming from your apartment," he said. "It sounded like you were moving your furniture around. I almost came up and offered to help but then the noise stopped so I figured you were done. And yeah, well, I fell back asleep. Of course, now I realize the moving furniture idea makes no sense, but hey, I was dead asleep when the noise started."

"Charlie, focus. You heard noise in my apartment?" Lindsey repeated. Her brain was whirring like the back tires on a car stuck in a bog.

"Really loud noise," he confirmed.

Lindsey began to run up the stairs, taking them two at a time. She turned the corner and jogged across the landing to her front door. It was open just a crack and her skin tingled all over her body. Charlie was right. Someone had been in her apartment and maybe they still were.

CHAPTER

19

BRIAR CREEK
PUBLIC LIBRARY

"Lindsey!" Charlie yelled as he ran up the stairs behind her. "Wait for me. It might not be safe."

He joined her in front of the door. They looked at it and then each other.

"We should call the police," he said.

Lindsey knew she couldn't do that. Not until she knew it wasn't Jack. Maybe he had gotten away. Maybe he was hiding in her apartment even now. She went to push open her door with hope pounding through her. Charlie stepped in the way and stopped her.

"Don't touch anything," he said, grabbing her hand before it made contact with the door. "Use your elbow or something."

Lindsey realized he was right. For all she knew, the big man from the beach could be in there. Heathcliff looked like he was ready to dash in, but there was no way she was going to let her baby lead the way.

She grabbed his collar and held him back. She looked at Charlie and said, "Hold him?"

Charlie squatted down and held Heathcliff. Lindsey stepped forward when Sully and Robbie stomped onto the landing. They were both huffing and puffing, looking as if they'd run a race.

"What's going on up here?" Sully asked between breaths.

"Yeah, it sounded like a bloody ruckus had broken out," Robbie wheezed.

"Someone broke into Lindsey's apartment," Charlie said. "I heard them about three fifteen last night. I thought it was her, but Lindsey said she spent the night at your place."

Charlie gave Sully an approving look with raised eyebrows, which Sully, in a show of singular good sense, ignored.

"Just as friends," Robbie clarified. He looked at Charlie and said, "Opposite ends of the couch, if you must know."

Now the look Charlie gave Sully was one of supreme disappointment and Sully rolled his eyes.

"Boys, enough," Lindsey said. She gestured to her apartment. "Break-in, remember?"

"I'll go first," Sully said.

"Like hell," Robbie said.

He moved to stand beside Sully, and Lindsey blew out a breath. The temptation to clonk their heads together and knock them out was becoming almost more than she could bear.

"If you don't mind," she said. "My apartment, I'll go in first. Charlie, keep Heathcliff out here, please."

Charlie nodded. Lindsey stepped between Sully and Robbie. They both shifted to the side, barely, and she could feel them both leaning in on her as if determined not to let her out of their reach.

Lindsey used her elbow to push open the door. A gasp escaped her as she took in the wreckage that used to be her home sweet home.

"Whoa!" Charlie said from behind them. He was crouched down with the dog and looking through their legs.

Lindsey couldn't think of a better word to describe the devastation. Chairs were turned over, cushions and throw pillows slashed. Her bookcase had been emptied with the books tossed to the floor in a careless heap like dead bodies after a natural disaster.

She covered her mouth with her hand to keep from crying out. She wanted nothing more than to scoop them all up and examine their boo-boos like a child's skinned knee on the playground, but Sully caught her elbow and held her still.

"You have to report this to the police," he said.

"But—" Lindsey began to protest, but Robbie interrupted.

"Much as it pains me, I have to agree with sailor boy," he said. "This is too serious to ignore."

Lindsey nodded. She knew they were right. She was being followed, someone had trashed her apartment, and her brother was still missing. It was time to call for backup.

"I'll check the bedroom," Robbie said. "And make sure our uninvited visitor isn't here."

"I'm coming with you," Sully said grimly. "If our bad guy is here, we can't have the famous thespian risking a punch to the kisser, although some might argue that it would be an improvement."

"Only the jealous ones," Robbie said as he led the way.

Lindsey stepped carefully around the room, taking in the damage. Every cabinet in the kitchen was hanging open, but she was relieved that no dishes had been smashed. They weren't of any value, but the thought of having to clean up shards of glass was not her idea of fun. A chill went through her when she realized if she hadn't stayed at Sully's, she might have been here when they broke in.

Sully and Robbie returned moments later. They both looked grim, and Lindsey wondered if they were thinking the same thing she was—that this could have gone very badly had she been home when the person decided to do their search.

"It doesn't look as if anything was taken," Robbie said. "Just more of the same mess."

"So it's safe to assume they were looking for something specific," Lindsey sighed.

"Come on," Sully said. "Let's go down to Nancy's and call the police."

Lindsey was about to protest when Robbie frowned at her.

"If you don't call them, we will," he said.

"All right, fine," Lindsey said.

She left the door open as they all trooped back down the stairs to Nancy's apartment. Freshly brewed coffee and some breakfast croissants awaited them, but Lindsey couldn't eat. Charlie took Heathcliff for a walk, which left Lindsey free to report the break-in.

Chief Plewicki, Emma, answered her call and she sounded overtired and cranky when Lindsey reported the situation. Emma said she would be right over, and Lindsey spent the time trying to figure out how she could tell Emma about her brother without telling her about her brother.

"You have to tell her," Sully said. Lindsey was standing by the living room window, keeping an eye out for Emma's car.

Panic made Lindsey's insides clench. "What if it gets him killed?"

"What if not telling gets you killed?" Robbie asked as he joined them. Lindsey looked at him and he gave her a small sad smile. "Maybe you could live with that, but me and the water rat would be devastated, and I'm pretty sure your brother would be unhappy with you, too."

"Water rat? Really?" Sully asked. "Spoken like a true canned ham."

"Hey—" Robbie began to protest, but the front door opened and in strode Emma Plewicki and she did not look happy.

"Show me," she ordered without greeting.

"Upstairs," Lindsey said. She exited the room, but when Sully and Robbie would have joined them, she said, "Stay," in much the same tone she would have used on Heathcliff.

Both men stopped and Emma nodded at her in approval. "The fewer bodies up there, the better."

The two women began up the stairs, and Emma unzipped her thick uniform coat and took a pad and pen out of the inside pocket. Lindsey took this as a sign to start talking so she began at the beginning with arriving home to find that her apartment had been trashed but nothing stolen.

When she mentioned that she'd spent the night at Sully's, Emma didn't even flicker so much as an eyelash. It occurred to Lindsey that one of the things she liked best about Emma was that she never judged, never gossiped and played it all pretty close to the vest.

She told Emma that Charlie had heard noises in her apartment and thought it was her. Emma surveyed the damage from the doorway and then called for one of her officers to come over and do a crime scene sweep.

"Officer Wilcox will photograph the damage, take fingerprints and look for any hairs or fibers left behind by whoever broke in," she said. "Nothing is missing?"

"Not that I could see," Lindsey said.

"Do you have renter's insurance?" she asked.

"Yes."

"Then I'll make sure you get a copy of the police report in case you need to file a claim."

"Thanks," Lindsey said.

They stepped into the room, being careful not to touch anything. Emma scanned the room and then did a cursory walk-through. When she finished, she stopped beside Lindsey and frowned.

"Why you?" she asked.

"What do you mean?"

"Why your apartment?" Emma asked. "It's not as easy as a ground-floor apartment. You don't seem to own anything of tremendous value. So why you?"

"Maybe they knew I was out," Lindsey said. "Maybe they saw me with Sully and just assumed I'd be gone for the night."

"Then why not take anything?" Emma asked. "Your laptop is right there. Your jewelry box has a few pawnable sparklies in it. It's like they were looking for something specific but didn't find it."

"Maybe they got the wrong address," Lindsey said.

Emma studied her. Her brown eyes were narrowed in suspicion as if she knew Lindsey was holding something back. Lindsey knew this was her opportunity to tell Emma about Jack, the kidnapping, all of it. And yet she kept hearing Jack's voice telling her that the fewer people who knew about him, the better, and she couldn't make herself do it.

She knew she could be in trouble for obstructing an investigation, but really, would she risk her brother's life just to stay out of trouble? Hell no.

"Yeah, maybe," Emma said. Lindsey knew she didn't believe it.

Together they left the apartment. As they walked down the stairs, Emma began a discussion about safety.

"It was a forced entry on your door," she said. "You may want to invest in an alarm system. Another great deterrent is leaving a light on."

"Do you think they'll come back?" Lindsey asked. She was pleased that her voice didn't shake.

"I don't know," Emma said. Her voice was sharp. "I can't really answer that, given that I don't know what they were looking for."

Lindsey remembered the state of ruin her apartment had been left in, and for the first time, a sense of violation swept through her, making her feel fragile on the inside as if the burglars had stolen something after all. Then she realized they had. They'd stolen her peace of mind and sense of well-being in her own home, and there was no way leaving a light on or even having an alarm was going to give that back.

When they reached the bottom of the stairs, Nancy and the others were waiting.

Nancy looked guilt ridden and she grabbed Lindsey's arm and said, "This is all my fault. I forgot to lock the dead bolt on the front door. They never would have gotten in here if I had remembered."

"No," Lindsey said. "I refuse to let you blame yourself. It could just as easily have been Charlie or me. Besides they forced their way into my apartment. If they were that determined, they would have forced the front door, too."

"And if you had heard them and come out to investigate, Nanners, who knows what they would have done to you?" Charlie said.

"He's right," Emma said. "I'm sorry Lindsey's apartment took a hit, but I'm relieved she wasn't there and that neither of you meddled. Charlie, I've got some questions for you. Can you walk me to my car?"

"Sure," Charlie said, and he rose to his feet and grabbed his jacket off its hook in the foyer and followed her out.

"Why don't you run upstairs and pack a bag?" Sully said.

Lindsey blinked at him. "Excuse me?"

"You're not staying here," he said.

"Where am I going to go?" she asked.

"My house," Sully and Robbie said together and then looked at each other in annoyance.

Nancy made a noise that sounded like she was choking on a chicken bone. Lindsey gave her a dark look and she stepped back into her apartment.

"Is that the timer on my oven?" Nancy asked no one in particular. "Yes, I do believe it is."

The door shut behind her and Lindsey faced the boys.

"Thanks, but I can find my own place to sleep," she said. Both men looked like they were about to protest, but she held up her hand to silence them. "That is all."

Sully heaved a put-upon sigh. "Fine, but English here and I are going to take turns babysitting, since you obviously did not tell Emma anything about your brother."

"I call the night shift," Robbie said with a quick grin.

"We'll split it," Sully agreed with a glower.

"No, you won't," Lindsey said. She saw the concern on their faces and she softened her tone. "Listen, I didn't tell Emma about Jack, but I have my reasons. The minute I know he's safe, I'll tell her everything. I promise. In the meantime, I really appreciate your concern, but I'll be fine. I'm sure there is a reasonable explanation for all of this."

Neither Robbie nor Sully said anything, and she knew they were just too polite to point out the obvious. This was hell and away from anything resembling reasonable.

CHAPTER

20

BRIAR CREEK
PUBLIC LIBRARY

Lindsey had not expected to have to call out of work to spend the day cleaning her apartment. Generally, cleaning ranked in the top five of her least favorite things to do and it was amazing how the chore of dusting could be usurped by a good book. Not today, however.

Thankfully, the crafternoon ladies all popped in and helped, and it wasn't long after Officer Wilcox left with his fingerprint kit and digital camera that order was restored. The most critical of all, of course, was making sure her books had not been harmed. Her first fear when she saw the pile on the floor had been that the person who had broken in had damaged the bindings and ripped the pages. After the bout of panicked nausea had passed and she discovered that they had thrown them on the floor in either a temper tantrum or to see if there was anything behind them, she felt like she could breathe again.

None of the books were rare editions or of any spectacular value beyond the sentimental, but they were hers and they comforted her and it hurt her to see them mistreated. As she placed the last of the books, an old edition of Dashiell Hammett's *The Thin Man*, back on the shelf beside her other favorite of his, *The Maltese Falcon*, she felt as if she were back in control of the situation.

"Lindsey," Stew Hardy called to her from the front door. "Here are the keys to your new locks."

Stew had moved to Briar Creek from Ansonia just a few months before Lindsey had been hired as the library director. He was somewhere in his sixties and lived alone with a parrot named Mojo, who liked to hang out on Stew's shoulder during the summer months and chat with the regulars at the bakery in town.

Despite being retired, Stew worked as a local handyman who specialized in locks. Lindsey knew he wasn't much of a reader, but he sure put the library DVD collection to good use, his favorites being superhero movies.

"Thanks, Stew," she said. She took her new keys and jiggled them. "Did I tell you we got the new Avengers movie in yesterday?"

"Sweet!" Stew said. "I know I'm first on the list."

"Yes, you are," she said.

"When do you think it'll be ready?" he asked.

"I'm going to put a rush on it tomorrow," she said. "Because I really can't thank you enough for this."

"Ha! Wait 'til you get my bill," he said. He laughed at his own joke, which made Lindsey smile, and then he nudged her with an elbow. "Just joshing. I'd never overcharge for something like this. Damn shame someone decided to pick on you."

"Thanks, Stew," she said.

"Listen." He looked serious. "My locks are good, but you need to be careful. Got it?"

"I promise," she said. She waved as he headed down the stairs, and then she turned to go back into her apartment. There were still gouges in the wooden door where it had been pried open. She quickly glanced away, realizing that was a chore for another day off.

Lindsey knew tonight was going to be a bit unsettling, but she was determined not to be freaked out in her own home, even though she was.

Mary Murphy hauled a garbage bag holding the remnants of Lindsey's couch pillows and dropped it just outside her front door.

"I think I got all of the pillow fill that was scattered," she said. "Heathcliff was a big help, really."

Lindsey smiled. She knew Heathcliff equated pillow innards with toys so she could only imagine what a help he had been.

"Dishes are washed," Violet said as she joined them. "And I took the liberty of making a pot of coffee."

"Terrific," Nancy said. She gestured to a plastic container on the counter. "I brought some macaroons."

Beth came out of the bedroom with a bucket and a sponge. "I think I got all the fingerprint dust residue off of your furniture."

Violet and Charlene had taken on the chore of washing Lindsey's bed sheets and blankets, which had been thrown to the floor. They came out of the bedroom behind Beth, having just remade the bed.

"Your place is no longer sullied by the break in," Violet announced.

"I truly can't thank you all enough," Lindsey said. "It would have been a very long and scary day for me if I'd had to do this all by myself."

"That's what friends are for," Nancy said. She opened the lid off the macaroons and passed out some napkins.

Mary plunked six mugs down on the counter and began to pour the coffee while Violet put out the bowl of sugar and a small pitcher of milk.

Lindsey felt as if her throat was too tight with emotion to choke down a macaroon, but she gratefully reached for a mug of steaming hot coffee.

"So now that we're all together," Beth said, "start talking."

Lindsey sputtered on her coffee. She gave her friend a wide-eyed look. She loved her friends, but she didn't think it wise to talk to the entire group about her brother or his possible connection to the dead man or the break-in.

"So a sleepover at Sully's last night?" Mary asked.

Mary was Sully's little sister, so to say that this was uncomfortable was putting it mildly.

"What book was I supposed to be getting for our next crafternoon?" Lindsey asked. "Beth, you were lobbying for *The Secret Garden*, weren't you?"

"Yes, and I already have copies for all of us," she said. "And that was the lamest attempt at a subject change ever."

Lindsey rolled her eyes. "Does the word *awkward* mean anything to you?"

"Please, I'm a children's librarian. It's hard to define *awkward* when you dress like Babar the Elephant and do finger plays and felt boards every week," she said.

"She has a point," Violet said. She blew on the steaming

169

coffee in her mug and asked, "So how did Robbie take the news?"

"What news?" Lindsey asked.

"That you and Sully are back together," Charlene said. Both she and Violet gave Lindsey reproving looks, no doubt because Robbie was a longtime family friend.

"You are?" Nancy asked, looking delighted.

"Hold the phone," Lindsey said. She held up her hands in a gesture to stop the crazy talk. "I fell asleep on Sully's couch. There is nothing, and I do mean nothing, else to report."

The looks of disappointment were almost comical, except of course, for Charlene and Violet. They looked hopeful.

"Stop that!" Lindsey said to them.

"What?" the mother and daughter asked in unison.

"Thinking that I am going to take up with Robbie and give him a reason to stay in Briar Creek," she said. "He's married, remember?"

"Kitty is just his business manager," Charlene protested. "I'm sure he'll file the divorce papers now, especially if he knows it bothers you."

Mild frustration had Lindsey biting a macaroon in two. "It doesn't bother me, because he and I are just friends."

Nancy and Mary exchanged a pleased look.

"Sully and I are just friends, too," Lindsey said, squashing their moment.

"Well, it must be nice to have two men interested in you," Beth pouted. "Heck, I'd be happy if one man looked my way and wasn't swept off by some exotic beauty . . . ouch!"

Lindsey kicked her ankle to stop her from saying any more.

"Oh, was that your foot?" she asked. "Sorry."

Beth frowned at her, but the others were already assuring her that she would meet someone someday.

"Beth, you are a wonderful woman," Charlene said. "Any man would be happy to have you."

"Really? Then I've been alone for over a year because why exactly?"

"Mostly because you picked a clunker and stayed with him for too long," Nancy said. Beth looked about to protest, but Nancy shook her head. "I know he died a horrible death but really, dear, you need to have your boyfriends vetted. He was not a keeper."

Beth sighed and rested her chin on her hand while she absently stirred her coffee. "You're right."

"What about using an online dating service?" Mary asked. "I know of two couples who met that way and they seem very happy."

"I tried," Beth sighed. "The first guy wanted to know how much money I made. The other guy wanted me to send him proof that I owned my house. I'm telling you, ladies, it's just weird out there."

"Maybe you could meet someone doing volunteer work," Charlene said. "You could be a baby snuggler at Yale–New Haven Hospital or a dog walker at the Humane Society."

"No," Beth said. "I've tried all of that. I even attempted to join an adventure club where you go hiking and boating and do all sorts of cool stuff. Everyone was coupled off after the first two weeks and the cheese stood alone. In case you're wondering, I am the cheese, the stinky kind apparently."

"Well, that's a good thing," Nancy said. They all looked at her and she explained, "Cheese gets better with age."

Beth burst out laughing. She hugged Nancy close and said, "And that is why I love you; you know just what to say."

When the crafternoon ladies left, Lindsey sank down on her sofa and Heathcliff jumped up beside her and planted himself on her hip. He was a cuddly dog by nature, but she wondered if his canine sensors had picked up on the fact that things were not normal and he felt a need to keep close.

She scratched his head. "It's okay, buddy, we'll stick together and be just fine."

But it wasn't fine. According to Emma, there was still no ID on the dead man in the library. Jack was missing, and no matter how many times she checked her phone, there was no text or e-mail from him to give her any peace of mind.

Now someone had broken into her home and they'd been looking for something. It certainly hadn't been a who, because they wouldn't have felt compelled to destroy all of her pillows and toss the place. No, this had definitely been a thing they were seeking, but what?

It was getting dark outside, and she knew she needed to feed Heathcliff and take him for a walk before settling in for the night. She sat staring out the windows that gave her a view of the bay and the islands, willing herself to get up.

A creak outside her door made her insides clench. Her pulse kicked into triple time and Heathcliff launched himself off the couch to charge the door with his ferocious barking growl fully engaged.

Lindsey crossed to the door. She figured she'd play it up just in case her destructive visitors had returned.

"Down, boy!" she ordered. "And don't go for the throat. If you kill again, they'll euthanize you for sure."

Heathcliff cocked his head at her in a look that said more plainly than words that she was overselling it. Lindsey shrugged.

"Lindsey Norris, that is quite possibly the worst performance I've ever heard," a man's voice with a distinctive British accent said through the door. "Now, let me in, I brought dinner."

Lindsey yanked the door open and there stood Robbie Vine, carrying a large pizza and a bottle of wine.

CHAPTER

21

BRIAR CREEK
PUBLIC LIBRARY

"Robbie!" She stepped aside to let him in. "What are you doing here?"

"Really?" he asked. "I thought the pizza box was a dead giveaway."

"Fair enough," she said. "Sorry, I'm not myself."

"No, but your place looks put back to rights," he said. "I was worried you might be nervous about being alone."

He put the pizza and wine down on her coffee table, and took the time to scratch Heathcliff's head. The dog stood on his hind legs and hugged Robbie around the knee. It was a gesture the dog reserved for those he particularly liked, and it made Lindsey smile to see the Englishman was one of them.

"You didn't have to go to so much trouble," she said. "I'm fine."

"It was no trouble," he said. "Dylan and I spent the

afternoon looking at Yale's theater program, so it was a quick stop at Wooster Square for pizza, one of which he and his friends devoured on the ride back while I guarded this one for you and me."

"I've seen teenagers eat," Lindsey joked as she handed him the corkscrew. "You were taking your life into your hands there."

"You've no idea," he said with a wink.

Lindsey went back to the kitchen for plates and napkins. When she rejoined Robbie, he was sitting on the couch while pouring two glasses of wine.

Although Lindsey could have sworn she wasn't hungry, the smell of the white pizza from the famous brick oven pizza joint in New Haven made her mouth water.

Heathcliff sat at full alert until Robbie shared his crust with him. Lindsey found it small wonder that the dog adored the men in her life; they both spoiled him rotten.

"So do the police have any idea who ransacked your place or why?" he asked.

"Not that I've heard," she said. She took a sip of wine and set her glass down.

"You're worried about your brother," he said.

"I'm beside myself," she admitted. "I just wish I could figure out who these people are that are after Jack, who the woman was who snatched him and the identity of the man who called me. I know that if I could just figure that out, then I'd have some sort of clue. I mean he's an economist, he's not James Bond."

"Are you sure about that?" he asked.

"I'm not sure about anything anymore," she said.

"What did he do for a living exactly?"

"I'm a book person, not a number person," she said

175

apologetically. "From what I understand, he consulted with companies and helped them drive sustainable growth using long-term strategy tools or something like that. The gist was that he was hired to boost the company's sales when it had stagnated."

"So he was a hatchet man?" Robbie asked. "That could make him very unpopular."

He took a bite of pizza and studied her face while she thought about his question.

Lindsey took another sip of wine. "No, he didn't go in and terminate employees. He mostly scrutinized the company's way of doing business, their leadership, the current market, and their profit margins. He then made recommendations on how they could improve."

Lindsey took a bite of her own slice and chewed while she pondered the possibility that her brother's business was more dangerous than she had realized.

"Was he part of a company?" Robbie asked. "Did he have an office? Anyone you could call and ask?"

"When he graduated, he worked for a firm in Boston, but my brother is a roamer. He enjoyed working globally because he said it gave him a better feel for how businesses operated worldwide. He enjoyed immersing himself in different cultures."

"Is there anyone who would know where he was most recently?" he asked.

"I—" Lindsey began but a fist pounding on her door interrupted whatever she was about to say.

"Expecting someone?" Robbie asked.

"No," she said.

"Maybe if we ignore them, they'll go away," Robbie suggested.

The pounding resumed.

"Or not," Lindsey said. "Excuse me."

"Certainly," Robbie said on a sigh and then downed his wine in one swallow.

Before Lindsey could reach the door, a familiar voice shouted, "Open up, Vine, I know you're in there."

Lindsey's eyes went wide. She knew that voice. It was Sully, and while he rarely ever lost his temper, she could tell he was not happy.

She turned to look at Robbie, who shrugged. For one of the world's most talented actors, he did not sell it very well, and she narrowed her eyes as she studied him.

"What did you do?" she asked.

"Innocent until proven guilty," Robbie said.

"Hang on, Sully," Lindsey said as she fussed with her new locks. "I'm opening up."

No sooner had she pulled the door open than Sully strode into the room.

"I knew it!" he cried. "You set me up so you could take advantage of my absence."

"Did you fall off your dingy and get water on the brain?" Robbie asked. "Whatever are you talking about?"

"I was on water taxi duty this evening, which is usually quite dead in the dark days of December, but no, I had three different calls for pick up out in the farthest islands in the bay, and, big shock, when I got to each one, no one had called for taxi service."

Lindsey turned from Sully to Robbie. "You didn't."

"I refuse to answer that on the grounds that I might incriminate myself," he said.

"Why you . . ." Sully lifted his hands like he was about to throttle the other man.

Robbie, being quicker on his feet than most, managed to keep the wide coffee table between them. "Hey, you got to spend a whole night with her. I was just evening it up a bit."

"I almost froze out there, not to mention the amount of gas I wasted for nothing," Sully said. He looked like he was going to lunge across the table but instead he snatched a piece of pizza from the box.

"Bill me," Robbie said.

"Oh, I will," Sully said. "But now you can leave, since I think it's my turn to watch Lindsey."

"The night's not half over," Robbie protested.

"It is for you," Sully said.

Lindsey rolled her eyes at Heathcliff. Enough was enough. She picked up the box of pizza and shoved it at Sully. Then she maneuvered so that she was behind both of them. With one hand on each of their backs, she applied a steady pressure until she had them out the door and into the hallway.

"I can't tell you how lovely it's been, really," she said. "Now good night."

She shut the door in their faces.

"Well, you certainly managed to bollocks that up," Robbie snapped.

"I managed to?" Sully argued. "What was the big idea sending me out on a fool's errand?"

"Your words, not mine," Robbie said. "I'm an actor. I can't help it if I'm no good at strategy."

Lindsey wondered if they would stand there and bicker all night. She opened her door a crack and said, "Good night, gentlemen."

With sulky glances, they obviously took her meaning and began to walk down the stairs. She noted they were sharing the remains of the pizza and took that as a good sign.

She did check the lock on her door once to make sure she and Heathcliff were safely locked in. Then she did a quick scan of all of her window locks. Yes, the break-in had given her a case of the wiggins. There was no doubt about it.

She finished her glass of wine and took the empty plates to the kitchen to be rinsed. She ran the conversation she'd had with Robbie through her mind. It bothered her that she didn't know as much about her brother's business as she should. What kind of sister had only the vaguest clue as to what her brother did for a living?

She went over to her small desk by the window. It was fully dark outside and the living room lights reflected the room on the window glass, making it hard to see out but easy to see in. A sense of caution zipped over her nerves. She reached over and closed the thick curtain.

She sat at her small desk and opened her laptop. She scrupulously saved all the e-mails she received from her brother in a file appropriately labeled "Bro." It took her computer a minute to get going.

Last year, Lindsey had attended a cybercrimes workshop put on by the state library association. Being providers of the Internet to the public at large, libraries were finding that some users knew how to hack the filters that were put in place to keep the computers in the library safe for all users.

One of the many things the detective teaching the class had taught them was how they could trace a criminal user back to the library by tracing the IP address, which stood for Internet Protocol address, a numerical label assigned to every computer, printer and other device within a network. Lindsey had never really thought the information would come into play in her life, but now she wondered. If Jack had been using a foreign network when he e-mailed her, she might be able to trace where he had been most recently by locating the origin of the IP address.

Lindsey opened the file from the workshop that listed the websites that could help her trace Jack's IP. Then she opened her personal e-mail and frowned. How was she supposed to figure out his IP address from an e-mail? She switched back to her notes. Sure enough, scribbled in the margin were notes for just that.

She chose an option she had never noticed before that read "show original." Bingo! A bunch of cybertext came up on her screen that read like gobbledygook to her, so Lindsey figured it must be right.

She checked her notes. She cut and pasted the gook onto the query screen of a website that said it would track the IP. It came back a second later with a message that said it was unreadable. She checked and trimmed her original cut from the recognizable words "return path" to "content." She sent the query again. This time a chart came up.

Lindsey had to pause to pump her fist. She was pretty sure any computer-savvy ten-year-old could have done this in half the time, but still she had managed it. She felt the need to let out a nerdy "Woot!" before she got back to work.

She checked her notes again and logged on to the website that could track an IP address. Success was short lived. The first few websites she tried couldn't find the IP. She tried another and another. No luck.

She needed something more to go on. She opened up her e-mail and read her brother's messages. Jack was not one to post much more than "Hey, I'm alive!" which, while reassuring when she hadn't heard from him, was also very annoying because it really gave her no details as to where he was or what he was doing.

Usually, the only way she discovered where he'd been was when her birthday or Christmas rolled around and a box that looked as battered as if it had walked all the way from its destination to her house arrived and inside she would find anything from a Tibetan singing bowl to a Costa Rican string bracelet.

"Jack," she said to the miserly list of e-mails in her Bro file, "when I see you again, we are going to have a very long talk about communication, your lack thereof, and how you will improve or face my wrath."

Finally, in the fifth e-mail she scanned, there was a kernel of information. His closing sentence read, *Linds, I'm south of the border consulting on plantas de café. Hope to be home for the holidays. L, Jack.*

Jack spoke at least four languages fluently and a smattering of others. It was one of the reasons he liked to be a global business consultant—he got to dust off his language skills. Lindsey had always thought that his use of the language of the country he was headed to was him showing off, but now she was grateful. It was the first solid lead she'd gotten. It fit, too, as the woman who'd absconded with him had an accent and she was clearly a beauty, a Latin beauty.

So Jack had to have been in a Spanish-speaking country and was there assisting with a company that produced coffee. At least, given her college Spanish, she hoped *plantas de café* meant coffee plants. She supposed she could use an online translator, but it seemed pretty obvious.

Lindsey rubbed her eyes. Sleeping on Sully's couch had been fitful, since she was worried about her brother, freaked out that someone had followed them, and frankly, distracted by how close Sully had been. Her exhaustion was catching up to her and she yawned.

She logged on to the library's website. She needed a quick business breakdown about the coffee industry. Ironic how much a cup of java would help her right now, she thought. She chose the "Business Insights: Essentials" option and typed in a search for the coffee industry.

Under the subheading "Roasted Coffee," she read all about the history of coffee, the difference between the arabica and robusta beans, the importance of storage and roasting, and a multitude of other facts. Finally, in a small paragraph toward the bottom, she saw the listing for the countries where it is grown, with Brazil leading the way by producing one third of the world's coffee.

Brazil. So maybe *plantas de café* was not Spanish so much as Portuguese. She sincerely hoped so. Either way, she knew her next step was to find and search a Latin IP address registry.

Heathcliff suddenly dropped on top of her feet, and Lindsey scratched his head while she waited for her search. Finally, it popped up with a Latin IP address registry. She cut and pasted the IP address into the search, and sure enough, the country of origin was verified as

Brazil. Jack must have been using one of the computers belonging to the Brazilian company he'd been hired by to send his e-mail.

The cybercrimes detective had talked to them about how some criminals use a proxy server to hide their IP and thus their specific location, but there would be no reason for Jack to do that, so she had to assume this address was legit.

She was afraid to look and see how many coffee companies were in Brazil. She had a feeling it would be like trying to locate one particular bean in a silo of coffee beans. Was there anyone in Jack's inner circle who would know?

Surfacing like a submarine from the depths of her brain, the name *Stella McQuaid* rose to the top. Lindsey logged on to the library's website, and from there she went into the newspaper databases.

She found an article written two years before about Stella McQuaid. At that time, she was still working for the consulting firm, New System Technologies, which Jack still worked for in a freelance capacity. She remembered that Jack had thought very highly of Stella. Lindsey wondered if they'd kept in touch. It was too much to hope that the Brazilian coffee company was a freelance gig for this company, but hey, she wouldn't know until she asked.

She glanced at the clock. It was closing in on midnight. She'd have to wait to call Stella's office in the morning. She tried to convince herself that she was okay with that.

She shut down her laptop. She turned off the lights. She wondered what had become of Sully and Robbie and then told herself it didn't matter. She was safe, she told herself. Perfectly safe.

She unlocked her front door and peeked out just to do one more visual sweep for peace of mind. It was a mistake. The sight before her gave her anything but peace. Instead her voice was full of ire when she asked, "What do you think you're doing?"

CHAPTER

22

BRIAR CREEK
PUBLIC LIBRARY

"I told you'd she'd get her knickers in a twist about this," Robbie said.

"Can't be helped," Sully said with a shrug. "Do you have any eights?"

"Go fish," Robbie said.

Sully sighed as he took a card off the top of the pile. The two men were sitting on the landing with a pack of cards and a bottle of brandy between them. The only light shone dimly from Charlie's landing below, and the draft that blew through the stairwell caused her to shiver.

"You're playing go fish?" Lindsey asked, knowing full well she was just verifying the obvious.

"Neither of us had enough money for poker," Robbie said.

"And war seemed inappropriate," Sully added.

"Could lead to fisticuffs," Robbie agreed.

"Go home!" Lindsey barked.

They both looked at her in consternation. Sully picked up the brandy and took a sip and then handed it to Robbie, who did the same.

"Nope," Sully said. "We're staying."

"But that's completely unacceptable," Lindsey said. "You can't sit in my hallway all night."

"It's a free country," Robbie protested. Lindsey noticed his British accent seemed thicker and he was slurring. "And coming from me, that's saying something."

"Are you all right?" Lindsey asked. She hunkered down in front of Robbie. One whiff and she knew he was not all right. "You're shnockered."

"Am I?" he asked. Then he keeled over onto his back with his arms out wide and a snore coming from his mouth.

Lindsey glanced at Sully. "This is your doing, isn't it?"

His bright blue eyes went wide with innocence. "I can't imagine what you mean."

"Let me take a wild guess," she said. "Robbie was a bit miffed about my sleeping at your house and was quite determined to even things out by sending you on a wild errand so he could be my shadow tonight."

Sully prodded Robbie with the toe of his shoe, but the Englishman didn't respond.

"When I tossed you both out," Lindsey continued, "I'm betting he planned to camp out on the steps and you joined him, bringing brandy and cards to pass the time. How am I doing so far?"

"Sounds reasonable enough." Sully brushed a bit of imaginary lint off his shirtsleeve.

"But"—Lindsey emphasized the word, hoping Sully

caught the double meaning—"you didn't actually drink any of the brandy, did you?"

"It's not really my thing," he said. "It's more of an Englishman's beverage, don't you think?"

"I think you got even for being sent on a wild-goose chase, that's what I think," she said. "Also, you should be ashamed of yourself. Look at him. He's a drunken mess!"

"Oh, I don't know. I think he's kind of cute when he's not flapping his lips."

Lindsey rolled her eyes. "Come on, help me carry him in."

"What?" Sully squawked.

"Well, he's got to sleep it off somewhere," she said.

"I'll give him a ride home," Sully said.

"You're going to carry a man down three flights of stairs?" she asked. She gave him a dubious look.

"I was thinking I'd roll him," he said.

"No."

"I'm sure he'd bounce."

"No."

"He'd better have one heck of a headache tomorrow," Sully said.

"I'm sure he will," she said.

She bent over and hoisted Robbie into a seated position. Sully took one arm and draped it over his shoulder while Lindsey took the other. Together they hauled the Englishman into her apartment and dumped him on the sofa.

"What if he's faking it?" Sully asked.

Lindsey held up the bottle of brandy to the light. It was more than half gone.

"Somehow I doubt it," she said.

"Still, he's an actor," Sully said. "This could just be a ruse to get into your apartment and be alone with you."

As if he heard them speaking, Robbie let out a grunt and a snore and turned over onto his side into the back of the couch. Heathcliff hopped up beside him and lay down next to him.

Sully frowned at the dog. "Hey, help a guy out."

Heathcliff put his head down on his paws.

"Robbie gave him pizza crust," she explained.

"I think I should stay just in case someone tries to break in," Sully said. "This one is going to be of no use to you."

"No one is going to try and break in," she said. "Why would they? It's like Grand Central Station around here."

She put her hand on Sully's arm and guided him to the door. "Thanks for looking out for me, but I'm good."

"But I—" he began, but she cut him off.

"Good night, Sully," she said. She closed the door on his frowning face.

Back in the living room, Robbie snored on. Lindsey was quite certain he wasn't faking it, as he didn't move when she put a quilt on him. He'd been known to catch her off guard with a surprise kiss before. Never would there be a better opportunity, but he slept right through it, for which she was relieved. She was not up for any more relationship shenanigans, not when she was so worried about her brother.

She headed to the bedroom with Heathcliff at her side. Amazingly enough, even though he wasn't in shape enough to defend a wet noodle, she felt better just having Robbie in the apartment. His presence, well, maybe his snoring made the shadows stay in the shadows and Lindsey was grateful.

My head," Robbie moaned. "I think that bloody pirate split me with an ax when I wasn't looking."

"No, you're in one piece," Lindsey said. "I promise."

She'd cooked up a breakfast of toast and tea, which Robbie was gingerly nibbling. She'd also given him some pain pills for his head, but she had a feeling only lots of water and a nap would set him right.

"I'd say you two are even now, wouldn't you?" she asked.

Robbie glowered. "I don't know. How's he feeling this morning?"

"Vindicated?" she asked. "After all, you did send him out into the cold."

"Not far enough," he said. "I should have sent him to Long Island."

Lindsey rolled her eyes and poured him some more tea.

"So tell me," Robbie said. "Because truly, I can't feel any worse than I do now—do I stand a chance with you at all?"

"Are you still married?" she asked.

"It's just a piece of paper," he protested. "You know Kitty and I are just business partners."

"Not to me," she said. "I don't date married men."

"What if I were free?" he asked. He lowered his head and was cradling it in his hands as if holding it together to keep it from separating. "What then, my lovely librarian, would I stand a chance with you then?"

His normally mischievous green eyes were studying

her so intently that Lindsey felt her breath catch. Even with a pitiful hangover, Robbie was a force to be reckoned with. It was as if he emitted his own electromagnetic field and no one was immune. Not even Lindsey.

She had always used his marriage as a buffer for her attraction to him. There could never be a them because she was not about to date anyone who was already spoken for, whether it was in name only or not. The thought of him being available was singularly disturbing because she really didn't know if she could resist his charm.

"I really can't answer that since it isn't the case, now is it?" she asked, skillfully dodging the question, or so she thought.

His green eyes flashed and his grin was wicked when he caught her hand and placed a kiss on her knuckles, which made her shiver.

"Then I have hope," he said.

Lindsey tugged her hand away and said, "No, you don't, because you're *married*."

A fist pounded on her door, and the fire went out of Robbie's eyes and he groaned, clutching his head.

"I'll bet it's the sodding seahorse here to gloat," he said.

Lindsey left him and went to open the door. Not surprisingly, Sully stood on the other side. He looked Lindsey over and then glanced past her to where Robbie was sitting at the table, the picture of misery.

"So all went well last night?" he asked. He looked pretty satisfied with himself.

"All went just fine," Lindsey assured him. She tossed her hair over her shoulders, placed her hand over her chest and gave a deep sigh. "I feel like a new woman. I had no idea it could be so life altering, so earth shattering—"

Her words were cut off by a low growl coming from Sully's throat.

"Ha! Serves you right," she said. "Now give the poor man a lift home. I have to get to work. Oh, and lock up after yourselves."

CHAPTER

23

BRIAR CREEK
PUBLIC LIBRARY

Lindsey hurried down the stairs with Heathcliff bounding after her. They stopped in at Nancy's, where Heathcliff would spend the day. Nancy attempted to pry information about Sully and Robbie out of Lindsey, but she resisted saying anything except that Sully would be giving Robbie a lift home.

When Nancy lifted her eyebrows in surprise, Lindsey did not elaborate. She had more important matters than her personal life to think about today, and she wasn't going to give any grist to the gossip mill. Just like her, they'd all have to wait and see how it played out.

She got her bike out of the garage and tossed her handbag into the basket in back before pushing off and pedaling toward town. The wind was brisk and she tucked her nose into her knit scarf. The tips of her ears were chilled, however, and she was relieved when the library came into view and she knew she was mere moments from a cup of hot coffee.

She locked up her bike and hurried through the back door, deactivating the alarm as she went. She was the first one to arrive today, which meant the opening procedures were all on her.

She stashed her purse in her desk and turned on her computer and then started a large pot of coffee. Next she began to turn on the lights and the computers for the rest of the building. While she was turning on the lights, Ann Marie arrived and began to unload the book drop and check in the materials that had been returned while they were closed.

Lindsey glanced at the clock. She had just enough time to pour a cup of coffee before she unlocked the front doors. She was manning the reference desk this morning until their library assistant, Jessica Gallo, came in to take over. Ms. Cole and Beth were due in any moment.

Lindsey took her coffee cup out to the reference desk. Today was not a day to be faced without java. She knew Ms. Cole would feel behooved to point out that her predecessor, Mr. Tupper, never let them drink beverages on the floor, and Lindsey would have to remind her that she wasn't Mr. Tupper and she wasn't giving up her coffee.

She left the small circular desk in the middle of the adult area and went to open the doors. Ms. Cole appeared behind the circulation desk from the back room, and Ann Marie gave Lindsey a nod that she was ready.

Lindsey unlocked the sliding doors and checked that the door counter was on zero. An automatic counter, it ticked every time someone came into or departed from the building. The staff took the total number each day and divided it in half to ascertain the number of people coming into the library that day.

Statistics were the town's way of summing up the library's worth with a number. How many people used the library? How many people checked out books? How many people came to the programs? How many people used the computers? All these numbers.

Did it really quantify the value of a place where information was free, where thoughts and ideas were stored and shared? Lindsey didn't think so, and she didn't believe the people who loved the library thought so either. Still, the town needed to justify their paychecks, and this was what they'd come up with.

She stepped back onto the rubber mat, and the automatic doors swung open. In rushed Beth looking harried as she raced by.

"Morning, boss," Beth said as she shot toward the children's area, dragging a rolling plastic bucket full of books and craft supplies behind her.

"Hi, Beth," Lindsey said.

A few customers shuffled in. An older gentleman set out for the day's newspapers that Ann Marie had just put on the racks; two more younger men headed right for the Internet computers. A third, an older woman, approached the circulation desk with an overdue notice in her hand and fire in her eye.

Mrs. Bane was the world's worst library borrower. She took out too much and could never manage to get it back on time. Naturally, Ms. Cole took this personally.

When Lindsey had first started, she had tried to mediate the situation, but it had come to her attention that both Ms. Cole and Mrs. Bane enjoyed their little go-rounds.

They never raised their voices or swore, and as far as she knew, no one had taken a swing at the other as yet; rather they really enjoyed the art of the veiled insult. Lindsey didn't want to impede their joy and so she left them to it.

"I suppose if I had a *job* working here, I would remember to bring my things back," Mrs. Bane said. She managed to make the word *job* sound like the equivalent of cleaning toilets.

"Don't fret, not everyone has the *intelligence* to have a marketable skill set," Ms. Cole returned.

Mrs. Bane let out a huff of indignant air, and Lindsey turned away before they caught her smiling.

She had taken her cell phone with her to the reference desk. Since there were no customers waiting, she decided to try calling her brother's old office in Boston. She picked up her coffee and paced over to the window, where she could look out at the street, the park and the bay beyond.

It took three transfers and five minutes of Muzak before she reached Stella's office.

"Stella McQuaid's office, this is Tracy, may I help you?" a pleasant voice answered.

"Yes, please, my name is Lindsey Norris and I'm calling to speak with Stella," she said.

"I'm sorry, I don't have you listed on her schedule," Tracy said. "If you'd like to leave your name and number and what this is regarding, I can have her call you back."

"No, I really need to speak with her for just a moment," Lindsey insisted.

Tracy's voice became firm and a teeny bit irritated. "I'm sorry but Ms. McQuaid is very busy."

"I appreciate that, but if you could just tell her that Lindsey Norris is on the phone and—"

"I'm sorry, Ms. Norris, I can't interrupt her right now but I'll be happy to—excuse me, hold on, please."

Splat! Lindsey felt as if she'd just run into the proverbial brick wall. By the time Stella got her message, assuming she even made the name connection between Lindsey and Jack, it could be hours or possibly days from now. Lindsey didn't think she was panicking to think that every second counted right now.

"Lindsey Norris? Jack Norris's sister?" a new voice spoke into the phone.

"Yes, yes, that's me," Lindsey answered.

"Where the hell is he?" the woman barked.

"Stella?"

"Yes, sorry, Stella McQuaid here. You're Jack's sister?"

"Yes, Lindsey Norris. Honestly, Stella, I was hoping you knew where Jack might be," Lindsey said. She didn't like that Stella's anxiety was ratcheting hers up. She'd been hoping the woman would calm her down.

"He hasn't been in contact in days," Stella said. "I know Jack is unpredictable, but even for him, this is irresponsible."

"He was here in Briar Creek," Lindsey said. Then she realized she was on a cell phone, which was not a secure line, and decided she needed to talk to Stella from her office. "Listen, can you call me back on my landline?"

"Good thinking," Stella said. "Give me the number."

Lindsey rattled off the numbers and hung up. She hurried around the circulation desk, noticing that Ms. Cole and Mrs. Bane were still going nose to nose.

"Ann Marie, if anyone needs reference help, I'll be right back," she said. "I have a call I have to take."

Ann Marie nodded and turned back to watch the battle of barbs between Mrs. Bane and Ms. Cole.

Lindsey paused and whispered, "What's the score?"

"The lemon seven, Mrs. Bane six," Ann Marie said.

Lindsey nodded. She figured Ms. Cole was due to win this round as Mrs. Bane had trounced her last time.

She hurried on to her office. She stepped through the door right as the phone started to ring.

"Hel—"

She didn't even get her greeting out before Stella started talking. Lindsey had never met the woman, but she was getting the feeling that Stella took her business very, very seriously.

"When was the last time you saw him?" Stella asked.

Lindsey paused. How much did she want to tell this woman? She wasn't certain she wanted to tell her anything. She had called looking for information, not to be grilled.

"That's not why I called," she said. Stella started to talk, but this time Lindsey went right over her. "No. I'm asking the questions. What do you know about who my brother was working for and in what capacity? Also, if you could confirm that he was working for a company in Brazil, that would be a big help as well."

"I'm sorry," Stella's voice was crisp. "I'm not at liberty to share confidential business information."

"Then this call is useless to me," Lindsey said. Now she was getting mad. She knew this woman knew something, and damn it, she wanted to know what.

"I feel the same," Stella snapped.

They were both stubbornly silent for a few moments.

Lindsey almost gave in, but not knowing what exactly she was dealing with kept her silent.

"All right, fine," Stella caved in. "I can tell you this. Jack was working on a strategic plan for a company in South America."

"What company?" Lindsey pressed.

"How can that matter?"

"Because he didn't just leave here," Lindsey paused. "He was taken."

"What?"

"And that was after a dead body was found in my library, which I think had something to do with Jack, but he was snatched before I could confirm," Lindsey said. "Now please tell me who he was working for."

"No," Stella said.

"Hey, I shared," Lindsey protested.

"And I'll share with you as soon as I get there," Stella said. "I'm leaving Boston now. I should be there in a few hours."

"Do you really think that's nec—" Lindsey began, but Stella cut her off.

"Yes. Where is a good place to stay in town?"

"The Beachfront Bed and Breakfast is about the only place to stay," Lindsey said.

"Excellent," Stella said. "I'll be in touch."

She hung up with a click.

Lindsey tried to work. She reviewed her quarterly budget three times, but the numbers meant nothing to her. Her eyes kept tracking to the clock and then the door. She knew it was ridiculous, but Stella McQuaid had sounded so frighteningly competent that she half expected her to just appear out of thin air.

She managed to get through the budget and was saving it into an Excel spreadsheet when a sharp rap sounded on her office door.

"Come in," Lindsey called.

A petite woman strode into the room, and Lindsey knew without a doubt that this was Stella McQuaid. Her dark brown hair was styled in a big donut-shaped bun on the back of her head. Her charcoal gray suit was impeccably cut over a crisp white blouse. Her platform shoes gave her an added five inches of height, which given how tiny she was, still made Lindsey feel like an Amazon standing next to her.

"Lindsey?" the woman asked.

"Yes. Stella?" Lindsey said as she held out her hand.

"Nice to meet you." Stella's hand was cold but her grip was firm and dry.

"Have a seat," Lindsey said. "Can I get you anything?"

"No, thank you," Stella said. "We ate on the train."

"We?" Lindsey asked.

"Tom Jarvis," Stella said and gestured behind her. A man in jeans and a weathered leather jacket entered the room. "He's in charge of security for our company."

"Security?" Lindsey asked.

"Our people go into many developing nations where there are unstable forces," Stella said. "Tom and his crew monitor them and go in to assist should it be required."

"Was it required for my brother?" Lindsey asked.

Tom had a short military-style haircut, a rugged build and a pair of brown eyes that missed nothing. He ran a hand over his close-cropped gray hair.

"We were just about to go in, when Jack disappeared," Tom said. "Jack was one of our more experienced consultants."

"Meaning he's been in some hot spots before?" Lindsey guessed.

Tom nodded with a rueful twist of his lips. "I've always told him if he wants to give up crunching numbers, he can work in my crew."

Stella rolled her eyes. "Back to the point."

"Jack disappeared," Tom said. "We never received a distress call, but one minute he was there and the next he wasn't."

Lindsey studied the two of them. They looked as worried as she felt, which did nothing to calm her nerves. She decided she had to trust them.

"Jack was here," she said. She went on to tell them everything. Stella listened, watching her with a scrutiny that made Lindsey want to pace but there was no place to go in the tiny room. Tom nodded a few times as if what she was saying was pretty much what he'd figured. They didn't flinch when she mentioned the dead body in the library.

When she got to the part about the woman taking the phone from Jack and telling Lindsey that they were lovers and her jealous husband was after them, Stella looked mad enough to chew through an aluminum can.

"That conniving little bitch," she spat.

Lindsey's eyes went wide and Tom gave her a level look. He took out his smart phone and tapped it a few times. He held it out to Lindsey.

"Is that her?"

Lindsey glanced at the small photo. With long dark

hair, a lush figure and sharp features, the woman was a ringer for the woman who'd taken Jack.

"Yes, that's her," Lindsey said.

"Damn it!" Stella pounded her fist into her open palm.

Jack had been breaking hearts his entire adult life. Lindsey wondered if Stella's anger was in part because she had feelings for Jack. She glanced at Tom. He was frowning at the picture.

"Does she own the coffee company in Brazil that Jack was working for?" Lindsey asked.

"Jack told you that much?"

"No, I pieced it together from his e-mails and I traced the IP address he used," she said.

"Looks like Jack's not the only Norris with some skills," Tom said. He gave her an approving glance.

"Who is she?" Lindsey asked.

"Antonia Murroz," Stella spat. "Heiress to the largest coffee company in Brazil."

"Oh," Lindsey said. "Which would explain why her husband is so upset."

Stella gave an undignified snort. "Antonia is not married. Moreover, she never has been."

CHAPTER

24

BRIAR CREEK
PUBLIC LIBRARY

"I don't understand," Lindsey said. "Why would she—"

"To keep you from reporting it," Tom said. "She was buying time."

"Buying time for what?" Lindsey asked. "What could she possibly want with Jack?"

"That's the question, isn't it?" Stella said. Now she looked grim.

"Jack has had some pretty crazy ex-girlfriends," Lindsey said. "You don't think she's a woman scorned, do you?"

Tom cast a quick glance at Stella, and Lindsey realized she was probably one of those girlfriends. She wished she'd phrased her question more carefully, but it couldn't be helped now.

"Could be," Stella said with a shrug. "But nabbing

him seems a bit extreme for a woman who can have any man she wants."

"I think it has something to do with the job," Tom said. "There is a suspected coffee cartel in Brazil, a commodity cartel if you will, that agrees to work together to keep the prices where they want them."

"Times have been tough on the Brazilian coffee growers," Stella added. "Other countries like Vietnam are beginning to cut into their profit, and they've been hit with an invasive fungus called coffee rust, which is decimating their crops."

"Jack's not a botanist," Lindsey said. "How could he help?"

"The Murroz family said they have a new plant that is resistant to the fungus, but they have to convince the market that it tastes just as good as the old," Stella said. "Jack was hired to advise them on that."

"Okay, so Jack shows up at my library, telling me to keep his presence on the down low," Lindsey said. "An hour later a dead man is found where Jack is supposed to be."

"Any ID on the victim yet?" Tom asked.

"None," Lindsey said. "Jack said he fell asleep on the couch, and when he woke up, there were two men, one of whom was supposed to be his contact. Of course, Jack didn't say contact for what. One of the men told him to run, so he did. I know he didn't think anyone was going to get killed; otherwise he never would have left."

"Are you sure Jack didn't kill him?" Stella asked.

"Yes!" Lindsey said. She couldn't believe that Stella would even suggest such a thing.

"It could have been an accident," Stella said.

"He was strangled," Lindsey said. "That's not an accident."

Stella shrugged. Again, Lindsey wondered if she had a bit of the woman-scorned thing going on.

"Did Jack say whether he recognized either of them?" Tom asked.

"No, but he suspected they were looking for him," she said. "What should I do? Since Antonia lied to me and there is no crazed husband, do I go to the police with this?"

"That won't be necessary," Tom said.

Lindsey glanced at him and saw he was looking through her office window out into the library. She followed the line of his gaze. Detective Trimble and Chief Plewicki were approaching.

"Oh, they're here," she said. "How convenient."

Knuckles rapped on the wooden door, and it was pushed open before she could issue an invite.

Chief Plewicki strode into the office and stopped short, surprised to see two people already there. Detective Trimble was right behind her, and he stopped just shy of slamming into Emma.

"Lindsey, if we could have a moment of your time," Emma said.

"Absolutely," she said. "But first there are some people I'd like you to meet. Chief Plewicki, Detective Trimble, these are my brother's work associates, Stella McQuaid and Tom Jarvis."

"Nice to meet you," Emma said. She gave Lindsey a confused look. "So can you spare a minute?"

"Actually, I think you're going to want to talk to

them," Lindsey said. "If you have an ID on the dead man, they may be able to help you further with it. You see, we think he was after my brother."

"Your brother?" Detective Trimble asked. He looked bewildered but Emma nodded as if suddenly Lindsey was making more sense.

"You've been holding out on me," Emma said. Her brown eyes looked disappointed, and Lindsey felt an uncomfortable twist of guilt squeeze her insides.

"Sometimes in the name of justice, full disclosure has to wait," Lindsey said. Emma had used the same line on her once.

She did feel bad about not telling Emma everything, but there was a time in the not too distant past that Emma had not disclosed certain information to Lindsey for a very good reason. Of course, Lindsey was a librarian and not a cop, but still.

Emma gave her a small nod, letting her know that her point had been grudgingly acknowledged.

"Explain," Trimble said. He was obviously not at grudging acceptance yet.

Lindsey told them about the day the body was found. How Jack had been in the room and then he was gone and a body was there. She explained about Jack escaping while the two men fought. She noted that Emma was looking unhappier by the minute but she pressed on. When she got to the part about Jack being taken by Antonia Murroz, Emma could obviously not contain herself any longer.

"And you didn't tell me?" Emma cried. "A citizen was in danger in my town and you didn't tell me?"

"Technically, when he was taken, he was on the water so he wasn't really in town," Lindsey said.

Emma was not pacified and Detective Trimble looked as if he was seriously thinking of charging her with impeding an investigation.

"Listen, the woman who took my brother made it very clear that I was to tell no one," Lindsey said. "And Jack said the same. I was not about to put him in danger for a man we can't even identify."

"Juan Veracruz," Emma said. "We were finally able to run him in an international database and the name *Juan Veracruz* popped. He works for a Vincent Carrego, who—".

"Owns a coffee company in Brazil," Stella said at the same time as Emma. "He is rumored to be a part of the commodity cartel with the Murroz family."

"Cartel?" Detective Trimble perked up at the word.

"Yes, but for coffee, not cocaine," Stella said.

"That doesn't make any sense," Tom said. "Why would one of Carrego's men be looking for Jack?"

"My guess would be trouble within the cartel," Emma said. She leaned against the wall and crossed her arms over her chest. "But it's only a guess, since I am so light on facts."

Stella took over this portion of the conversation. She explained about their consultant business and how Jack had been hired in a freelance capacity to go to Brazil to help them promote the new type of coffee plant.

Detective Trimble was not impressed. "I still think Norris had something to do with the dead guy. We only have his word secondhand"—he paused to stare at Lindsey—"that there was a second man in there. Why didn't he come to the police right away?"

"My brother had nothing to do with Veracruz's death," Lindsey insisted.

"I agree," Stella said. "We're economists, not killers."

Trimble looked unmoved, but Emma seemed willing to listen.

"The crime scene techs got several prints we haven't been able to match. If we run Jack Norris's, that will eliminate one more and let us focus on identifying the others. That may lead us to the second man."

"If there is one," Trimble said.

Lindsey frowned.

"Ms. McQuaid and Mr. Jarvis, I'd like you to come to the station and give statements," Emma said. "I want to know everything you know about the members of the coffee cartel in Brazil."

"What about Jack?" Lindsey asked. "A man called here, the day before yesterday, looking for him. At the time, I thought it was Antonia Murroz's husband, but now I realize it could have been Vincent Carrego. Maybe he's looking for Jack because he wants to know what happened to his man Veracruz. He said he'd be in touch. He's probably the one who tossed my apartment looking for Jack. If Antonia isn't running from a jealous husband, what does she want with Jack? What's to keep her from killing him if he doesn't do what she wants, whatever that is?"

No one answered her, and Lindsey assumed it was because the answer was not one she would like.

"When did you receive the call exactly?" Emma asked.

Lindsey wrote down the date and time, which she handed to Trimble. "Can we try and trace the number?"

"We can try," he said. He sounded doubtful. "I'll bet it was from a throwaway cell phone, but we'll give it a go."

Emma and Trimble exchanged a look that Lindsey didn't like. She felt compressed with fear as if her skin were shrinking and she didn't fit inside it anymore.

"Lindsey, it seems as if your brother got involved in something dangerous," Emma said. "With two factions of the cartel going after him, I have to figure he's got something that they both want."

"We'll do everything we can to figure out what it is," Tom said. He rose from his seat as did Stella.

"Do you need a statement from me, too?" Lindsey asked.

"Have you told us everything you know?" Emma asked.

"Yes," Lindsey said. She couldn't help but feel as if it was horribly inadequate and that she really knew nothing at all.

"Then I think we're good," Emma said.

"Oh, all right." Lindsey nodded. "You'll keep me informed?"

Emma gave her a small smile. "Every step of the way."

Lindsey sank back into her chair as she watched them leave. The panic that she had been firmly squashing down was threatening to overwhelm her. She bit her lip and tried to think positive thoughts. Jack would be okay. He was always okay. Their whole life he'd gotten into scrapes and then landed on his feet, only to do something equally stupid the next time around.

She glanced at the picture of her and Jack that she had on the shelf behind her desk. She remembered when they were eight and nine and Jack got the big idea to add sails to their skateboards. They'd cut up a pair of bedsheets without asking their mother, and using tree branches, they had fashioned some spectacular sails. They'd been sailing across the vacant parking lot of the church at the end of their street when their father pulled up in the family minivan.

He'd been impressed with their aerodynamic skill but not thrilled that it was their mom's best sheets for guests that they'd sacrificed. Jack had convinced their dad to try it, however, and after one sail across the lot, their dad was hooked. When their mom showed up to call them all to dinner, their dad was the one in the soup, and when Lindsey looked at Jack, she knew that had been his plan all along.

She tried to work to keep her mind off what the police and Jack's colleagues were talking about. She hated feeling left out of it all, but she knew she had made herself persona non grata and really didn't have much leverage to demand to be included.

At quitting time, she opened her desk drawer and grabbed her handbag out of it. She took her coat off its hook and wrapped her scarf around her neck. She knew it was going to be a cold bike ride home, but she planned to stop at the police station for an update first, so it wasn't as bad as a straight shot.

She left her office and found both Sully and Robbie waiting for her. They stood leaning on either side of the circulation desk, looking like a matched set of badass. Lindsey figured if someone was watching her, they were definitely going to be discouraged by her entourage.

"Hello, boys," she said. "I figured you two would have worked out a rotation by now."

"Yeah, we have a little problem with that," Robbie said.

"Neither of us trusts the other to be alone with you," Sully said.

"So you're stuck with the two of us," Robbie said.

"Well, you can declare yourselves off duty," Lindsey said. "I'm headed over to the police station."

The men exchanged a look of surprise.

"You went to the police?" Sully asked.

"No, they came to me," she said. Her tone was rueful. "But you'll be happy to hear that I told them everything."

"Well done," Robbie said with obvious relief. "What brought you to your senses?"

"My brother's colleagues in Boston have come to town with new information," Lindsey said. She told them about the cartel and Antonia not being married as well as the theory that Jack had stumbled into something he shouldn't have.

Sully gave a low whistle, which caused Ms. Cole to give him a quelling glance, which made Robbie smile.

"That's not all," Lindsey said. She told them that the dead man had been identified, and it didn't look good for Jack to have disappeared just before the man's death with no other witnesses to the second man.

"That is a nasty pickle," Robbie said.

"I just wish I knew where Jack was right now," Lindsey said. "I wish I knew if whatever he discovered was enough to get him killed. He sounded so reassuring on the phone, teasing like he always did when we were about to get in trouble . . ."

Lindsey thought about her last conversation with her brother and frowned. Had he been joking with her? He'd referenced their favorite book as kids, *A Wrinkle in Time*. She'd assumed he was trying to make light of what happened, but what if he'd been trying to leave her a clue?

CHAPTER

25

BRIAR CREEK
PUBLIC LIBRARY

"Oh, man, I just thought of a thingy I have to do before a meeting with the mayor tomorrow," Lindsey said.

She turned and tossed her purse back in her office and shrugged off her coat and tossed it into the small room as well. She hooked a hand through each of their elbows and half led, half dragged them to the door.

"You two are just the sweetest of the sweet," she said. "But it looks like I'll have to work late. Tell you what, I'll call Nancy or Charlie for a ride so you don't have to come back here. Great. Awesome. K'bye."

She all but shoved the two men out the sliding door and then spun on her heel and raced into the young adult reading section. Beth had been building a corner of the children's area into a sweet teen hangout space with video games, manga and loads of music, magazines and DVDs. Lindsey frequently wished she'd had a space like this when she was a teen. It was, in their words, epic.

She hurried over to the fiction shelves and searched for the book Jack had mentioned by the author's last name. Please do not let it be checked out, she thought. She dove into the *L*'s and followed them to L'Engle. One copy of *A Wrinkle in Time* was on the shelf, and she grabbed it and hurried back to her office.

Jack had said, "Don't worry. It's not like I've been taken to Camazotz—" just before he'd been cut off by Antonia.

Camazotz was the dark planet mentioned in the novel, and when Lindsey and her brother were little, they used to play in their parents' walk-in closet, locking themselves in with the lights out and pretending it was Camazotz and "IT" was trying to control their minds. In their game, one of them was always controlled by "IT," and the other had to perform a daring rescue to save them.

So why had he mentioned it? Was it a clue? Had he just been trying to put her at ease by referencing their favorite book? Or was he being held in a closet somewhere? Lindsey felt tears of frustration well up in her eyes.

Where are you, Jack? What's happening? What did you get mixed up in? Around and around the questions pummeled her brain.

Lindsey rubbed a hand over her eyes. She had to get a grip and pull it together. She thumbed through the book. Had Jack scribbled a note in it somewhere? The librarian in her didn't even care about damage to materials if it meant she could find her brother.

There was nothing. No errant piece of paper wedged

inside the pages. Nothing written in Jack's distinctive blocky scrawl. She paged to the part of the book that mentioned Camazotz. Again, nothing.

She turned the book over. She looked for anything odd on the cover. The labels were all in place. The paperback book was in perfect condition, despite a little wear on the binding.

She put it down on her desk and rested her hand on it. Maybe Jack's words had been just that, words. She drummed her fingers on the cover. Under her ring finger, she felt a ridge.

She ran her fingers over it. Sure enough, on the back cover there was a tiny little bump. It could be nothing, but she flipped open the book and checked. The square of adhesive that held the book's RFID—radio frequency identification—tag in place in the book was the only thing she saw.

The library had switched to the RFID method of checking out a few years before. It was a microchip radio frequency mash-up that replaced the barcode and combined the ability to check out and prevent theft all in one. Ms. Cole had been resistant to the new technology, but Lindsey had been insistent and she noted that Ms. Cole had ceased complaining once the new system was installed and operational. Lindsey suspected that the lemon really enjoyed the antitheft properties of the RFID.

Lindsey examined the tag. A corner was peeling as if it had been tampered with. Lindsey carefully pulled it back and gasped. Sure enough, tucked under the tag was a micro SD card the size of the fingernail on her pinky and as thin as a piece of poster board.

Her hands shook as she carefully took it out of its hiding spot. Jack *had* been leaving her a clue. This card had to be what the cartel members were seeking.

Lindsey reached for her phone. She had to tell Emma right away. Before she touched the receiver, her phone rang. The noise made her jump and she tightened her grip on the tiny little card.

"Briar Creek Public Library," she answered, hoping to get rid of her caller as swiftly as possible. "This is Lindsey, how can I help you?"

"You're holding what I want," a woman's voice said. It was thick with an exotic accent, and Lindsey knew she was talking to Antonia Murroz.

"Where's my brother?" she asked.

Lindsey's eyes scanned the windows. Where was Antonia? How could she see her? Dread trailed its cold clammy hand up her back to rest on the nape of her neck.

"He is unharmed—for now," Antonia said. "If you want him back, you will exchange the micro card in your possession for him. We will be at the pier at ten o'clock. Don't be late and don't go to the police or I will have no choice but to kill your brother."

The woman hung up and Lindsey realized she was shivering and sweating at the same time. She glanced at the clock. She desperately wanted to go to the police and make this their problem, but that wasn't an option. She had no doubt that the woman would kill Jack and not even chip her nail polish while doing it.

Lindsey closed her eyes. She needed to think. The most important thing to do was keep the micro card safe. She took her phone out and popped out her tiny memory card and put this one inside it. She then put her phone in her pocket for safekeeping.

She figured she might as well help close the library and then she could go to the Anchor and wait until the appointed meeting time with Antonia.

She rose from her desk and headed out front. Ms. Cole had most of the building shut down while Ann Marie was checking out the last borrower. When that person left, Ann Marie went to lock the door after them.

Lindsey swept the adult area, the meeting rooms and the bathrooms. She was just rounding the corner to go back to the front desk when a man stepped out from between the stacks.

He was built big and strong with a thick neck and a square jaw. The woolen cap on his head made him look like a dock worker who would be just as comfortable cracking skulls as he would be unloading barges. Then Lindsey noticed the gun he held. It was pointed at her. His hand didn't shake, letting her know he was perfectly capable of pulling the trigger with no hesitation.

She gulped. "I'm sorry, the library is closed."

The man frowned at her. He held out one beefy hand and gestured to her impatiently. His voice was thick with an accent much like Antonia's when he said, "Give it to me."

"I'm sorry," Lindsey said. Her mouth was dry and her tongue was sticking to the roof of her mouth. "Did you need something?"

Yes, she was going with the tried-and-true play stupid method of stalling for time. She knew she couldn't give him the micro card. If she did, Jack was a dead man. On the other hand, if the guy killed her and took it, they would both be dead. She wondered if she could grab a book and smack the gun out of his hand. It seemed unlikely. She glanced at his arms and wondered if they were the same arms that had choked the life out of Juan Veracruz. It seemed probable.

"Give it now!" the man demanded, and he snapped his fingers in her face.

"Listen—" she began but was interrupted by the sudden arrival of Robbie.

"Lindsey, the sea serpent and I were talking—" Robbie began but was cut off when the man turned and fired at him through the stacks.

"Bloody hell!" Robbie cried as the bullet whizzed past his ear and lodged itself into a section of Nicholas Sparks's books.

Lindsey knew she had one chance to get away. She raced around the shelving unit and started shoving the books through the shelves with all her strength. Robbie ran to her side and started to do the same. The man was hammered by an avalanche of books.

"What the hell is happening?" Sully shouted as he appeared at the end of the row. "You were supposed to convince her to let one of us give her a ride home."

"Yeah, well, winning the coin toss to talk to Lindsey was not great!" Robbie answered.

"Man with a gun!" Lindsey shouted.

Sully was in action before her words even registered. He went down low and started firing books through the shelves like rockets. He must have gotten in a particularly good shot, because Lindsey heard the man grunt and saw him double over.

She heard the gun clatter to the floor and Robbie grabbed her hand and shouted, "Run!"

They raced out of the stacks with Sully bringing up

the rear. Ms. Cole and Ann Marie stared at them until Lindsey waved for them to run, too.

"Go! Go! Go!" she cried.

Ms. Cole and Ann Marie dashed through the workroom to the back door. They pushed through it, not slowing down until they reached the parking lot.

"Go to the police station!" Lindsey ordered. "Hurry!"

In a tight pack, with Robbie and Sully on the outside trying to cover the ladies, they hustled down the sidewalk toward the station. Robbie jerked the door open and pushed each of the women into the main room.

"Get away from the window," Sully ordered. He ushered them all to the back of the room.

"What is going on out here?" Emma Plewicki entered the room from the offices in back.

"There's a man with a gun in the library," Lindsey said.

"Was the building clear?" Emma asked.

"Yes, we were the only people left in it," Ms. Cole said. She gestured to the five of them.

Emma went right to her radio and began calling all of her officers in. Detective Trimble came out and Emma briefed him on what was happening.

"We have to secure the building," she said. She and Trimble headed out with Tom Jarvis right on their heels.

"I work security," he said. "I can help."

"Are you licensed to carry?" Emma asked.

"Of course," he said.

The three of them left and the room grew quiet.

"What do we do now?" Ann Marie asked. She looked scared and nervous and Lindsey felt bad for her.

"You go home," she said. "Call your husband and have

him come get you. If Emma needs to speak with you, she'll call you in."

Just then the front doors banged open and Milton Duffy strode in. He crossed right to Ms. Cole and wrapped her in a hug.

"My dear, I was at a historical society meeting when Bill Sint popped in to say he'd been listening to the police scanner and heard there was a shooting at the library," Milton said. He glanced at them all and then back at Ms. Cole. "Are you all right?"

Ms. Cole patted his arm. "I'm fine, dearest, just fine."

In a world that had gone utterly mad, Lindsey couldn't help but feel an "*aw*" bubble up inside her. Milton had been a widower for several years, and Ms. Cole was the town spinster, but after performing in a play together a few months before, they seemed to have found something special together.

"Are you needed here, or can I escort you home?" Milton asked. "I imagine a nice spot of tea would calm your nerves."

"That would be lovely, among other things," Ms. Cole said.

Lindsey saw Ann Marie's jaw drop, and it was all she could do to keep hers firmly in place. Had Ms. Cole just made an innuendo-laden proposition to Milton? Judging by how red the tips of his ears got, Lindsey was pretty sure she had.

"G'night," Milton said to them in a hasty and distracted manner as he hustled Ms. Cole out of the station.

"Damned octogenarian is making better time than either of us," Robbie muttered to Sully.

"Please, my ego is battered enough," Sully said.

"Excuse me," Lindsey said. If Antonia had been watching her in the library, she had to assume that Antonia was still watching her. Then again, if the man with the gun had been watching Lindsey for Antonia, maybe she was in the clear.

That didn't make sense, however, because why would Antonia have set up an exchange with her if she was sending a thug into the library to muscle the micro card away from Lindsey? Because just like she had lied about being married to keep Lindsey from reporting Jack's kidnapping, she had arranged a meeting with Lindsey to exchange the card for Jack, knowing full well that her thug would take it from Lindsey before the arranged time and place.

Unless, of course, Antonia was on the up and up and the thug had been sent by one of the other cartel members like Carrego. Either way, Lindsey had a feeling she was not supposed to come out of tonight's meeting alive and neither was Jack.

Lindsey felt as if her brain was contracting. She was tired of letting the bad guys call the shots. She needed a new plan.

Lindsey searched the contacts in her phone. Nancy picked up on the second ring.

"Can you come and get me at the police station?" Lindsey asked.

"I'll be right there," Nancy agreed and hung up.

There was no hesitation, no questions asked. That was the power of true friendship.

CHAPTER

26

BRIAR CREEK
PUBLIC LIBRARY

Lindsey sent off a few texts to the other crafternoon
ladies. She had a feeling she was going to need a backup
plan.

Stella was grilling Robbie and Sully about the man in
the library.

"How was he in the library when it was closed? Did
you get his name?" she asked.

"Really didn't stop to introduce myself while he was
using my ear for target practice," Robbie said.

Sully snorted and Lindsey glanced up to see that the
two men were practically bonding while Stella peppered
them with questions.

"I'd assume he hid in the building somewhere," Sully
said. "When he saw Lindsey alone, he must have figured
that was his chance."

"Chance for what?" Stella asked. "What did he want from you?"

"No idea," Lindsey lied. She kept pacing, which conveniently kept her from having to make eye contact with any of them. "He just asked me to give 'it' to him, but I don't know what 'it' was."

Her voice cracked on the words, and she hoped they attributed that to her rocky emotional state and not the fact that she was a terrible liar. She raised her eyebrows in an effort of stop herself from crinkling her nose.

"I just don't understand," Stella said. "None of this makes any sense."

"Agreed," Robbie said.

"Oh, here's my ride," Lindsey said. "Tell Emma to call me if she has more questions. I'm assuming they'll lock up the library once they have it secured."

"You mean you're not going to wait and see if they catch the guy?" Sully asked. His blue eyes were wide with disbelief.

"Nah, I'm really beat," Lindsey said. "Must be an adrenaline crash."

"You're going to leave the library without checking on it?" Robbie sounded as shocked as Sully.

"I'm sure it'll be fine with all of the police there," she said. "Good night."

She shoved through the doors and hurried down the walk. She heard Sully call her name, but she yanked open the door to Nancy's powder blue Mustang and jumped in, pretending she didn't hear him.

"Make it look like we're going home," she said to Nancy. "But then double back to the Anchor. I have everyone meeting us there."

"Oh, a covert op," Nancy cooed. "I'm on it."

She hit the gas and they took off down the street toward home. Nancy drove past the Blue Anchor and Lindsey hoped they'd managed to fool Sully and Robbie into thinking she was just having a stress meltdown and was going home.

Nancy pulled over onto a side street and they waited while the heater cranked out warmth over their toes.

"Okay," Lindsey said. "I think we're good now."

Nancy pulled out of the side street and parked in the small lot on the other side of the Anchor. It wasn't visible from the street, and Lindsey hoped it kept Nancy's distinctive car hidden from view. She could not afford to let Sully or Robbie know what she was doing. Primarily because she had a feeling that, like most men, they would feel compelled to jump in and help her.

This wasn't a problem anyone else could fix. She had to face Antonia alone and try to bargain to get her brother back. That being said, she wasn't stupid and she knew she needed a backup plan.

She and Nancy hurried into the Anchor. Mary met them at the door.

"Are you okay?" Mary asked.

"I will be," Lindsey said.

"Come on," Mary said. They followed her through the restaurant to the far corner, where the ladies' room was located.

Nancy stopped and looked at Mary. "Seriously?"

"Trust me," Mary said. She pushed open the door and they saw that Violet, Charlene and Beth were already hanging out in the big square room. Beth was sitting on the edge of the sink while Violet lounged against the wall and Charlene was wedged between the sink and the toilet.

"Why on earth are we meeting in the ladies' room?" Nancy asked.

"Because . . ." Mary paused to reach around Lindsey and flip a switch next to the light switch. The grind of an overhead fan kicked in. It sounded like a motorcycle, revving its engine. "It will cover our conversation if anyone is listening."

Lindsey nodded. It made sense, given that she had no idea who Antonia might have sent to follow her. It was a wise precautionary move, and she had to admit Mary had some skills in espionage.

"So does this have anything to do with your apartment being trashed?" Violet asked.

"Yes," Lindsey said. She exchanged a glance with Beth, who gave her a slow nod. It was time to tell all and hope her friends weren't too irritated that she'd left them out of the loop. She began with finding Jack in the crafternoon room and ended with the man in the library with the gun.

The crafternooners were silent. Lindsey felt her insides twist while she waited for them to absorb what she'd said. Were they going to be mad? Reject her? Storm out? What?

"What do you need us to do?" Nancy asked.

Lindsey glanced around the room, and the relief that swept through her almost took her out at the knees.

"Come here, honey," Violet said, and she opened her arms.

Lindsey didn't hesitate. She let Violet enfold her in a

hug that comforted as well as bolstered. The others joined in, and in short order they had a massive group hug going. Lindsey felt the lump in her throat start to burn. Everyone should have the pack of friends that she had.

The sound of flushing broke up the hug.

"Sorry," Charlene called out. "I hit the handle with my butt."

This made Beth snort, which cracked up the group. Lindsey felt the burn in her throat ease with her chuckle.

"Okay, we're going to get Jack back from the she-devil," Mary said. "What's the plan?"

"Antonia, the woman who took my brother, wants to broker a deal for him," Lindsey said. "She was watching me, and she knew when I found what he'd hidden in the library and called me immediately. I have to make an exchange on the pier at ten o'clock tonight."

"No police?" Violet asked.

"She was very clear that law enforcement would be a bad idea," Lindsey said.

"What about the shooter in the library?" Charlene asked, ever the reporter. "If he was working for her, then I say her deal is null and void."

"I've been thinking about that," Lindsey said. "I think he might have been working for her but he could also have been from one of the other cartel members. Either way, she still has Jack so I don't have much leverage to call foul."

Violet shivered. "Sorry," she said. "The whole cartel angle spooks me no end."

"Agreed," Mary said. "A coffee cartel—who even knew something like that existed?"

"Jack did," Lindsey said.

Her voice was grim, and she could feel the fear that she wouldn't be able to save her brother rear up inside her like a hairy beast. She swallowed hard, trying to beat it back down. As if sensing her distress, Nancy put a bracing arm about her and gave her a solid half hug.

"Don't," she said. "We'll get him back. Period."

Lindsey drew in a shaky breath. That was exactly what she needed to hear.

"Okay, here is my plan, if you're willing," she said. She paused to glance up at the tiny room full of women, her friends, the strongest ladies she knew. They each met her gaze with no fear, no uncertainty, just the knowledge that one of their own was in trouble and needed help and they would be there to do what needed to be done.

Lindsey almost laughed. Who would have guessed that a love of books, food and crafts would forge a bond so strong among such a disparate group of women? The gratitude she felt almost overwhelmed her, but there was no time.

She shook her head and cleared her throat and began to outline her plan. With input from the others, it was fine-tuned and tweaked down to the last detail.

A poor woman came to use the restroom in the middle of their session, and Mary stuck her head out the door and told her to keep her panties on.

They were all staring at her when she closed the door to return to their meeting.

"What?" Mary asked.

"Do you think that's good business, dear?" Nancy asked.

"*Pffthbt.*" Mary made a short raspberry sound. "That was Bubble Hubbell."

"Ah," they said in collective understanding.

Bubble was a nickname Mary used for Heather Hubbell, who had been Ian's girlfriend before he met Mary. Heather had tried repeatedly over the years to win him back, and although Ian had been clear that he had less than no interest, Heather kept trying.

"I loathe that woman," Mary said.

"She is a nasty piece of work," Beth agreed. "But she's not worth getting upset over. You know Ian would never—"

"Oh, I know," Mary said. "It's just the nerve of her to keep trying. *Argh.* It's maddening."

"Maybe we can interest Bubble in a nice cartel member," Charlene said. "How does she feel about Brazil?"

Mary looked thoughtful. "That might be far enough away."

"Excellent, I'll just pencil that in at the bottom of our plan," Lindsey said. "Okay, let's go over it one more time."

They finalized the plan, and then one by one they left the bathroom. The tiny space was down the hall from the main restaurant, but Lindsey wondered if they had fooled anyone by staggering their departures.

There was no sign of Heather Hubbell waiting in the hallway, and Lindsey was relieved. The last thing they needed was to navigate a smack-down between Mary and Ian's ex.

Lindsey waited in the hallway while the others slipped out the back door. Lindsey watched the clock on her cell phone, willing the minutes to slow down so that her friends had enough time to do what needed to be done. All the same, she wished it were a half hour later so that she could be at the meeting place, getting her brother back.

As Lindsey paced in the narrow space, she thought about the events of the past few days. A dead man in the library. Her brother's return and subsequent kidnapping. Threatening phone calls and people following her. Sully opening up about his past and a drunken Robbie sleeping on her couch.

Lord-a-mercy! No wonder her nerves were shot.

Ian poked his head around the corner. "Lindsey, have you seen my wife?"

"Recently?" Lindsey asked. Yes, she was stalling.

"Yeah," he said. "Heather Hubbell stormed out of the café, no loss there, but she said Mary wouldn't let her in the bathroom and told her to keep her panties on. Is that true?"

"Um, yes, I do believe there was a conversation to that effect," Lindsey hedged.

"I can't believe she didn't tell me herself." Ian sounded mystified. "Mary loves getting all worked up about Bubble . . . er . . . Heather, which is crazy because anyone with eyes in their head knows I am berserk for my wife."

Lindsey glanced down at her hands. She had a feeling *berserk* would surely describe his reaction when he found out what Mary was doing right now. What to do, what to do. Should she tell him?

She did a quick risk assessment in her head. If everything went according to plan, then Mary would be perfectly safe for her part of their plan. If things didn't go as planned . . . Lindsey shook her head. She refused to even go there.

"Well, if I see her, I'll let you know," Lindsey said.

Ian gave her a considering glance. "You okay, Lindsey? You don't look yourself."

"I'm good," Lindsey said. "I am *thoroughly* good."

CHAPTER

27

BRIAR CREEK
PUBLIC LIBRARY

Okay, probably she had just oversold it, as Ian's eyes narrowed even more as he studied her. "I'm going to get you a glass of wine. It'll be at the bar when you're done waiting for the restroom."

"That'd be great," Lindsey said.

He turned and walked away, and Lindsey blew out a long, slow breath. He'd thought she was waiting for the restroom. That would buy her some time. She glanced at the clock on her phone. It was five minutes until show time. She may as well get a head start.

She hurried down the short hallway and pushed through the unalarmed emergency exit that let out in back of the restaurant. The cold December air hit her like a slap, and she pulled her coat tightly about her. She paused, noting the security light that illuminated the Dumpsters to her left and tuned her ears to listen over the sound of water lapping against boat hulls, but there was nothing.

She walked away from the café, feeling very much alone on her mission even though she knew it wasn't true. The wooden planks gave under her feet. The boards creaked. The sound of a buoy's bell rang out in the bay, warning boats that they were entering a rocky channel.

She walked to the end of the pier, staying half hidden behind a tall wooden pile on the corner of the massive dock. She was glad her sweater was black but still she couldn't help but feel as if she had a big bull's-eye painted on her. She checked the time on her phone again. She still had three minutes.

Now was the final part of her backup plan. She opened the micro card on an app on her phone. It was encrypted. Damn. It looked like a mess of random symbols. She should have expected no less from Jack.

She attached it as a file to an e-mail and mailed it to herself. Maybe it wouldn't work. Maybe no one would be able to get into her e-mail or decipher the encryption should everything go horribly wrong. And maybe her phone would now self-destruct in five seconds. She gripped it in her hand as if it might catch fire. Nothing happened.

Okay. She stretched her neck, letting it crack in an effort to ease the tension that had her drawn as tight as a guitar string. She exited out of her e-mail. Antonia should arrive any minute.

"*Psst*, hey, what's a girl like you doing in a place like this?"

Lindsey whirled around. There, leaning against a wooden rail, was Robbie.

"*Gah!*" she shrieked. "What are you doing here?"

"Oh, come on, love," he said. "We've already established that I know your tell. Big fat lies don't really become you even when you're trying not to crinkle your nose."

"You have to get out of here," she cried. "They can't see you."

"Who's they?" another male voice asked.

Lindsey whipped around and there on the opposite side of the pier was Sully.

"Murroz," she hissed. "They're coming with Jack. You can't be here. I have to meet them alone."

"Lindsey, you can't trust her—" Sully began but she cut him off.

"No, this is my brother's life you're playing with," she snapped. It felt like terror had her in a stranglehold. "Now go!"

A light shone out on the water. It grew steadily closer. Lindsey knew it was Antonia. She hurried to the gangway that led to the small dock below.

"Oh, God, they're here. Do not follow me," she hissed through gritted teeth. "And stay hidden!"

She scurried down the ramp. The smaller dock bobbed on the water. She had a hard time keeping her balance, but she managed to pop the micro card out of her phone while the light grew in size and brightness until it was shining right in her eyes. Lindsey held up her hand to shield her eyes. She was desperate to see Jack.

Finally, as the boat neared, she caught a glimpse of her brother's blond tousled head. Her heart leapt in her chest and her throat squeezed tight. He was alive and he was here. She knew if Antonia demanded a kidney from her at this point, she would gladly give it up for the safe return of her brother.

The driver angled the boat so that it stopped smoothly at the dock. Another man reached over the side and grabbed a metal post to keep the boat in place.

Jack sat on a bench with his hands tied behind his back, a thin shirt was all he wore, and even in the darkness Lindsey could tell he was battered and bruised. Rage thumped through her, but she knew now was not the time. She had to get him back first.

The person beside the driver stood and approached Lindsey. Throwing back the hood on her coat, Antonia faced her.

"Did you bring what I want?" she asked.

"Yes," Lindsey said through gritted teeth.

"Give it to me," Antonia ordered.

"After you let Jack go," she said. Her voice shook, which irritated her. She didn't want to sound weak, damn it.

"Do you really think you're in a position to bargain with me?" Antonia asked.

Lindsey took the micro card out of her pocket. Now she was mad. She glared at the other woman.

"Actually, yes, I do," she said. "You've gone to an awful lot of trouble to get this; it'd be a pity to lose it. Now give me my brother."

"Don't do it, Linds," Jack said. His voice was weak and his speech slurred as he spoke through swollen, cracked lips.

"At the same time?" Antonia asked.

"Fine, on three," Lindsey said.

The man who'd been holding the boat hauled Jack up to his feet by his elbow. Lindsey recognized him as the man who'd held the gun on her at the library. Obviously, he had escaped the police, but even worse, his presence

233

made it clear that Antonia had no intention of turning over Jack; otherwise, why would she try to double-cross Lindsey by stealing the micro card before their meeting?

Lindsey only had one chance for this to go her way. She watched Jack limp up onto the step that led out of the boat.

"Don't give it to her, Linds," Jack pleaded. "Please don't do it."

While Antonia and the others looked at Jack, Lindsey took her opportunity. Reaching forward, she grabbed the front of Jack's shirt in her fist and yanked him forward.

All hell broke loose. The man in the boat shouted as Jack was yanked out of his grasp. Lindsey turned to help Jack when Antonia grabbed her arm and yanked her half onto the boat. The micro card was snatched out of Lindsey's hand and she tried to rear back from the edge of the boat but the big man grabbed her by the back of the coat and dumped her on the floor.

"Lindsey!" Jack scrambled to his feet just as two men dropped from the pier above onto the dock below. Sully and Robbie. Lindsey saw them for a only second, but they both looked pasty pale with fear.

"Do not follow or I will kill her!" Antonia yelled.

Lindsey saw the gunman wave his firearm in the air. All three men froze. The driver jammed the throttle into high gear and Lindsey skidded across the floor at the sudden motion.

She glanced up, thinking she might be able to jump. Antonia anticipated her move and planted a boot heel on Lindsey's shoulder. The spiky heel impaled her muscle and bone in a shot of nerve-twisting pain that made Lindsey's eyes cross.

She went limp, hoping to make it stop. Antonia laughed.

Her teeth gleamed feral in the moonlight and the whites of her eyes glowed. For a beautiful woman, she looked purely evil, and Lindsey felt herself begin to shake with fear.

"You have what you want," Lindsey said. "You don't need me. Now let me go."

She wanted to sound tough and demanding, but her voice cracked, making her sound like a child afraid of the dark.

"Oh, I don't think so," Antonia said. She leaned over Lindsey, grabbed a fistful of her blond hair and pulled her close while grinding her heel into Lindsey's shoulder. "Keeping you will assure your brother's cooperation. In fact, I probably should have grabbed you from the start."

Lindsey felt the sweat bead on her upper lip. It was taking every bit of self-control she had not to whimper like a whipped puppy. She would rather bleed out than give Antonia the satisfaction.

The driver shouted and Antonia's foot eased. She hurried to stand beside him. Lindsey felt her heart hammer in her chest. Could she jump now? A heavy hand landed on her shoulder, holding her in place.

The gunman was behind her. Lindsey wondered if he had his gun trained on her right now. Probably. At least he was holding her by her uninjured shoulder.

They were nearing the channel markers. Lindsey sent a silent prayer that her friends had been able to set up in time.

"Go faster," Antonia demanded. "We have to get out of here."

The driver opened up the engine and the boat gained speed, churning up a big wake and smacking hard against the water's surface. As they neared the two largest channel markers, Lindsey slumped down onto the floor of the boat as if she'd fainted. Surprised, the man let her go.

"I think she's hurt!" he called to the others.

"So long as her brother thinks she's alive, who cares?" Antonia said, shrugging.

Lindsey curled up into a fetal position. She had no idea what was going to happen, if their mad plan would even work, but she figured she'd best protect herself either way.

She knew the moment they hit the fishing line tripwire. The men grunted and Antonia shrieked as they fell into the ocean. The boat got knocked hard as if someone had hit it on their way out. Several big splashes sounded, and Lindsey bolted up from her spot on the floor. The boat was slamming out into Long Island Sound at top speed.

Thank goodness she had ridden with Sully enough to know how to control the throttle. She used the back of the chair to haul herself forward, feeling like she was riding a bull in a rodeo. The wind snatched at her hair and clothes as if trying to throw her into the briny sea.

Lindsey eased back on the throttle and the engine slowed. She turned the boat around and headed back. She didn't want Antonia and her thugs to get away.

As she headed for the channel markers, she saw the blue lights of the Briar Creek police boat, flashing brightly in the night sky as if signaling that everything was going to be all right.

She steered the boat to the channel marker on her right. Sure enough, Mary was there. Her kayak was bobbing in the water as she had climbed up on the big red structure. She was cutting the lines she and Beth had strung between the two markers.

Lindsey slowed her engine to a crawl so that she could shout over it.

"You need a lift?" she cried.

Mary grinned at her. Her eyes sparkled, her cheeks were bright pink and her nose was damp with snot, which she gloriously wiped on her coat sleeve.

"Did you see? It worked! It freaking worked!" Mary shouted.

Lindsey laughed. "I sort of missed it from my spot on the floor, but yeah, and thank goodness."

Mary sliced through the wire, which fell into the water with a plop.

"Where's Jack?" Mary asked, looking in the boat behind her. "And why are *you* here?"

"Small change of plan—they took me instead," Lindsey said.

"No way!" Mary gaped.

"Way. So how about that ride?"

"Nah, I'm good," Mary said. She gestured to her kayak. "I have my ride."

"Is everyone else okay?" Lindsey asked.

Mary gestured to the rocky shore nearby, and Lindsey could see Beth with her kayak huddled with Violet, Nancy and Charlene.

"All good," Mary confirmed.

Lindsey raised her arm and waved at the ladies. They waved back and Beth let out a whoop of joy.

Lindsey glanced back at where Antonia and her thugs had been clotheslined into the water by the fishing lines that Mary and Beth had rigged across the channel markers. She scanned the water but she didn't see anyone. She wondered if they had gotten away, but then the police boat slowed and Lindsey watched as someone was fished out of the water. Judging by the high-pitched shrieking, it was Antonia.

"Looks like they got her," Mary said. She climbed back into her kayak. "Give me a push?"

"Sure," Lindsey said. Mary held out her oar and Lindsey gave it a shove, moving Mary toward the shore. "Meet me at the pier."

"You bet!"

Lindsey moved her throttle past idle and began to work her way to the pier. She kept an eye out for the men that had been in the boat with Antonia, not wanting to run either of them down, well, not much at any rate.

She pulled up to the police boat, and a searchlight snapped onto her face.

"Hands in the air!" the terse order came.

CHAPTER

28

BRIAR CREEK
PUBLIC LIBRARY

Not wanting to tempt fate, Lindsey popped her hands into the air. She tried to shield her eyes from the glare as she yelled, "It's me, Lindsey!"

Abruptly, the light was lowered. "Damn it, Lindsey, what the hell is going on?"

It was Emma and she sounded highly stressed.

"There were three of them," Lindsey shouted. "Two men and a woman, did you get them all?"

"No, we're missing a man," Emma said. "Sully, double back."

It was then that Lindsey looked over at the driver. Sully was manning the controls, and the look he gave her was one of pure and utter relief.

"You all right?" he shouted.

"Never better," she said. Then she smiled at him to try and validate the lie. The truth was her hands were shaking and she felt a bit like vomiting, but she didn't want to let it show and cause him to worry.

"Get the boat to the dock," Emma ordered. "And try not to touch anything."

She was curt and dismissive and Lindsey couldn't blame her. Her case had blown wide open and she had been out of the loop. Lindsey imagined this was going to impact their friendship and not for the better.

Lindsey puttered past the police boat while they did a search for the missing man. When she neared the dock, Robbie grabbed the boat and steadied it, tying it up with the line Lindsey tossed to him.

Jack, looking the worse for wear, grabbed her and squeezed her tight. When Lindsey gave him the pat on the back that indicated it was time to let go, he didn't. In fact, after three reassuring pats, he still clung, making her worry that he'd hit his head or something.

"Jack, you're strangling me," she croaked. Jack stepped back and then he grabbed her arms and studied her face with an intensity usually only seen on their mother's face when they broke curfew and didn't call.

"Are you crazy, Linds?" he cried. "That had to be the dumbest, most lamebrained stunt I've ever seen anyone pull. What the hell were you thinking?"

Then he hugged her again. He was hugging her so tight, Lindsey's face was smashed into his shirt front and she couldn't answer.

"Just wait until I stop hugging you," he said. "I'll shake you until your teeth rattle."

"Get in line, mate," Robbie said. "Me and sailor boy have dibs."

"Jack, you need someone to look at you," Lindsey said.

She pushed out of his arms and shrugged off her sweater. She draped it around his shoulders and rubbed his arms in an attempt to warm him up. "The black, swollen eyes and lumpy nose look you've got going is not attractive."

"Oh, I don't know, I think he looks pretty badass," Stella said as she hurried down the ramp from the pier above to join them.

"Stella!" Jack cried. He stepped away from Lindsey and grabbed Stella then he planted a kiss on her that, judging by the way she twined her arms around him, was not unwelcome. Lindsey wondered if Stella was as much of an ex of Jack's as she'd thought.

"Hey, a little help over here," a voice cried.

Beth and Mary had arrived in their kayaks. Lindsey grabbed one while Robbie grabbed the other. Beth glanced at Jack and Stella still in their clinch and sighed.

"Always a runner-up," she said to Lindsey.

"Not to me," Lindsey said. "Besides, you don't want to date Jack. He's an economist, for Pete's sake."

"Yeah, whatever was I thinking?" Beth asked. She looked Lindsey in the eye and asked, "Are you okay?"

"Bumps and bruises but otherwise fine," she said. "Thanks to you and Mary."

"Can you believe we pulled it off?" Beth asked.

"Honestly, no," Lindsey said. "I feel like most of it was sheer dumb luck."

"I'll say," Emma said. The police boat, which was Sully's water taxi with a blue light slapped on the front, pulled up to the dock.

Emma hopped out and Lindsey noted that behind her were three soaking wet people, who were handcuffed and miserable looking. Antonia raised her head and glared at

Lindsey. As Tom Jarvis helped her out of the boat, she spat at Lindsey, who had the quick reflexes to dodge.

"Now, now, Antonia, is that any way to behave?" a man asked from the pier above.

Lindsey knew that voice. She grabbed her brother's arm, pulling him away from Stella. "That's him!"

"Who?" he asked.

"The man who called me looking for you," she said. "I'd recognize his voice anywhere."

"He's—"

"I'll nab him," Robbie said, and he dashed up the ramp to the pier above.

"No!" Jack cried. "Lindsey, he's the man I'm working for."

"What?" she asked. "I thought you were working for Antonia."

"It's a long story," Jack said.

"And you'll have plenty of time to tell it at the station," Emma said.

"But you have no evidence," Antonia snapped. "Your little micro card was lost in the sea."

"Good thing I e-mailed all of the data to myself then," Lindsey said.

Antonia's face tightened and turned a vibrant shade of red.

"That's my brilliant librarian sister," Jack said. His battered face looked gruesome when he smiled, but Lindsey couldn't help but smile in return.

"Got him!" a shout sounded from up above.

They all glanced up to see Robbie wrestling the older gentleman in a sort of bear hug.

"Robbie, it's okay," Lindsey cried.

"What?" he asked.

"You can let him go!" she yelled.

"No, I—" Robbie's next words were cut off by a solid clip on the jaw from the older man.

Lindsey watched in horror as Robbie went down like a sack of cement. Mercifully, Detective Trimble caught him by the collar and eased his fall.

"Oh, he's going to have a nasty bruise tomorrow," Sully said as he stepped out of the boat and came to stand beside them.

"What did he grab me for?" the older man asked as he shook out his hand.

"I'm getting a headache," Emma said. "Trimble, take them to the station. We'll follow with this group."

Lindsey and the others waited for the officers to escort their suspects up the ramp before falling in line behind them. When they reached the pier above, it was to find Nancy, Violet and Charlene waiting along with a very unhappy-looking Ian.

He glowered at his wife. "Since when have you taken to kayaking in the middle of the dinner shift?"

"It was a spur-of-the-moment idea," she said. "Beth and I felt the need for some fresh air."

"Really?" he asked. "And it had nothing to do with chasing bad guys or any other dumb ideas?"

"Dumb?" she asked. Her temper snapped in her blue eyes. "I'll have you know it was brilliant. Beth and I rigged a line across the channel markers, and sure enough, when they came speeding through, it clotheslined them, *bam*, dumping them right into the water. It was awesome!"

"You could have been killed!" Ian roared.

Never in all the time she'd known him had Lindsey heard Ian raise his voice. He was always quick with a joke and had an easy can-do attitude.

"Oh, quit being so dramatic," Mary said. Ian scowled and Mary cupped his face with her hands. "I would never take a risk that would take me away from you."

The anger went out of Ian like a puff of smoke. He wrapped his arms around his wife and pressed his forehead to hers.

"Do me a favor," he said. "Next time, tell me you're going to scare five years off of my life, would you?"

"I will keep you duly informed," she said.

Arm in arm, they made their way back to their restaurant.

Lindsey saw her brother shaking hands with the man that Robbie had tried to subdue. He was a distinguished-looking man with a thick head of gray hair and a neatly trimmed goatee.

"Vincent, it's good to see you," Jack said.

The man clapped Jack on the shoulder and said, "Not as good as it is to see you, I promise you."

He and Jack exchanged uneasy smiles, and Lindsey got the feeling that Jack had been involved in something even more dangerous than she had supposed.

"Vincent Carrego, I'd like to introduce my sister, Lindsey Norris," he said.

"Carrego?" Emma spun around with her hands on her hips, gun at the ready. "The same Carrego who employed Juan Veracruz?"

"That's me," Vincent said.

"Hands in the air," Emma said. In a blink, Emma had her gun pointed at Carrego's head.

"Whoa!" Jack cried. "Everyone calm down. I can explain everything."

"I certainly hope so," Trimble said. "In the meantime, Mr. Carrego, we'll be taking the necessary precautions."

He moved behind Carrego and cuffed his wrists. Antonia glanced over her shoulder, and sent Vincent a malicious grin.

"Who's laughing now?" she asked.

He gave a careless shrug. "Now doesn't matter, since I will be . . . in the end."

CHAPTER

29

BRIAR CREEK
PUBLIC LIBRARY

The police station was standing room only. While the rest of the crafternooners had gone with Mary and Ian to the Blue Anchor for a hot beverage and a celebratory dessert, Lindsey had been ordered to the station.

Lindsey was just happy that it was toasty warm. While Antonia and her thugs were taken in back to be processed, Emma and Trimble wanted to hear Jack's story in the main room before they talked to Antonia.

They gathered around one of the police department computers, but because the town had so many firewalls to safeguard information, Lindsey was forced to use Stella's personal tablet to access the e-mail where she had copied Jack's micro card.

She brought up the file with all of her brother's data. Both he and Vincent looked weak with relief that it was still there. Lindsey might have felt that way if it didn't look like a bunch of wingdings and other junk. A part of her worried that the file hadn't transferred correctly.

"It's encrypted," Stella said as if reading her mind. "Here I'll decode it for us."

"While she's doing that, you can explain," Emma said to Jack.

Lindsey noted that Trimble turned on a digital recorder just before her brother began to speak. She nudged Jack to make sure he knew, and he nodded.

"It's okay," he said. "Really, we're the good guys."

The group settled in to listen. Lindsey noticed that Stella frequently glanced up from the tablet and watched Jack with a fierce look as if she was overwhelmed that he was here and she was determined that he would stay. Lindsey wondered if the woman knew that her feelings for Jack showed so plainly on her face. She suspected not.

She glanced around the room until she found Robbie sitting on one of the hard plastic chairs by the window. One of the officers had given him a bag of ice for his jaw, and he sat holding it to his face. She realized she hadn't thanked him properly for taking on what he thought was a dangerous stranger. She crossed the room and looked at the purpling bruise on his chin.

"Thank you for what you did out there," she said. "You were very brave."

To her surprise, Robbie actually looked embarrassed.

"It was nothing," he said.

"No, it was something," she corrected him. "And I really appreciate it."

When his green eyes met hers, they sparkled with his usual mischief. "Does this mean you'll date me?"

"I—" Caught off guard, Lindsey hesitated.

"You still married, Vine?" Jack asked as he appeared beside Lindsey.

"Technically speaking," Robbie said with a frown.

"Then the answer is technically no," Jack said. He took Lindsey by the elbow and led her away.

"Heh heh heh," Sully chuckled as they walked by.

"She's not dating you either, buddy," Jack said. "You broke her heart once. That's enough."

"Ha!" Robbie chortled while Sully looked distinctly uncomfortable.

"Jack," Lindsey said. "I love you, I really do, but you need to mind your own business."

"What?" He looked offended.

"She's right," Emma said. "Especially since we're waiting for the rest of your explanation. I'm sure your friend would like to get it under way, so we'll take his handcuffs off."

Jack looked at Vincent, who still had his hands behind his back.

"Oh, sorry, family stuff," Jack said. Vincent nodded as if he completely understood or maybe he'd like for Jack to get on with it. Hard to say.

"All right," Jack said. "Have any of you heard of coffee rust?"

Lindsey glanced around the room. Judging by the blank stares, they were all as baffled as she had been before Stella and Tom had told her what it was.

"It's a fungus that is devastating the coffee crops in Central and South America," Jack explained. "About a year ago, Vincent called me in to strategize about what to do, since his crop was getting hit so hard. I recommended he diversify into soybeans and oranges."

"I took his advice, but it was very difficult. My family has grown coffee for five generations," Vincent said. "So I tried to keep my coffee crop going."

"Then I got a call from Antonia Murroz," Jack said. "She wanted advice on how to market a new type of coffee plant, but when I went down there, I discovered that she had very little contamination from coffee rust at all."

Emma and Trimble exchanged a look as if they were trying to follow him but couldn't.

"It was odd," Jack said. "Why diversify to a new plant if your crops aren't suffering? With coffee, next season's berries are borne on this season's shoots, so rust on this season's growth reduces next season's yields. With little contamination from coffee rust, the Murroz family, who has one of the biggest coffee plantations in Brazil, would have had a high yield the following year. On the other hand, the loss of revenue while the new plants were being introduced would be significant."

"Okay, that does seem odd," Trimble said.

"Exactly, so I got in touch with Vincent and we had a frank discussion about the coffee cartel," Jack said.

Officer Wilcox entered the main room from the break room with a coffeepot and a tray full of mugs.

"It seemed appropriate," he said.

"Good call," Emma said. Officer Wilcox began to pour and Lindsey noted that everyone had a cup, probably in an effort to warm up their insides.

"Explain about the cartel," Trimble said.

"It is essentially a group of coffee growers who agree to fix the prices of the commodity so that they all profit," Jack said. "Both the Murroz and the Carrego families were long-standing members in the cartel."

"Isn't belonging to a cartel illegal?" Emma glared at Carrego as if sizing him up for a prisoner's onesie.

"In my grandfather's day, it was a matter of survival, but in mine," he paused and spread his hands wide, "I found I was better served to be the undercover cartel member for the Brazilian Federal Police."

"That's brave," Trimble said. Emma looked at him and he said, "What? It is."

"It was dangerous, but clearly imperative as one by one the members in the cartel were losing their crops to the fungus," Vincent said. "Since Antonia had hired Jack, I convinced him to be our inside man and find out what she was doing."

"And I found out," Jack said. "That document"—he pointed to the screen on Stella's tablet—"shows how Antonia and her hired thugs used the wind to spread the fungus to her competitors' crops. At first, I assumed she had so many charts and graphs about the weather for her own crops, but I soon realized she wasn't just tracking the wind. She was harnessing it to spread the fungus to destroy the competition with the added bonus that she wouldn't be tied to the cartel's agreed-upon pricing and could charge a small fortune for her coffee, since no one else had enough of a crop to give her any competition."

Vincent muttered something in Portuguese that sounded very unflattering.

"Come and look," Stella said. "It's all here."

Trimble and Emma peered over Stella's shoulder while she explained the document to them.

Satisfied, Trimble straightened up and turned to Jack. "That's all very well and good, but it doesn't tell me who killed Juan Veracruz or why?"

"Juan worked for me," Vincent said. "He was to meet Jack in the library, and Jack would give his information to Juan, who would bring it back to me to share with the rest of my . . . associates. We knew it wasn't safe for Jack to try to meet with me. We suspected that Antonia was already onto him."

"I had a hard time getting out of Brazil," Jack said. Lindsey knew him well enough to know he was understating how dangerous it had been. She glanced at Stella and saw that she knew it, too. "Antonia's people caught up to me right as I was downloading the information. She had figured out what I was doing and had ordered them to kill me. I got out of Brazil with the micro card and the clothes on my back. I didn't even have time to email the information or back it up. I figured once I handed the chip off, I would be safe, but no."

"You should have called me," Tom said. He was frowning at Jack. "That's what I do."

"I know you," Jack said. "You'd have gotten yourself killed trying to help me. I couldn't have that on my conscience."

Tom made an impatient noise and looked at Stella. "It's like he forgets that security is my *job*."

"When I arrived at the library, I was pretty wracked, running on no sleep or food for two days," Jack said. "Lindsey let me use the back room and I fell asleep waiting for my contact. When I woke up, two men were grappling and one of them yelled for me to get the hell out of there."

Jack's eyes took on a faraway look. "I never would have left if I'd known he was going to be killed. I thought they were just beating each other up, and when one was unconscious, the other would come after me. I knew I couldn't risk losing the information, so I hid it in one of the library books."

"*A Wrinkle in Time*," Lindsey said. "Clever."

Jack bowed his head. "I was hoping you'd figure out the clue if I didn't make it back."

"Wait. Rewind," Emma said. "What clue?"

"When Antonia nabbed Jack, she put him on the phone with me for a moment," Lindsey said. "He told me not to panic, that it wasn't as if he was being taken to Camazotz."

"Oh, that's the dark planet," Trimble said. He looked cheered that he'd figured it out. Emma frowned at him and he said, "It's a great book. You should read it."

Emma dug her fingers into her hair as if to keep herself from wrapping them around someone's neck. "So who killed Juan Veracruz?"

"At a guess?" Jack asked. "I'd say one of your thugs back there. You may want to start squeezing them to roll over on Antonia."

Emma studied him. She gave a nod to Trimble, who released Vincent from his cuffs. As he rubbed his wrists, Lindsey stepped forward and poured him a cup of coffee.

"It may not be as good as you're used to," she said.

"I'm sure it's fine," he said as he took a bracing sip.

"Was it one of your men?" she asked. Vincent met her gaze, and she knew that he knew what she was talking about.

"Yes, one of my men followed you on your beach walk," he said.

"Did he also toss my apartment?" Lindsey asked. She was feeling a head of steam beginning to roil.

"No, they followed you to make sure you were safe,"

Vincent said. "I was afraid Antonia meant to harm you in order to get to Jack."

"Wait! Someone searched your apartment?" Jack asked.

"Yes, luckily, I was spending the night at Sully's," Lindsey said. "Or it could have gone very badly."

"What?" Jack squawked in an alarmingly high-pitched voice.

"Really?" Lindsey asked. "You're shocked?"

"But you . . . but he . . ." Jack stuttered.

"Oh, quit worrying," Lindsey said. "Being with Sully kept me safe the night my place was ransacked, and then Robbie spent the next night at my apartment with me, also keeping me safe."

Jack went wobbly in the knees. "I think I need a drink."

Lindsey laughed at him. "You're an idiot."

"An idiot with heartburn," he said. "I'm glad I'm staying through the holidays. Obviously, a visit to check out your relationship situation is long overdue. Ha! Get it? Overdue."

Lindsey and Stella groaned and then shared a small smile.

"We'll check the fingerprints we took in your apartment against our guests and see if anything hits," Emma said.

"I'll bet we have a match with one of Antonia's goons," Trimble said.

"Am I free to go then?" Vincent asked.

"You are released on your own recognizance," Emma said. "But don't leave town—yet."

Lindsey noticed that Jack was looking a little shaky. She wondered what had happened to him while he'd been held by Antonia. Judging by the bruises she could see, he hadn't had an easy time of it.

"I think you need medical attention now," Lindsey said.

"Well, it's been a few days since I ate or slept," he said.

"I'm sending for a doctor. I want photographs taken of all of your bruises and a professional's description of your condition," Emma said. "If I can't get Antonia on murder, I want to make damn sure I can get her on kidnapping and assault."

"I'll order you some food from the Blue Anchor," Lindsey said. "Clam chowder okay to start?"

"That would be heaven," Jack said.

She watched as Stella helped him to a back room in the station house. Again, Lindsey was swamped with relief that her brother was here and he was okay.

She turned to face Emma and Detective Trimble, who were again studying the file on the computer.

"Do you think you'll be able to stop her?" she asked.

"We'll do our best," Emma said. "It's international so it could get dicey."

"I'm calling in some help from headquarters," Trimble said. "We'll nail her. Don't you worry."

Lindsey nodded. She felt better seeing the determined expressions on their faces.

The room began to empty as everyone else had been cleared to go home. Lindsey was just pushing through the front door when Emma called her name.

"Yeah," Lindsey answered.

"Nice work on the micro card and stopping Antonia from escaping," she said.

"Thanks," Lindsey said. She was almost out the door when Emma added, "And when everything calms down, we'll be having a meeting with the mayor about the library director's exact job description."

Lindsey wasn't sure if it was a threat or a promise, but she scurried outside, pretending she hadn't heard her.

CHAPTER

30

BRIAR CREEK
PUBLIC LIBRARY

"This is a first," Beth said as she entered the room carrying a bowl of spinach dip in one arm and a plate of cubed bread in the other.

"What is?" Lindsey asked. "A crafterevening?"

The crafternooners had decided to bump their lunch meeting to a festive evening shindig. It was the first time the room had been used since Juan Veracruz had been murdered, and Lindsey figured it was the best way to dispel the awful memories.

The fire was roaring in the fireplace; soft holiday music played out of an iPod plugged into some speakers. They had read Frances Hodgson Burnett's *The Secret Garden* per Beth's request, and Lindsey was glad they had. It had been nice to read about springtime in Yorkshire when outside New England was in the frosty grip of winter.

"Well, yes, but it's also the first time I've made it to

crafternoon, er, evening not in a story time costume," Beth said.

Lindsey glanced at her friend in her professional blouse and skirt and cute pumps.

"You're right," Lindsey said. "You look like a grown-up."

Beth laughed. "See? First time for everything."

"Hot meatballs! Hot meatballs!" Violet charged into the room with her Crock-Pot while Charlene arrived right behind her carrying thick paper plates and bowls and plastic dinnerware.

"Plug it in right here," Lindsey said. She gestured to the buffet table they had already set up, which was sagging under two punch bowls, one for eggnog and one for a sherbet-lemon soda concoction of Nancy's, a cheese and cracker platter and a large veggie tray.

"Oh, this is a party!" Charlene cried. "I'm going to be as big as a house if I eat my share of all of this."

"Fritters, get your clam fritters and crab salad," Mary said as she entered carrying two large bags. "Oh, this is cozy. The weather is just beginning to turn out there, but they're not predicting much snow on the ground, just flurries."

Lindsey glanced out the window at the town park and saw the falling snow illuminated in the streetlamp's golden light. It was beautiful.

"Okay, I couldn't make up my mind what sort of cookie to bring, so I brought a little of everything," Nancy said. She had a large tray of cookies piled six deep, and she plopped it onto the edge of the table with a thump.

The ladies gathered around the table and finished arranging their dishes. When they were done, they all stepped back to admire it.

"It's lovely," Violet said.

"Too pretty to eat," Charlene agreed.

"Nah!" Beth said. "Let's dig in!"

With a chorus of agreement, they all began to fill their plates. Beth reached for cookies and Nancy gave her a look.

"Life is uncertain," Beth said. "It is best to eat dessert first."

They all chuckled, and when their plates were fully loaded, they turned to take their seats, except their seats were full of men.

"Ian Murphy!" Mary cried. "What are you doing here?"

Ian glanced up from the copy of *The Secret Garden* that he clutched in his big square hands.

"My friends and I are enjoying our crafterevening," he said. His expression was bland as he added, "If you'll excuse me. Now, gentlemen, where were we?"

"I was sharing my information that the book's working title was *Mistress Mary* in reference to the nursery rhyme *Mary, Mary, Quite Contrary*," Sully said.

He gave his sister a pointed look, and Mary stomped her foot and said, "Quit looking at me. I am not contrary . . . much."

"Wasn't it published in serial form first?" Martin, Charlene's husband, asked.

"It was," Robbie confirmed. "And given that Hodgson Burnett moved to America when she was sixteen, she did a bang-up job capturing the broad Yorkshire accents."

"I find the character that I most enjoyed was Dickon," Jack said. "I admired his adventuring spirit."

"We do get to eat, too, right?" Charlie asked as he strode

into the room with Heathcliff, who bounded at Lindsey as if he hadn't seen her in weeks instead of hours.

"What are you all doing here?" Nancy asked. "This is for crafternooners. You know, you read the book—"

"Done," the men all said together.

"You do a craft," Mary said.

Suddenly, tote bags stuffed with yarn and crochet hooks appeared. Robbie fished out some sort of lengthy rope he was working on.

"I've almost got the hang of it," he said. His bright green eyes were sparkling with mirth.

"And food," Charlene said. "You're supposed to bring food."

"On it!" Martin jumped up and exited the room. He came back carrying five large pizza boxes.

"Well, it looks like they've covered it, ladies," Beth said. "Shall we take a vote on it?"

"Seems only reasonable," Lindsey said.

"All right, those is favor of letting the men stay—" Violet began but was interrupted by Mary, who added, "This time only."

"Say 'Aye,' " Violet said.

The women all glanced at one another and then at the men and then back. As one, they all said, "Aye."

"Any nays?" Violet asked. When no one responded, she turned to the men and said, "Okay, but just this one time."

From there the crafterevening turned into the most rockin' gathering the crafternooners had ever had. Beth helped Robbie with his crochet while he coached her for her upcoming audition in the next community theater production. Charlie and Heathcliff circled the buffet five or six times, snacking all the way. Martin and Jack talked about world economics, which no one else understood except Charlene, but they all smiled and nodded as if they did.

Ian and Mary debated putting a brick oven into their restaurant, thinking that as they got old, owning a pizza joint with a set menu might be easier to manage than a full-scale restaurant.

Violet and Nancy talked about the next self-defense class they were going to take. Someone had recommended they sign up for tai chi, but they had gotten it confused and signed up for tae kwon do instead, so instead of calm soothing meditation, they were learning to kick ass. Somehow, that seemed about right.

The party was half over when Lindsey realized she'd left the cheesecake she'd brought in the refrigerator in the staff break room. She excused herself from the party saying she'd be right back with cake.

She was halfway down the hall to the main library when Sully caught up to her.

"Need a hand?" he asked.

She stopped and turned to look at him. "It's cake. I think I've got it but thank you."

Sully lifted a hand and smoothed back one of her long blond curls. The gesture was so familiar it made Lindsey's throat tight.

"I haven't had a chance to tell you that I'm glad you're all right," he said. "The other night when Antonia and her crew grabbed you, I . . ."

As if he'd run out of steam or words, Sully stopped talking and looked at her as if he could never express how truly awful that moment had been.

"I know," Lindsey said. "Even with a plan in place, it was scary on my end, too."

They glanced at each other, and Lindsey knew that this was Sully trying to open himself up and let her in. She grinned. He was doing pretty well, too. She felt a bubble of hope float up inside her.

She looped her hand through his arm, and they walked down the hall together.

"Oh, hey, look here," he said. He stopped walking and pointed up at a holly bough hanging in the doorway. "Is that—why, I do believe it is. Mistletoe."

Lindsey raised one eyebrow and looked at him suspiciously. "Funny, I don't remember that being a part of the garland when I put it there."

"Must be fate," Sully said.

"Oh, no, I'll tell you what it is," she said. "It's disgusting."

Sully's eyes widened in surprise.

"Every year I field reference calls about what exactly mistletoe is," Lindsey said. "It's nasty, that's what it is. It's a parasitic plant that chokes the life out of its host by taking its water and nutrients, oh, and if that isn't enough, guess how it moves around?"

"No idea," Sully said drily.

"Bird feces," Lindsey said and wrinkled her nose. "Mistletoe moves from host to host by having birds poop the seeds out after they've eaten the berries. Gross."

Sully glanced from the plant overhead to Lindsey and smiled.

"Funny, you would think that would be more off-putting than it is," he said.

Then he leaned forward and kissed her, and Lindsey forgot all about reference questions and cheesecake and kissed him back with every bit of longing she'd felt over the past few months. The bubble of hope inside her swelled to bursting.

When Sully leaned back, he looked at her with a heat that warmed her all the way down to her toes.

"I'd say it's shaping up to be a happy new year after all," he said. Then he grinned.

"Yes, yes, it is," she agreed and gave him a saucy wink.

The Briar Creek Library
Guide to Crafternoons

Book talk, food and crafting—is there a better way to spend a lunch hour than this? The Briar Creek crafternooners think not. Lindsey and her friends always look forward to their time together even if the talk is sometimes more personal than just about the book they've read that week. Here are some ideas from the ladies to kick-start your own crafternoon to share a book, a craft and good food with good friends.

Readers Guide for
The Woman in White
by Wilkie Collins

1. *The Woman in White* is considered one of the first true mystery novels ever written. Do you agree with this and why?

2. There are multiple mysteries entwined in this novel, such as switched identities, falsified records and secret societies. Which one is your favorite and why?

3. Because there are several mysteries, there are also a couple of amateur sleuths. Which do you believe is the better detective: Marian Halcombe, the heroine's half sister and companion, or Walter Hartright, the heroine's art teacher and love interest?

4. The author, Wilkie Collins, was a close personal friend of Charles Dickens. Do you see any similarities in their work, and if so, in what way?

5. Critics suggest that the theme of the novel is an examination of the unfair position of a married woman at the time. Do you agree with this, or do you see a different theme?

Craft: Recycling Candles

It does not get much easier than this. Even if you're like Lindsey, who is not very good at crafts, melting wax is pretty simple and can be a lot of fun.

Supplies:

Cotton string
Pencils
Clean canning jars (or any substantial glass container)
Old half-used candles
Small pot
Electric warming plate

CRAFT: RECYCLING CANDLES

Cut the string a few inches longer than needed to reach the bottom of the jar. Tie the string to a pencil, and balance the pencil on the top of a canning jar. The string should touch the bottom. Melt the old bits of candle wax in the pot on the warming plate until the wax can be poured easily. Carefully pour the wax into the jar. If using different-colored candles, consider melting the wax in alternating colors, and when one layer is cool, pour a new layer on top. When the candle is as high as you want, trim the string, leaving just enough to be a wick for the candle.

Recipes

BETH'S SPINACH DIP

1 (10-ounce) package frozen chopped spinach
1 (16-ounce) container sour cream
1 (8-ounce) can sliced water chestnuts, drained and
  chopped
1 cup mayonnaise
1 package Knorr vegetable soup mix
3 green onions chopped (optional)

Mix all the ingredients in a large bowl and let chill for 2 hours.
Serve in the bowl with dipping options such as bread cubes,
crackers or fresh veggies on the side. You can also hollow out
a large round loaf of sourdough bread and put the dip inside.
Tear up the removed inside of the bread for dipping. Yum.

RECIPES

VIOLET AND CHARLENE'S MEATBALLS

2 (16-ounce) cans tomato sauce
2 (16-ounce) cans diced tomatoes in water
2½ tablespoons oregano
1½ tablespoons rosemary
1½ tablespoons basil
1 tablespoon onion powder
Several pinches thyme
⅓ cup extra virgin olive oil
6 cloves pressed garlic
½ tablespoon ground black pepper
1 bag frozen Italian meatballs, fully cooked

Mix all the ingredients except the meatballs in a large pot and heat to a boil. Reduce the heat and let simmer for three and a half hours, stirring occasionally. Add the meatballs and cook at medium heat for another half hour until the meatballs are hot.

NANCY'S FRUIT CAKE COOKIES

1¾ cups flour
½ teaspoon baking soda
¼ teaspoon salt
1 cup packed light brown sugar
6 tablespoons butter, softened
2 tablespoons shortening
1 large egg
1 cup pitted prunes, chopped
1 cup golden raisins
½ cup red candied cherries, chopped
½ cup sweetened shredded coconut
3 ounces white chocolate

Preheat oven to 375°F. Grease a large cookie sheet. In a large bowl, combine flour, baking soda, salt, and set aside. In another large bowl, with mixer on low, beat brown sugar, butter, and shortening until blended. Add egg and mix until creamy. Add flour mixture, prunes, raisins, cherries and coconut until just blended. Drop dough by rounded teaspoonfuls onto cookie sheet two inches apart. Bake 10-12 minutes until golden around edges. Allow to cool. Arrange cookies in one layer on a large sheet of wax paper. In a small saucepan, melt the white chocolate over low heat until smooth. Using a fork, drizzle white chocolate on top of all of the cookies and allow to set. Store in a tightly sealed container. Makes about 3 dozen.

Turn the page for a preview of Jenn McKinlay's
next Hat Shop Mystery . . .

AT THE DROP OF A HAT

Coming February 2015 from Berkley Prime Crime!

I stood at the counter of *Mim's Whims*, the hat shop I inherited from my grandmother, Mim, along with my cousin Vivian Tremont, and I gazed out the window. All I could see was gray.

Gray clouds, gray sheets of rain, gray fog filling the streets and alleyways, gray, gray, gray. Or, as the Brits like to spell it, grey.

Our shop is nestled in the midst of Portobello Road and takes up the bottom floor of the three-story white building that our grandmother bought over forty years ago. I've always loved it and found the bright blue and white striped awning and matching blue shutters on the windows above to be cheerful, but even they couldn't defeat the never-ending gloom that seemed to descend upon our section of London.

As I was raised in the States and hailed most recently

from Florida, this weather was pushing me just to the right of crazy.

Three solid weeks of rain will do that to a girl. Besides, I was quite sure I was going to sprout mold if I didn't get some sunshine and soon.

"It's the last one," Fee said. "You should have it."

"No, no, I insist you take it," Viv said. She tossed her long blond hair over her shoulder as if the gesture added weight to her argument.

Fee is Fiona Felton, my cousin Viv's apprentice. She's a very nice girl with a tall willowy build, a dark complexion courtesy of her West Indies heritage and a bob of corkscrew curls that she liked to dye new and different colors. Currently, she was rocking green streaks, which I thought was pretty cool but would look hideous in my own auburn shoulder-length hair.

Viv is my cousin Vivian Tremont. She's the mad hatter of our little trio. Growing up down the street, she trained to be a milliner beside Mim. My own attempts at millinery were encouraged, but it became readily apparent that I did not have the family gift for twining ribbons into flowers or shaping brims or anything artistic or even crafty.

Viv and Fee were standing on the other side of the counter, taking a break from their current creations in the workroom. They were pushing a plate back and forth between them which contained one rogue piece of Walker's Toffee, which was the last of the package we had been nibbling on all day.

"After such a large tea this afternoon, I couldn't eat another bite," Fee said.

"Fee, honestly, I insist you take the last piece of toffee," Viv said. She sounded very bossy about it.

"No, you absolutely must have it," Fee said. She blew a green curl out of her eyes.

"Oh, for goodness sakes," I said. "I'll eat it just to end this."

I scooped up the last piece of toffee and popped it into my mouth. Viv and Fee both turned to look at me with wide eyes.

"What?" I asked while chewing.

"Nothing," Fee said and glanced away.

"It's fine," Viv agreed.

I stopped chewing. I knew the stone-sinking sensation of committing a social gaffe when I felt it.

"Aw, man," I said. "I messed that up, didn't I?"

"It's fine, honestly," Viv said.

Which is how I knew it really wasn't.

"What did I do?" I asked. "Did I not force it on you two enough?"

"You're making fun of us," Viv said.

I swallowed the last of the toffee. "No, my American brain is just trying to figure out how pushing something that you apparently really want onto others makes sense? If you want it, take it."

"That's not our way," Fee said. "There are just certain things we do out of politeness, like saying 'Cheers' when you step off the bus."

"The toffee push could have gone on all day," I said.

"It probably would have," Viv agreed.

"See? You did us a favor," Fee said.

"And now you're trying to make me feel better for being a clumsy American," I said.

"You're half British," Viv reminded me. Like I could forget my charming mother, Viv's mother's little sister, that easily. The woman had all but demanded a vow of celibacy out of me after my last relationship implosion went viral on the Internet and had my dad, a pacifist, looking into buying a gun to shoot the rat bastard who hurt his baby girl.

"I still don't get it," I said.

"It's just one of the many idiosyncrasies of being British," Viv said. "You indicate you're longing for something by rejecting it. Repeatedly."

"Now I see why you're both single," I said.

"Was that nice?" Viv asked. "We're just very polite."

"One might say cripplingly polite," I said.

"Huh, enjoy that toffee, yeah?" Fee said.

I smiled. Maybe I was too brash and forward for my cousin's sensibilities, but at least I didn't spend my time pining or pretending I didn't want things that I actually did.

The doors to the front of the shop opened and in strode Harrison Wentworth. My heart did a little toe tap against my ribs, but I refused to acknowledge it. Okay, so maybe I did pretend I didn't want something that I really did want just a little.

"Afternoon, ladies," he greeted us as he stood in the door and shook out his umbrella.

"Hi, Harrison," Viv and Fee greeted him in unison.

"Hiya, Harry," I said.

His bright green eyes glittered when they landed on me.

"It's Harrison, Ginger," he corrected me.

Little did he know I liked hearing him call me Ginger, especially in that swoon-worthy accent of his. Although I had tried to get everyone to call me Ginger over the years, Harry was the only one who'd kept it up from childhood. Yes, I'd known him that long.

Most of my school holidays had been spent in Notting Hill in Mim's hat shop. My mother had insisted that I be well versed in all things British and palling around with Viv was never a hardship. She was two years older than me, and given that we were both the only children in our families, she was the sibling I had never had.

Harry had been one of our brat pack, the kids whose families lived or owned businesses on Portobello Road, who ran amuck in the neighborhood. His uncle had been Mim's bookkeeper just as Harry was ours. Of course, I had recently come to find out that he had bought a share of the business and was now technically my boss. Yeah, I was still chewing on that one.

I couldn't fault Viv, though. She'd gotten into financial trouble over a haul of Swarovski crystals, yes, like me she has impulse control issues. Unfortunately, I'd been so caught up in the drama that was my life at the time that she'd forged ahead and had Harry save the business when I should have been there to help. I still had guilt about it, but I was working through it.

"What are you doing here?" I asked Harry.

He raised his eyebrows at me and I realized my American rudeness was rearing its ugly blocky head—again.

"Sorry," I said. "Was that too abrupt?"

"One does generally start with a comment about the weather," he said. "Then you slowly segue into a softly pedaled interrogation."

I glanced at the window. "After three weeks of gloom, I am thinking any conversation about the weather would be redundant, but if it makes you feel better . . . ruddy wet out there today, isn't it?"

He grinned and then looked at Viv. "There's hope for her yet."

Fee snorted. "Not if there's toffee involved."

I was about to protest when the bells on the door jangled and a woman in a blue hooded raincoat entered the shop carrying a large plastic bag.

She stood dripping on the doormat, and I took it as my opportunity to escape the discussion of my manners or lack thereof. I left the group at the counter and crossed the shop.

"Hi, may I help you?" I asked.

"Oh, I hope so," she said.

She opened the dripping plastic bag and pulled out an old hat box. It was white with thick blue stripes and a blue satin cord. On the top of the box in a swirling script were the words *Mim's Whims*.

I heard a gasp and realized that it came from behind me. I knew without looking that it was Viv and I knew she was reacting to the same thing that I was. This box was an old one of Mim's before Mim had updated the shop's boxes in the nineties.

"Is there a hat in there?" Viv asked as she joined us on the mat in front of the front door.

"Yes, it's an old one that belonged to my mother," the woman answered.

She pushed back the hood on her raincoat and I was struck by how dark her hair was. It was an inky black color, thick and lustrous, the type you'd expect to see on a model. After I recovered from my spurt of hair envy, I noted that she was quite pretty with big brown eyes and an upturned nose. Mercifully, she was spared from being perfect, as her lips were on the thin side and she wore glasses, a nerdy rectangular pair with thick black frames.

"I don't want to drip all over your shop," the woman said.

"No, worries," I said. "Here I'll take the bag and your coat."

She handed me the dripping bag and shrugged out of her coat, freeing one arm at a time as if afraid to let go of her hat box. I hung her coat and the bag on our coat rack by the door. Usually we kept it in the back room, but so many people had been coming in with wet coats that we'd moved it out front for the interminable rain fest we had going.

I hurried after them as Viv led the woman over to the counter where Fee and Harrison were watching the happenings with curious expressions.

"Ariana, is that you?" Harrison asked. He looked delighted to see the young woman, and I felt the prick of something sharp, like the spiny point of jealousy, stab me in the backside.

She looked up at him in surprise and then laughed. "Harrison, fancy meeting you here!"

He stepped around the counter and swept her into a friendly embrace. "I wondered why Stephen asked me about this place? Was it for you?"

This place? I turned to exchange a dark look with Viv, but neither she nor Fee was looking in my direction. Did they not see that Harrison had just insulted our shop?

"Yes, I knew you did the books for a hat shop on Portobello and was so hoping it was the same one, and then Stephen said that you bragged that it was the best in the city and that the girls who owned it were—"

"Yes, well," Harrison interrupted her by coughing loudly into his fist.

He glanced at me and I narrowed my eyes at him. What had he said about us? I opened my mouth to demand to hear it when Viv spoke first.

"Do you know what year your mother purchased the hat?" Viv asked Ariana.

"I do, it was 1983, in fact," she said. "The hat was a bridal hat for her wedding."

"1983? Oh, that was a very good hat year. John Boyd was designing for Princess Diana. I loved the turquoise hat he made for her first foreign tour to Australia. It was a cap framed by matching ropes of silk with a net over the top and a matching flower at the back. I tried to re-create it during my apprenticeship but I could never match his artistry."

"He is a genius," Fee agreed. "I adore the red boater that she wore perched to the side with the matching jacket."

"None of us were even born in 1983," I said. "How is it you know what the hats looked like back then?"

"Every milliner studies John Boyd and Princess Diana," Fee said.

"That and I did an apprenticeship in his Knightsbridge shop," Viv said. "Mim loved his work. They were friends, you know."

I didn't, but I didn't say as much, mostly because I was too embarrassed to admit that although the name John Boyd sounded familiar, I wasn't really up to speed on his work. The truth was I didn't know much about the millinery business. I had studied the hospitality industry in college and my gift was more with people, which brought my attention back to the woman in our shop.

"I'm sorry, Ariana, I didn't catch your last name," I said. I glanced meaningfully at Harrison, but he didn't look embarrassed in the least.

"Oh, of course, forgive me," he said. "Ariana Jackson, these are the owners of Mim's Whims Scarlett Parker and Vivian Tremont and their apprentice Fiona Felton."

"Ariana, what a pretty name," I said. I gave her my most winning smile. "It suits you. Do you and Harrison go a long way back?"

Harry raised his eyebrows, no doubt surprised that I hadn't used his nickname. Well, just like he didn't know that I liked the name Ginger, he also didn't know that I considered Harry my personal name for him and I really didn't want to share it.

"Not at all, just a few rugby seasons," Ariana said. She and Harrison exchanged a smile. "My fiancée Stephen plays on the same league team and when I said I wanted to get my mother's hat fixed for our wedding, Stephen asked Harrison about Mim's Whims. I was thrilled to find out you're still here."

She put the old hat box on the counter. "I was hoping you might be able to help me. My mother's hat needs some refurbishing and since it originally came from this shop . . ."

"Let's see what we've got here," Viv said. She gestured to the box. "May I?"

Ariana gave her a quick nod and Viv eagerly pried the lid off. Nested amid layers of pale tissue paper was a wide-brimmed white confection. Viv carefully reached into the box and gently pulled the hat free.

I gasped. It was beautiful; a wide-brimmed, white silk hat swathed in tulle with a large silk bow and a lush organza rose nestled in the center. As Viv lifted it, a long organza train fell down from beneath the bow and spilled over the brim. Fee reached out and pulled the train free. It was long and delicate with embroidered edges. Even I could see our grandmother's handiwork all over it.

"Oh, Mim," Viv said. Her voice sounded wistful and I knew just how she felt. To hold something our grandmother had made over thirty years ago brought her right back to us.

The sweet scent of Lily of the Valley filled my nose. I glanced at Viv at the same moment she glanced at me. *Mim.* It was the distinct scent Mim had always worn. I glanced around the shop as if expecting her to appear, but of course she didn't. Still, she was here or the essence of her was here. I was sure of it just as I was sure she wanted Viv to restore the hat.

"I'd be happy to try and fix the hat," Viv said. "No, I'd be honored."

Keep reading for a preview of Jenn McKinlay's
next Cupcake Bakery Mystery . . .

DARK CHOCOLATE DEMISE

Coming April 2015 from Berkley Prime Crime!

66 He looks really good in there," Angie DeLaura said. "Peaceful even."

"You can't say that about everyone," Melanie Cooper agreed.

"It's all about the casket," Tate Harper said. "You want to choose a lining that complements your skin tone in the post mortem."

Mel and Angie turned and gave him concerned looks.

"How could you possibly know that?" Mel asked.

"The funeral director at the mortuary told me," he said. He threw an arm around Angie. "Since we're engaged and all, maybe we should pick out a doublewide so we can spend eternity snuggling."

Angie beamed at him and giggled. Then she kissed him. It did not maintain its PG-13 rating for more than a moment and Mel felt her upchuck reflex kick in as she turned away.

She was happy for her best friends in their coupledom, really she was, but sometimes, like now, it was just gag worthy.

"Really you two, how about a little decorum, given the gravity of the situation?" she asked. She knew she sounded a bit snippy but honestly, some days they were just too much.

"Of course, you're right," Tate said. "Sorry."

He and Angie untangled themselves from one another. He smoothed the front of his shirt and straightened his jacket while Angie fluffed her hair and shook out her skirt. Duly subdued, the three of them stood beside the casket that held their friend and employee Marty Zelaznik.

Marty looked particularly spiffy in his white dress shirt and his favorite bold blue tie. His suit was black and Angie had tucked a blue pocket square into his breast pocket so that just the edge of it was visible. His features were relaxed and his bald head was shiny as if it had been waxed to a high gloss.

"Hey." Oscar Ruiz, a teen known as Oz, who worked alongside Marty in the bakery Fairy Tale Cupcakes that Mel, Angie and Tate owned, joined the trio by the casket. "So, we're going with an open lid, huh?"

"We think it's for the best," Mel said.

"His tie is crooked," Angie said. "We should fix that."

"Yeah, and his make-up is a little on the heavy side," Tate said. "He has angry eyebrows."

"Anyone have a handkerchief?" Mel asked. "A little spit will take care of that."

At this, Marty's eyes popped open and he sat up in his

coffin and glared. "What am I, five? You are not spit-shining me!"

"Ah!" Angie yelped and leapt back with her hand clutching her chest. "Gees, Marty, you scared me to death!"

"Nice one." Tate laughed as he and Oz high-fived and knuckle-bumped Marty.

"What? Did you think I was really dead?" Marty asked, sounding outraged.

"No!" Angie snapped. "I thought you were napping. You had a little drool in the corner of your mouth."

"I was, but that doesn't mean you get to swab my decks," Marty said as he shifted around and rubbed the dried spittle off of his chin. "You know, I have to say it's pretty comfy in here. I may have to look into putting a deposit on one of these for the future."

"*Way* in the future," Mel said.

Marty glanced at the four of them. "So when do we leave for the zombie walk? I want to catch a few more Z's. Oh, and by the way, the undead look you've all got going, yeah, I don't want to wake up to that ever again."

Mel glanced at her friends. Tate and Angie were doing the undead bride and groom. In requisite tux and white wedding gown, they had topped off their look with gray make-up and faux partially rotted flesh. Tate had a fake knife lodged in his skull, while Angie had an axe sticking out of her back. They had already taken bogus wedding photos that Angie was seriously considering making their official wedding portrait.

Being single and thinking this was going to become a permanent state, Mel had decided to go as an undead chef complete with her toque, double-breasted white coat and checkered pants. She wore her pleated hat back on her head to enhance the amazing latex scar Oz had adhered to her forehead. It was pretty badass.

Oz had decided to wear his chef whites as well, but had changed it up by making the side of his face appear to be rotting off. Every time Mel saw his fake putrid skin flap in the breeze, she had to resist the urge to peel it off.

Being the body in the casket, Marty had chosen to be less undead than the rest of them. He was pasty pale and sunken eyed but that was about it. Mel suspected because he was closer to his actual expiration date than the rest of them, dressing up as a dead man had less appeal for him. Overall, she had to admit, they were fabulously gruesome.

"Sorry, Marty, but no napping," Mel said. She grabbed him by the elbow and hauled him out of the casket, which was sitting on a trailer on the back of the cupcake van. "We've got to load up the van and get over to the Civic Center Park and set up our station before the undead descend upon us."

"Ooh, that sounded nice and grisly," Angie shuddered.

"It did, didn't it?" Mel said. She let go of Marty, ignoring the look of longing he gave the coffin. "Let's move, people."

She hurried to the back of the bakery, where she'd left her rolling cart loaded with boxes of cupcakes. She pushed it beside the service window of the van and began to hand them off to Oz, who was inside.

"What flavors did you create for zombie cupcakes?" Tate asked.

"No new flavors," Mel said. She flipped open the lid of one of the boxes to show off the cupcakes. "Just new names. In place of the usual suspects we have the Marshmallow Mummy—"

"Hey, you made the frosting look like bandages on a mummy's head," Oz said from the window. "Cool."

"And it has a marshmallow filling," Mel said. "We also have Vanilla Eyeballs, Strawberry Brains, and Dark Chocolate Demise just to round out the flavors."

"The eyeball one is staring at me," Marty said. "I don't think I could eat that."

"How about the brains?" Tate said. "How did you pipe the frosting in the shape of a pink brain?"

"Fine pastry tip," Angie said. "It was fun."

"Are those little candy coffins on the chocolate ones?" Oz asked. "I dig those. Get it?"

"Aw, man, that stunk worse than rotting flesh," Marty said. He closed the lid on the box, took it from Mel and handed it through the window. The others stared at him and he asked, "What? I'm just getting into the spirit of things."

"Fine, but please keep the rotten flesh remarks to a minimum when selling the cupcakes," Mel said.

"This from the woman who ruined a perfectly good cupcake by putting a bloodshot eyeball on it," he said. He shook his head as if he couldn't fathom what she'd been thinking.

Mel lowered her head to keep from laughing. She didn't want to offend Marty, as he took his vanilla cupcakes very seriously.

"Melanie!" a voice called from the bakery. Mel glanced up to see her mother, Joyce Cooper, stride out the door. Joyce took three steps and stopped, putting her hand to her throat. "Oh, my!"

"We look amazing, right?" Mel asked. She spread her arms wide to include her entire crew.

"*What* are you?" Joyce asked.

"The baking dead," Oz said from the van.

"Niiiice." Tate nodded.

"Yeah, I'll give you that one," Marty agreed and exchanged a complicated handshake with Oz.

Mel approached her mother, who only flinched a little when she drew near. "Thanks for watching the bakery so we could work the zombie walk, Mom."

"No, problem," Joyce said. "But, honey, really I just have to say that white foundation you have on, well, it's really not terribly flattering and now that you're single, you really might want to consider a little blush and maybe a less prominent eye shadow."

"I'm supposed to look like a zombie," Mel said. "I'm pretty sure they don't wear blush or eye shadow."

"Lipstick?"

"No," Mel said.

Joyce heaved a beleaguered sigh, turned and walked back into the bakery.

"Really?" Mel said to Angie. "She's worried about my pasty foundation but she blithely ignores the fact that I have a gaping wound on my head."

"She's just looking out for you," Angie said. "Maybe you'll meet a nice undead lawyer at the zombie walk and she'll stop worrying."

"There's only one lawyer I'm interested in," Mel said. "And as far as I know he is alive and kicking."

Angie gave her a half hug as if trying to bolster her spirits. The love of Mel's life was Joe DeLaura, the middle of Angie's seven older brothers. A few months ago, Joe had rejected Mel's proposal of marriage even though he had already proposed to her and she'd said yes. As Mel explained to her mother, it was complicated.

The truth was that Mel had gotten cold feet at the "until death us do part" portion of the whole marriage package, but she had worked through it. Unfortunately, when she had gotten over her case of the wiggins and proposed to Joe, he'd just taken on the trial of a notorious mobster, who was known for wriggling off justice's barbed hook by murdering anyone who tried to lock him up.

Joe had walked away from Mel to keep her from being a target. To Mel it still felt like rejection. She didn't handle that sort of thing well and in the past three months had gained fifteen pounds from comfort eating. For that alone, she hoped Joe brought his mobster to justice.

"Come on, ladies, it's 'time to nut up or shut up,'" Tate said as he dropped an arm around Mel and Angie's shoulders and began to herd them to the van.

"*Zombieland*," Mel and Angie identified the movie together.

The swapping of movie quotes was one of the foundations of their friendship. Mel and Tate had met first in middle school, but then Angie had come along and the three friends had spent weekends in Tate's parents' home theater watching old movies and eating junk food. Ever since they had played a game of stumping one another with movie quotes.

These days just the memory of those happier times made Mel glum. Why did it seem like everything was so difficult now?

"Chin up, Undead Chef," Tate said. "We're going to go sell cupcakes to the shambling masses and make an arm and a leg in profit."

"*Ba dum dum*," Angie made the sound of a drummer's rim shot.

Mel rolled her eyes. "I guess that's better than making a killing."

"That's the spirit," Angie said with a laugh.

"Aw, come on. It's a zombie walk finished off with an outdoor big screen showing of the *Night of the Living Dead*," Tate said. "How could we have anything but a good time?"

From *New York Times* Bestselling Author
Jenn McKinlay

DEATH OF A MAD HATTER

A HAT SHOP MYSTERY

Scarlett Parker and Vivian Tremont, co-owners of a London hat shop, are creating the hats for an *Alice in Wonderland* themed afternoon tea. The tea is a fund-raiser hosted by the Grisby family, who wants a new hospital wing named after their patriarch.

When the Grisby heir is poisoned, evidence points to Scarlett and Viv, and the police become curiouser and curiouser about their involvement. Now the ladies need to find the tea party crasher who's mad enough to kill at the drop of a hat...

"A delightful new heroine."
—Deborah Crombie, *New York Times* bestselling author

jennmckinlay.com
facebook.com/TheCrimeSceneBooks
penguin.com

FROM *NEW YORK TIMES* BESTSELLING AUTHOR
JENN MCKINLAY

-The Library Lover's Mysteries-

BOOKS CAN BE DECEIVING
DUE OR DIE
BOOK, LINE, AND SINKER
READ IT AND WEEP
ON BORROWED TIME

Praise for the Library Lover's Mysteries

"Fast-paced and fun...Charming."
—Kate Carlisle, *New York Times* bestselling author

"A sparkling setting, lovely characters,
books, knitting, and chowder! What more
could any reader ask?"
—Lorna Barrett, *New York Times* bestselling author

"Sure to charm cozy readers everywhere."
—Ellery Adams, *New York Times* bestselling author
of the Books by the Bay Mysteries

jennmckinlay.com
facebook.com/TheCrimeSceneBooks
penguin.com

M1145AS0514

Due or Die

"[A] terrific addition to an intelligent, fun, and lively series."
—Miranda James, *New York Times* bestselling author
of the Cat in the Stacks Mysteries

"What a great read! I can't wait to go back to the first title in this cozy, library-centered series. McKinlay has been a librarian, and her snappy story line, fun characters, and young library director with backbone make for a winning formula. Add a dog named Heathcliff and library programming suggestions—well, it's quite a value-added package!"
—*Library Journal*

"McKinlay's writing is well paced, her dialogue feels very authentic, and I found *Due or Die* almost impossible to put down."
—*CrimeSpree*

Books Can Be Deceiving

"When murder disturbs the quiet community of Briar Creek on the ocean's edge, librarian Lindsey Norris springs into action to keep her best friend from being charged with the crime. A sparkling setting, lovely characters, books, knitting, and chowder! What more could any reader ask?"
—Lorna Barrett, *New York Times* bestselling author
of the Booktown Mysteries

"With a remote coastal setting as memorable as Manderley and a kindhearted, loyal librarian as the novel's heroine, *Books Can Be Deceiving* is sure to charm cozy readers everywhere."
—Ellery Adams, *New York Times* bestselling author of
the Books by the Bay Mysteries

"Fast-paced and fun, *Books Can Be Deceiving* is the first in Jenn McKinlay's appealing new mystery series featuring an endearing protagonist, delightful characters, a lovely New England setting, and a fascinating murder. Don't miss this charming new addition to the world of traditional mysteries."
—Kate Carlisle, *New York Times* bestselling author
of the Bibliophile Mysteries

Tops

Read It and Weep

"Jenn McKinlay never disappoints. Each story is better than the last. She creates awesome characters and plots an engaging story around them that just keeps those pages flying . . . [A] wonderfully plotted mystery full of twists and turns."
—*Escape with Dollycas into a Good Book*

"*Read It and Weep* will have Jenn McKinlay fans enthralled. This is a great example of what a cozy mystery should be . . . Written to perfection . . . McKinlay is one of the best in the genre."
—*Debbie's Book Bag*

"With a strong cast of characters added, it's no wonder this series has landed on the *New York Times* bestseller list . . . [McKinlay] brings together the best elements of a small-town mystery in this latest enjoyable entry in the series."
—*Lesa's Book Critiques*

"Any time a writer can surprise a reader, it's a good thing. The surprise in this book is a dandy and caught me totally off guard."
—*Kings River Life Magazine*

Book, Line, and Sinker

"Jenn McKinlay skillfully mixes libraries and small-town life in her . . . entertaining series. *Book, Line, and Sinker* is an outstanding cozy mystery . . . featuring engaging characters and an intriguing story."
—*Lesa's Book Critiques*

"[A] quickly paced, tightly plotted, intricately crafted mystery that is action-packed and will keep you guessing until you've reached the final chapters."
—*The Season*

"Oh man, what a great book, and that ending, wow . . . A great read that I wish could have gone on forever, and now I look forward to the next book in this delightfully charming series."
—*Dru's Book Musings*

continued . . .